MW01169977

Waking Up Eve

For Deb ~

All My Best,

Darci J. Knowles

*This book is dedicated to
freedom from the shadows.*

Darci Knowles

Waking Up Eve

JB

JUPITER BRAHMS
PUBLISHING

Portsmouth, New Hampshire

Published by Jupiter Brahms Publishing
a division of ISIS 2000, LLC
Portsmouth, NH 03801
www.isistudios.com

The text of this book is set in Galliard.
Book design by Karen Merk.

Library of Congress Cataloging-in-Publication Data

Knowles, Darci.
Waking Up Eve / by Darci Knowles.
ISBN 0-9679857-0-6
00-131771 CIP

Printed in Canada
Hignell Book Printing

Acknowledgements

As with any journey, this one has introduced me to many individuals whom I may never have known had I not taken the path of novelist. It has also asked something new from my relationships with the people who were in my life before "the book." I wish to thank everyone who has encouraged the completion of this work, but I would specifically like to acknowledge the following people for their precious contribution to this achievement:

Ernest Hebert, for his painful yet powerful illustration of the importance of plot.

All the writers who attended that workshop with me at St. Paul's School back in the summer of 1994. And, especially Deborah Regan who led me, most graciously, to Kelley Conway.

Kelley Conway for her kindness, her encouragement and her commitment to guide writers in finding their own true voice without prejudice or judgement.

Bill Appel of EditInk who helped restructure and fine tune the manuscript in its early stages of development.

The handful of readers who were brave enough to say yes when I asked them to read the manuscript at various points along the way. Each of them offered invaluable encouragement and insight: Richard Cyr, Kymn Rutigliano, Kathy Parlier, Barbara Perkins, Dan Gair, Kiyra and Ansara Page, Karen Merk and Jennifer Stone.

My mother, Bette Knowles, for showing me the meaning of passion and for passing her love of language on to me.

My father, Elton Knowles, who has taught me by his example the courage to believe in myself against any odds.

Special thanks to Karen Merk for designing a book jacket that beautifully reflects the story, for her professional dedication and unwavering friendship.

Last and far from least, I thank my children Chad and Danièle whose wisdom reaches far beyond their years and whose presence in my life fills me with hope and the determination to make a difference.

The Lake Isle of Innisfree

I will arise and go now, and go to Innisfree,
And a small cabin build there, of clay and wattles made:
Nine bean-rows will I have there, a hive for the honeybee,
And live alone in the bee-loud glade.

And I shall have some peace there, for peace comes dropping slow,
Dropping from the veils of the morning to where the cricket sings;
There midnight's all a glimmer, and noon a purple glow,
And evening full of the linnet's wings.

I will arise and go now, for always night and day
I hear lake water lapping with low sounds by the shore;
I hear it in the deep heart's core.

~ William Butler Yeats

PROLOGUE
March 11, 1995

J USTIN TEMPLETEN KNEW he had lived many lives before. Three hundred and thirty-two to be exact. And because this was his three-hundred and thirty-third lifetime in human form, he knew this was an important one. He knew this because three times three equals nine and any true mystic knows that the nine vibration indicates completion. His past life history was so rich and so varied that it was rare for him to travel any place new without an old memory being triggered. He had an acute ability to recall past lives, both his own and those of others. Sometimes his clairvoyant sight was so vivid, so sensorial that he felt transported to another time altogether. This flicker in the time-space continuum could easily be ignited by the particular scent of someone's skin, the glare of sunlight on a quiet lake or the swift flight of a cormorant, things often unnoticed by the average person.

Justin had been invited to the East Coast from his home in San

Francisco by his dear friend Doris Stanley. She had just moved to Innis, Connecticut three months earlier and while she had found a job working for a local attorney, she had not yet managed to become part of the community. That's why when Doris begged Justin to come and escort her to the ball named for her boss' father, he had not hesitated.

On this crisp evening in early March, as Justin and Doris stood among the well-dressed elite of Innis at the annual Whitman's Way Gala, Justin scanned the room. He was not fooled by the masks they wore.

He knew that his dark good looks paired with Doris' red curls and pink gown made them hard to ignore. And even though the guests couldn't place the couple within their closed society, they all did their best to be polite.

"There," Doris said, trying to point with her nose.

Justin looked across the room.

"Ah," he said, and inhaled deeply as he focused his vision on the young dark-haired woman poised carefully between the two older men. The tall man wearing silver wire-framed glasses seemed uncomfortable in his skin, the other man, attractive and very fit for his apparent years, enjoyed the spotlight. The young woman, he noticed, was smiling, but he sensed she was not fully present in the room.

"I told you," Doris said, nodding proudly. "Gorgeous, isn't she?"

Justin smiled.

"You'll want to keep an eye on her," he said.

"What do you mean?" Doris said, gazing seriously into his dark eyes for the answer.

Justin placed his hand gently on her back.

"Just that. About a year from now everything will come to a head, until then just observe and let things unfold as they will."

CHAPTER ONE
February 29, 1996

P AUL JASON JORDON THANKED the dark-eyed man for helping him prepare to die. He said goodbye and closed the door. The two men had only met a few weeks earlier at the hospital when Paul's heart had grown so heavy with remorse that he couldn't take in a full breath. The dark stranger had just appeared beside his bed one day and introduced himself as Justin Templeten. Curiously, from that moment forward Paul had found it easier to breathe.

Paul turned away slowly from the pain that chewed away his insides. He shuffled over to the stove and picked up the kettle. His hand shook so much now that he could only fill the kettle with enough water for a single cup of tea. Paul had never much cared for tea before but now he found something sweet and kind inside the cup. He reached for the black knob to the far right on the back of the stove and clicked it onto high. When he placed the kettle on the burner there was a small ting.

He moved carefully through the kitchen and headed for the other room. When he finally reached his writing table he eased himself down onto the chair. He sighed heavily and brushed a trembling, eternally-tanned hand over the top of his bald head. It still surprised him that he had no hair. Just six months ago he'd had a full head of thick white hair; a sailor's hair, wavy and unkempt. The chemotherapy had seen to it, though, that he would take leave of this world much the same way he'd come into it sixty-nine years ago: skinny and bald.

The old man (it was his body that had grown old, not his mind and least of all, his heart) chose not to answer the insistence of the tea kettle's whistle. Instead, he just listened to the screeching, which drifted and swooped like the familiar far cry of a seagull.

Paul had spent the last twenty-two years at sea, carried from shore to shore by life's ever changing winds. He had been happy in spite of the high cost of his choices. He remained very still, watching the sun ease its way down beneath the horizon. He recalled something Justin had said to him when they first met: *It takes courage to follow your heart, most people never follow their dreams.*

The creamy orange, pink and purple shades of the late winter sky intoxicated him. He drank the colors in boldly knowing this would be his last sunset.

Innis, Connecticut was a decent place to die. The simple, quiet lifestyle of this small New England town had helped bring peace to Paul's heart. But then, any place near the sea would have been fine.

His fingertips roamed the ridges of the old desk from Bali he'd always treasured. He could almost see the sweet face of the man who had made it for him. *Special for you, sa,* the man had said over and over again while Paul sat contentedly in the cool shade of the palm tree and watched him carve. Paul smiled, a single tear rolled down his weathered cheek. He felt each ridge of the desk top, each scar, with a slow and sacred awe.

He placed the pen down across the last page of the letter he'd been writing for days to his only living child. Somewhere out there Paul had a son whom he had left twenty-two years ago.

Too tired to get up and turn off the tea kettle, he lowered his head to rest on the surface of his desk. He began to slip away; it felt good, this letting go. The face of his one true love began to emerge through the mist in his mind's eye. His hand slid off the edge of the desk bouncing slightly a couple of times from its own weight. His arm hung there swinging slightly, back and forth, back and forth.

By the time the land-lady had opened the door to turn off the smoke detector from the burning tea kettle, Paul Jordon was gone. His arm hung stiffly now as if frozen in midair, and there was a strange, crooked smile across his face.

CHAPTER TWO

DORIS STANLEY WAS quietly knocking on the door. It took a few raps for Eve to notice that her secretary was standing in the doorway to her private office. Eve looked up at Doris with raised eyebrows.

"Paul Jordan passed away late yesterday afternoon," Doris said.

Eve frowned. She nodded and turned her chair to gaze out the window to the harbor below.

"Well, at least he won't have to live with all that pain any longer," she said, and then she swiveled her chair back around to face Doris.

Eve was distracted by the elaborate earrings that Doris was wearing. Big, long dangly constructions that nearly reached her shoulders. Her wild crimson hair entangled them like snakes, reminding Eve of Medusa. She dropped her pen and began rubbing her forefinger and thumb together in small circles. She cocked her head to one side and looked squarely up at Doris.

"How's the search for his son coming? Anything?" she said.

"The agency found two men named Kyle Jordan who match the profile, one lives in Northern California, the other in the Virgin Islands. They're working on positive ID for us now," Doris said.

Eve nodded.

"Go ahead and prepare the letter; give the agency a call and let them know we need confirmation by the end of the day."

THE NEXT DAY was Wednesday again, and it was six o'clock in the morning. Eve yawned quietly and sat down on the rust velvet couch. She stroked the softness of the fabric as she waited for her psychiatrist. Every week she stepped into the soothing darkness of this room and became weightless. While she was here, gravity seemed to disappear and take all her worries and fears with it.

The soft, dusty colors of the room filtered the early morning light. She turned her head towards the heavily draped window when she noticed sounds of chirping. When did the robins arrive? She hadn't heard them at home. They always came to her house first in the spring. She frowned, then turned to Peter who was closing the door to his private office.

Except for the singing robins and the swish of Peter's careful footsteps on the thick oriental carpet, the room was hushed. This room swallowed sounds and muffled them. Eve laid down on cue, enfolded by the quiet. She adjusted her skirt and crossed her slender legs at her ankles. Her weight fell deeper into the cushions as she let go of the tension in her muscles and the chatter in her mind. It was easier to do this so early in the morning; she wasn't really awake.

Eve glanced at Peter who seemed more friend than doctor. He was her father's friend really, but she liked to think he was her's too. His hair had turned white in the past few years and he wore silver rimmed glasses now. Sometimes Eve thought Peter knew her better than she knew herself. She couldn't imagine her life without their private weekly visits.

She'd never been treated by any other doctor; there had never been a reason to because Peter had never missed a week. Ever since her mother died when Eve was six, Peter and her father had agreed that a weekly routine was necessary to keep her mood stable. It was plain to see how the treatments had helped her live a better life. Who knows if she would ever have become a lawyer if Peter hadn't helped her recover from the trauma of her mother's death. Eve understood that this was for her own good and she felt lucky to have two men who cared for her so much.

"All settled in?" Peter asked.

Eve nodded.

"It's the sound of my voice that brings you to that secret place, that private place within, where we must go to keep you safe. Are you moving there now?"

"Yes," Eve said.

"That's right Eve, keep going, all the way down the path—."
The unexpected click of the door handle caused Peter to turn abruptly toward the entrance of his private office. He watched Robert step through. It was easy to see where Eve got her beauty. Judge Robert Whitman was still strong, fit and very handsome even at sixty-five. Although Peter was not expecting him for this session, he wasn't surprised.

Peter stood up and stepped toward Robert. The scent of expensive cologne permeated the room.

"Anything unusual I should know about?" Robert whispered.

"No."

"Let's keep it that way," Robert said, and raised his thick eyebrows.

Peter turned away, his throat constricting.

"Peter?"

"May I continue?" Peter said, turning quickly to face Robert.

Robert waved his hand through the air and bent forward at the waist like a court jester.

Peter walked back over to his chair. He breathed deeply hoping to release the constriction in his throat and slow the racing adrenaline that pumped through his veins.

Eve waited peacefully, unknowingly.

"Bring yourself into your secret hiding place, Eve, and tell me when you're there," Peter said, gently. "There you are, you're all alone now, but you're not afraid. I'm here, and I'll keep you safe."

Robert's body brushed the back of Peter's head as he paced back and forth behind him. Peter inhaled deeply, taking more of Robert's cologne in through his nostrils. He stiffened. Both men paused to watch for the signs of Eve's deep hypnotic state to appear.

Her left foot dropped off the couch landing with a thud to the floor. She planted it firmly, causing her legs to spread open slightly. She had regressed to a state of pre-pubescence. Peter saw Robert's eyes grow narrow and become fixed on Eve's thigh where her skirt had risen. His stomach tightened. He looked back at Eve, to him she was still a child. She did have the legs of a dancer, a narrow waist and...he looked away from the curve of her calf muscle to watch for the next sign.

Eve clasped her hands and placed them on her abdomen. Finally, the third sign — a small sweet smile spread across her lips.

"There we are, Eve. How do you feel?"

"Fine," she said. "It's very nice here this time of year. Mommy loves springtime, too. She loves to listen to the birdies sing, especially the robins. The air is so crispy, but the sun is getting stronger. I think it's growing me like a flower. Mommy says I'm going to make a beautiful blossom some day, big and sweet like a peony. That's what she says... ."

Peter brought Eve through the treatment in the usual way, once again sealing the box that contained her past. Her sad voice and the deep crease between her eyebrows told Peter she needed to linger in her safe place awhile longer, but he could not bear another moment in the same room with the Judge.

Peter reminded Eve that she would always have access to her Mommy in her secret garden, but that when she wasn't there, she had him — and, of course, her father who loved her very much. He paused to clear his throat then told Eve that any time she felt sad or angry, afraid or uncomfortable in any way, all she had to do was rub her thumb and forefinger together and all those bad feelings would disappear.

Peter heard Robert quietly close the door on his way out. His shoulders relaxed; his vocal chords loosened.

"It's time to come out now. Follow my voice back to our special room where I'm waiting for you. That's it, follow the path back this way."

While he spoke, he watched for the three signs in reverse now. First, the smile vanished leaving her face expressionless, almost lifeless. She unclasped her hands and let them fall to her sides and finally she returned her leg to the couch, crossing her feet at the ankles.

"There we are Eve, all ready for a wonderful day, and a nice week ahead. You can open your eyes now, come gently back."

Blinking a few times, Eve stretched her arms over head, revealing a white silk camisole beneath her cropped gray suit jacket. Arching slightly, she let out a small sigh. She looked over at Peter and smiled gratefully.

"I love this room. I always feel so safe here. Thank you, Peter."

"There's no need—."

"No, really. I felt unsettled before. I feel so much better now. What would I do without you?"

Her eyes glazed over. She rubbed her thumb and forefinger together. Peter smiled and stood up. He lifted Eve off the couch from her elbows. Arm in arm they walked through the doorway, into his office.

Peter looked at Eve. She was so innocent. He couldn't take in a full breath. When Eve saw the sadness in Peter's eyes, she slumped. But she quickly straightened her spine, rubbing her thumb and forefinger together in tiny rhythmic circles.

Peter patted her hand.

"How's your practice going? Any interesting cases?" he said.

"It's good," she said. "I really enjoy estate planning, as much as Daddy thinks it's drab. But I could never follow in his shoes as a trial lawyer, can you imagine? Me up there manipulating and provoking witnesses, performing for the jury?"

Peter shook his head.

"I like things quieter, it's more intimate, I really get to know my clients. I guess that's why I'm kind of sad today, one of my clients just passed away."

"I'm sorry," Peter said.

"Thanks. We just found his son. He lives in the Virgin Islands. I guess he's been kind of a drifter, ever since his mother died four years ago."

Peter watched Eve shift her weight from one foot to the other, death was not an easy subject for her, particularly the death of someone's mother. He waited for the familiar gesture they relied on. There, she was making tiny circles now, it would be alright. Peter smiled.

"Finally, we located him working as a captain on a charter boat down there," she continued.

"What kind of relationship did they have? This man and his father?"

"I don't know. One day Paul Jordan just wandered in asking for assistance in writing out his will. Someone I don't even know sent him over. Maybe you know him, Justin Templeten?"

Peter frowned. "Sounds familiar... ."

"Well, anyway, he'd already been diagnosed with cancer when we met which was only a few weeks before he died. Paul was a charmer, though, even when he was dying. He had traveled all over the world. The only time he even mentioned his son was when he named him in the will. And then once again when he asked me to take him to see his boat."

"Did you?"

"Yes, it's an amazing schooner docked over at the Windward Yacht Club. He'd sailed everywhere on it, the *Kyle Jordan,* he actually named it after his son."

"So, is he coming to town to settle his father's affairs?" Peter said.

"Yes...he's supposed to be arriving next week."

"Really? Is he married?"

"No," Eve said, scowling. "Why?"

"No reason," Peter said. "I'm glad you found him, now let's get you out of here before the morning staff starts filing in."

Eve kissed Peter on the cheek just as she had her whole life, gathered her things together and left for her own office across town.

CHAPTER THREE

THE FOLLOWING WEDNESDAY after her regular session with Peter, Eve raced through her morning's work with intense concentration. She grabbed reference books down from shelves and jotted copious notes onto yellow legal pads. She worked straight through lunch and was so embroiled that she was jolted when her phone buzzed.

"Kyle Jordan is here to see you," Doris said, through the speaker phone.

Eve frowned. "Who?" she said.

"Paul Jordan's son? He's just in from St. Thomas to discuss his father's will... ."

"It's two o'clock already?"

"Hello? Eve, where are you? Earth to Eve, come in?" she said.

Eve giggled.

"I'm sorry Ms. Stanley," she said, in an exaggerated tone, "please do, send the gentleman in."

"Very good," Doris said, then whispered, "wait'll you see him—."

Eve gathered the paperwork together and stacked it in a pile on her desk. She slid open a drawer to pull the PJ Jordan file.

When Kyle Jordan entered her office, Eve was looking down into her file cabinet. He cleared his throat. Eve looked up, her chin froze in midair. He stood stiffly just inside the doorway. He was taller than her father...that meant he was over six feet. He was casually dressed in a white polo shirt which pointed her to his tanned, sinewy arms. He wore khaki pants and deck shoes without socks. He had sailor's hair, dirty blond, wavy and windblown. And he had a distinctively square jaw.

When Eve realized she was staring, she lost her breath for a split second. She rubbed her thumb and forefinger together in tiny circles.

She rubbed harder, creating more vigorous circles until the sensation passed, setting her free to stand up and move toward him.

"Mr. Jordan, I'm Eve Whitman. Thank you for coming," she said, and extended her hand. He took hold in a strong, respectful manner. Eve felt a wave of electricity pass through her. She held onto his hand for a moment then, releasing it, spoke again in a detached professional tone.

"I'm sorry about your father's death. It must have come as quite a shock." Eve paused. There was a hardness in his clear blue eyes. "Please, come in and have a seat."

Eve watched as Kyle looked around her office. She noticed the effects of sunlight streaming through the handcut Baccarat vase. She wondered what he was thinking as he took in the rows of leather bound books artfully placed between Aztec sculptures, pots from Bali, vases from the Orient, and all the other artifacts from around the world. Eve had traveled a lot with her father over the years and always made it a point to bring home something of her own.

Kyle walked straight past the appropriate chair for guests, directly over to the arched windows behind Eve's desk. He peered out at the scenic harbor below.

"I haven't seen my father in twenty-two years. He ran out on us when I was eight." He turned to face her. "So...is it Miss, or Mrs?"

"Oh no," Eve answered, without moving at all, "I've never been married, although sometimes I feel that—." She lowered her eyes. "You know, to my work."

"Looks like you're doing something right."

"Please, take a seat," Eve said, smiling awkwardly. She moved quickly over to the chair behind her desk. "Your father instructed me to read this letter to you, before reviewing the aspects of his estate."

She held up a sealed envelope for Kyle to acknowledge. Her hand trembled slightly.

He reached for the letter, Eve pulled it back.

"I'm afraid he was quite literal in that request, Mr. Jordan. He specifically required me to *read* the letter to you."

"That's not necessary, Ms. Whitman. I'm perfectly capable of reading the letter on my own."

"I'm sorry. I realize this is a sensitive matter. However, as an officer of the court, I am legally bound to follow your father's instructions."

He looked away from her. Eve swallowed. She rubbed her thumb and finger together urgently. Before Kyle looked back she had reached for a pen with her right hand while discretely pressing the intercom button with her left. She pushed the button a second time canceling the connection so Doris would have to buzz her back.

The phone rang. Eve excused herself, glanced quickly at Kyle and then grabbed hold of the receiver.

"Yes, Doris?"

"Yes, yourself. You buzzed me, doll."

"Oh? What's the time frame on that?"

"The time frame? About thirty seconds ago. Eve, what are you doing?"

"Well then, I guess we have no choice. Tell Mr. Carlisle I'll meet with him at the Court House at three-thirty, and please arrange an appointment for Mr. Jordan to return tomorrow, on his way out."

"Oh, you want him out of there...I get it. You don't really want me to contact Carlisle, right?"

"No, that won't be necessary."

"Okay, honey, but I've got to tell you, you're scaring me."

"Thank you, Doris."

Eve put the phone back in its cradle and looked at Kyle. His eyes had grown narrow.

"Forgive me, Mr. Jordan. I'm afraid I've got an emergency situation that I must attend to for one of my clients. Doris will assist you in rescheduling a meeting for tomorrow."

"Look," he said, still frowning, "I've come all the way up here to get this thing over with. The last thing I want to do is drag it out and hang around this sleepy, little town any longer than I have to. I understand that things come up, but meanwhile, I pay for another night in a hotel—."

"Of course, allow me to take care of that for you. Please let Doris know where you're staying and we'll cover the extra expenses."

Kyle eyed her suspiciously.

"No," he said, clicking his tongue inside his mouth, "that's okay. But if it happens again, I might just take you up on it."

He stood up and left the room without another word.

Eve watched him walk out of her office. His long legs swept swiftly across the floor. She realized she'd stopped breathing and concentrated on taking slow, even breaths. She needed more air. Her body was vibrating strangely from the inside, out.

She had forgotten about the familiar habit of rubbing her thumb and forefinger together. She rubbed tiny rhythmic circles, round and round.

She closed her eyes, tried to enter the dark room of her safehouse until her breathing began returning to normal.

She called the clinic to speak to Peter, but was told that he was in session; he'd left strict instructions not to be interrupted. Trying to disguise her agitation, she told the receptionist she would be at the clinic at five o'clock sharp and that she expected Dr. Weiss to be prepared to see her.

In the meantime, she moved erratically around her office. She had to get out. More circles, harder, faster.

"I'm really beat," she said to Doris on her way through the reception area. "I think I'll go home and take a nice long swim."

"Are you going to tell me what that was all about?"

"You mean with Jordan?"

Doris nodded.

Eve shrugged. "He seemed uncomfortable hearing from his father after all this time, you know, he hadn't seen him since he was eight...do you realize it's been exactly twenty-two years since my mother died?" Doris raised her right eyebrow.

"It's just odd, that's when his father left him. Twenty-two years ago...anyway, I just thought I'd let him off the hook. You know, give him a little time to prepare for whatever's in that letter."

"Oh, I get it," Doris said, coyly. "You have the hots for him and you're just trying to keep him around here a little longer so you can—."

"Doris, really," Eve said. But then she smiled. "He is kind of cute, isn't he?"

"Aha," Doris said, shaking a finger at Eve. "I knew it!"

Eve laughed as she turned away from Doris and said goodbye. She stepped out of the building into the fresh spring air; she did not feel well at all. There was a circus troupe practicing inside her head. Jugglers were throwing things around, trapeze artists were flying back and forth yelling 'hup,' lion trainers cracked their whips incessantly. Throughout the chaos a high-pitched pulsating sound kept fading in and out. Her body trembled. She sat down on a park bench, closed her eyes and let herself be comforted by the tiny rhythmic circles. She concentrated on breathing normally. Slowly, the aching in her stomach reminded her that she hadn't eaten all day.

She walked calmly over to the corner deli and went inside to order a sandwich. The smell of meat almost made her gag. She tried to make sense of the list of sandwiches behind the counter.

A voice from behind her said, "Is everything alright Miss Whitman?"

Eve gasped when tiny puffs of breath moved the hair on the back of her head. A chill crawled across her body. She spun around. Kyle Jordan was facing her, just inches away. Touching her hand to her heart she laughed uncomfortably.

"Mr. Jordan. You startled me. I'm sorry. Haven't you eaten either?"

They stood alone in the middle of the black and white checkerboard floor like two pieces in a game. Eve thought she was shrinking, like Alice. She fought a driving urge to turn and run out the door. She curled her left hand behind her back to rub her finger and thumb together.

"I saw you over at the park," Kyle said. "I was going to say hello, but you seemed upset. You okay?"

"You did? At the park? Just now?"

He nodded.

"Really? I didn't even see you. I'm fine. I just, well — sometimes I get these terrible migraines," Eve said, then raised the fingertips of her right hand to her forehead keeping her left hand behind her back.

"Is that why our meeting ended so abruptly?"

"Oh, no. I do have to be in court, I just needed to get some air, and something to eat before I went downtown. What are you doing?"

Eve wondered if he was following her. She shifted her weight and looked over her shoulder to smile awkwardly at Jim Olson, the man with the white apron who watched them from behind the counter. Kyle reached out gently, and touched her shoulder. He looked into her eyes.

"It's okay. Can I call you Eve?"

She nodded quickly, her pale green eyes opened wide.

"I've heard that migraines are really nasty, that light makes it even worse. Are you sure you're going to be alright?"

"Yes," she said, stepping away from his touch. "Thank you for your concern, but I really have to go." She tried to smile. She looked down at her shoes and noticed they were covered with dust from the park.

"Can I give you a ride," he asked, "I've rented a car, it's right outside."

"No. Thank you, though, really." She turned to leave too fast and almost tripped.

She paused then scrambled for the door. When she reached it, she glanced back to look at him. As soon as their eyes met she turned away quickly and stepped through the door.

"What about your sandwich?" he called.

"No time," she said.

Outside, Eve looked one way, then the other. Maybe she should find a bathroom. She looked at her watch and kept walking. She strolled through the park, the daffodils were in bloom, they looked so happy. The tulips were up, but had not yet blossomed. She turned onto the street lazily inspecting the windows of the art galleries and gift shops that flanked the small Innis waterfront. She didn't remember anything she saw. She had been transported to a place strange and unusual; it was like being inside Peter's room, but outside.

It wasn't until she heard the big clock in the square chime five times that she remembered her appointment with Peter. She ran past the entrance to her office, beneath the gold leafed, hanging carved sign which read EVE WHITMAN, Attorney at Law.

She didn't notice that Doris was about to lock up the front door.

And she didn't hear her when she called out or see the way Doris watched her as she fumbled frantically with her car keys to unlock the door before hurriedly driving away.

KYLE PULLED OVER to the side of the road under the shade of an ancient oak tree. He watched as Eve swerved into the parking lot surrounding the Weiss-Whitman Clinic. He could see her tapping fingertips on the steering wheel as she waited for another car to back out of a nearby parking spot. She stopped with a jerk and rushed toward the entrance.

Kyle sat in his blue rental car, watching as Eve marched through the glass doors of a psychiatric clinic. She held her head high. Her last name *was* on the sign... maybe one of her parents was a psychiatrist. One thing was certain, this was not the Court House. He put on his sunglasses and reached down to turn the key in the ignition. He paused, compelled to wait for a few minutes. He leaned back into the seat. Migraines can really fuck you up, he thought.

At least once a week while he was growing up he'd come home from school to find his mother laying flat on the bed as if strapped down, unable to move, all the curtains drawn. The house felt small like a closet on those days and the stench of smelly boots hung in the air. It was the light, she would say, the light of day that made the pain unbearable.

He leaned over to rest his forehead on the steering wheel. Why was he sitting there? What did he care that some lawyer hired by his father was suffering from migraines, pathological lying, or any other problem? The last thing he needed — or wanted — was any complications in his life. His fiancée was waiting for him back in St. Thomas, they were going to run a charter boat business together. He sat up and looked at himself in the rear view mirror. Their wedding was in six weeks.

Kyle looked over his left shoulder to check the doors of the clinic.

The hum of an approaching car grew louder and he saw a gold Mercedes weaving toward him through the late afternoon shadows. He slouched; expensive cars had rich, snobby drivers. His body jiggled from the pull of the passing car. He felt foolish. Even if she came out right then, so what? He looked at his watch. Twenty minutes he'd wasted. He started the car and drove away.

As he drove the winding country road back into town, Eve's eyes kept floating across his brain. He tried thinking of his father, what had made him land here?...of all the places in the world. He turned toward the waterfront, it was edged with brick buildings and specialty shops. He looked around but still he saw her eyes, the way they seemed to plead for help. He had plans. Her eyes were the soft green of a milkweed pod right before it bursts. She was like a china doll, fragile, and that made him want to protect her. But he wouldn't, it was ridiculous, he couldn't. He had plans.

The town Kyle saw was like most any New England town, brick buildings, white clapboards with black or green shutters, quaint, not much variety. Then he spotted the church, the center of every rural American town. Tall and proud, on a grassy plot, a village square or a noble hill. Its doors were usually arched, but always closed. The steeple up above promised a connection with God.

But, Kyle knew that being inside a church had little or nothing to do with God. He remembered the way people whispered and snickered after his father had left, gawking at his mother and him from their places on the pews. Every Sunday Kyle's mother had forced him to sit through the humiliation, then she'd take him home and read *The Ugly Duckling*. Even when he was sixteen years old, he would still let her read it to him.

He kept driving until the church was completely out of sight.

CHAPTER FOUR

E
VE DESCRIBED THE CONFUSION
she had experienced throughout the afternoon.
Peter nodded, listening intently.

What had gone wrong?

The programming had always succeeded in allowing Eve to repress any type of sexual attractions and sensations. Of course, Peter knew that what he'd accomplished with Eve was the epitome of unethical behavior. It was, in fact, the exact opposite required for overcoming trauma. Under normal conditions when helping a patient, Peter relied on memory retrieval, role playing and his own variation on something called the Mozart effect which utilized the power of music to heal.

Eve's treatments were the chains that kept Peter bound to Robert and his secrets, and if he'd had the key to unlock them he would have done so years ago. Now, as he grew older, the weight of these chains seemed a heavier burden than he could carry.

Peter's stomach twitched as he reviewed all the careful steps he had taken over thousands of sessions with Eve. After twenty-two years he was still convincing her psyche that physically she was a child of six.

Until now.

Peter knew he would have to handle this repair on his own. It would be a mistake to bring Robert in on what was happening too early. He would only overreact, and Peter would be blamed.

First he had to find out what had gone wrong. He would use narcohypnosis, with sodium amytal, to free up her subconscious mind. It was risky — it could bring forward aspects of Eve's personality which had been repressed and lay deeply dormant within her. But, if he could get at her sexual self, he might be able to prevent this from happening further.

"Okay, Eve. Here's what we'll do. First, I'd like to give you a vitamin B-twelve shot, it will help you fight against the stress —."

"I've had those before," she said.

"You have? When? Who administered them?"

"Well, Daddy, actually. He says I need it if he thinks I'm getting overloaded, showing any signs of stress, you know, that sort of thing. We relied on them a lot to get through college and law school."

Peter turned away, he was fidgeting with the papers attached to his clip board. What was the Judge doing giving Eve any kind of shots without his knowledge — vitamins, or otherwise? He cleared his throat and walked closer to Eve. His voice was soft when he spoke.

"What I'd like to give you today is a more complete vitamin solution. It has more than just vitamins, it also has some plant extracts which will help you to relax and feel better."

"Whatever you think." Eve shrugged. "I could barely function at work today."

"We'll take care of that. Do you have plenty of time? This may take a while."

Eve nodded.

"What about your father?"

Eve looked down at the floor.

"You know he always insists that we have dinner together," she said. "He expects me home by seven every night."

"Why don't you call him, tell him you won't be able to make it home for dinner...and that you have to...work late."

Eve shook her head.

"I'll just tell him I'm with you," she said, "and that you're going to give me a treatment."

"You know how he can be," Peter said. He straightened his back and smiled. "He gets very upset when you have the slightest relapse. Let's just get it under control, see what we can find out, and then, if you think we should, we'll tell your dad. But I really think it would be better if we could keep this between us for now."

"I can't lie to him."

"Is Doris at the office?" Peter suggested. "Maybe we could have her call."

"Then I'd have to ask her to lie for me, that's worse. Besides, I already told her that I was going home for the day." Eve stood up and said, "I'll call."

When she phoned home to the Whitman mansion, her father wasn't there. She left word with Mrs. Bristol, the housekeeper, that she would be home later...after dinner...she would be involved in researching a case at the legal library. She asked Mrs. Bristol to be sure to tell her father that she would miss him, but that this couldn't be avoided and she would see him for breakfast in the morning.

As she spoke into the receiver, Peter watched her rub her forefinger and thumb together in a tiny circular motion. But the strain in Eve's voice, the constant tapping of her foot, told him that the effects of that technique were not holding up. He was more convinced upon seeing this that his decision to use sodium amytal was a sound one. Eve was fighting for some reason, and Peter relied on narcohypnosis for patients who resisted hypnosis in general. Even though Eve was an extremely willing patient, something was brewing outside her normal patterns of behavior. He would also incorporate post-hypnotic suggestion so he could distinguish these results from her regular sessions.

Eve began walking toward the door of the room where she always felt so safe, the one she'd just been in eleven hours earlier. Peter quickly took hold of her elbow. She turned and looked at him quizzically.

"In order to administer the vitamin shot," he said softly, "we have to have our session in a different room, this way, just down the hall."

Eve hesitated, but then followed him.

Peter knew this room was much more sterile, much less soothing than Eve was accustomed. It smelled of cold, metal instruments, bleached linens and salty solutions. Eve turned to Peter, she looked at him with the uncertainty of a child.

"It's alright, Eve," he said, and put his arm around her. "I won't let anything bad happen to you."

Eve lowered her chin and stared at the shiny speckled floor. Peter asked her to remove her suit jacket and shoes and to lie down on the white sheeted bed. He reached inside a cabinet to get a blanket for her. When he turned back, her skirt had risen enough to expose a large bruise on the side of her leg, a few inches above her knee. He hadn't noticed it earlier this morning, then realized he'd only seen her other leg.

"How'd you get that nasty bruise?" he said, slowly spreading the blanket over her.

"Oh, that's nothing. That's the place where Father injected the last couple of B-twelve shots."

Peter's heart beat faster. If Robert Whitman had really been giving her B-twelve he would have known that it was always given into the buttocks, and if ever it was given into the arm — or, as in this case, the leg — it would be given into the muscle, not the vein.

"Does he always give it to you in the leg?" Peter said, trying to unclench his jaw.

"No, we switch back and forth between my arm and leg, to avoid bruising and sensitivity."

"That looks pretty bruised."

"I've been working so hard lately that Daddy gave me three shots last week. Most of the time we never do it more than twice."

Peter's jaw clenched again. He remembered when Eve was six, the way she shook, how she would curl up and not speak. Whitman had sworn he'd never touch her again. He had even cried. Peter had believed him. He started working with Eve, helping her to contain and then forget the memories that had prevented her from speaking and playing like children do. Peter thought he was helping, but later when he questioned the need for ongoing hypnosis, Robert would always reach back into the past and remind Peter why he would continue to do as he was told.

Peter wanted to ask if she was using birth control, but couldn't. He turned away so Eve wouldn't see his face. The sick feeling in his stomach was rising into his chest. He tried to swallow it down.

"How long have you been taking these shots?"

"I would have told you," Eve said. Her eyes flooded with worry. "I just never thought it was important. They're just vitamins."

"How long, Eve?"

"I don't know. I guess it started right before I went away to Boston for college. Daddy would come visit, or he'd send for me on the weekend. He was so worried about my studies and stress level. I don't see anything wrong with that. Do you?"

Peter took her left hand and guided her thumb and forefinger into the familiar circular motion. He held her hand in his while she continued rubbing. Then he gently stroked the hair away from her face and told her everything was fine. He hadn't meant to upset her, he said. But as her doctor, it was imperative that he be fully aware of any health measures with which she was involved. Anything at all. He just needed to be certain that the work they did together would remain compatible.

Nine, maybe ten years. Peter's head filled with a raging pressure. This time he didn't know if he could control the damage.

Peter told Eve to keep her arm very straight while he inserted the intravenous needle. He asked her to count with him backwards ...six...five...four...three...two, until she was fully under the influence of the drug. He carefully removed the needle and was quietly rolling the metal rod away from the bed when he heard an unfamiliar voice.

"Back so soon, lover boy?"

The voice was deep, husky. Peter reeled toward the door to see who was there. There was no one in the room besides him and Eve.

"Hey, I'm talking to you," she said. "What's the matter? Cat got your tongue?"

She laughed.

"Who are you?" Peter said, and stepped closer to the bedside.

She laughed again.

"I said, who are you?"

"What kind of question is that?" she said, snorting. "I'm your one and only. Are we going to play another game? What should we call this one, Bobbie goes under cover? Or, how about, the interrogation of Bobbie Whitman — then if you don't like my answers, you can do whatever you want to me. Would you like that?"

In spite of the twisting in his gut, Peter followed his patient's lead. He knew that this type of drug-induced hypnosis meant that Eve was unable to discern Peter from her own father. And because he suspected that this voice was the result of a programmed personality, not one of Eve's own making, she would have no reason to believe otherwise. He would have to play the role of Robert Whitman if he was going to learn anything.

"Let's play," he said. "The only rule is that you have to tell me the truth."

"You mean you don't want to pretend you're back in the CIA, where everybody lies?"

She laughed again, a little louder.

The strange laughter and the scorn in her voice was so disturbing that Peter almost ended the session. Yet he knew if he was going to devise a plan to deal effectively with what appeared to be a planned dissociative disorder, he needed to go further.

"No, I don't think so," Peter said, "this time I'd just like to talk straight. No bullshit. Let's talk about all our time together, how does that sound, Bobbie?"

"Pretty goddamned boring," she said.

"Where's Eve?"

"Don't be ridiculous." She grimaced. "You know very well where she is. She would never show up here, she hates you for creating me. You're just going to have to be satisfied with one of us. It's her you've always wanted though, isn't it?"

Peter rubbed his forehead trying to stop the hammering.

"I just want to make sure she's alright," he said.

"Sure. Your dick is probably hard just saying her name. What do you think, I don't know? I don't like this game, let's play one of our other ones now."

Eve turned her head away. Since Peter had not given her the command of opening her eyes, they remained closed.

"Okay. I just felt bad about hypnotizing her. That's what I did, isn't it?"

"Losing your memory, are you?"

She laughed again.

Peter forced a laugh, too.

"Maybe I am, Bobbie. But I did hypnotize her?"

"So?"

"You know that, right?" Peter said.

"Of course, I know it."

"I probably couldn't hypnotize you though, could I? You're too strong."

"I am a product of hypnosis, baby."

"Are you happy about it, that I created you like this?"

"I'm not happy, I'm not unhappy. It's just a fact, that's all. What's the matter with you tonight anyway? You don't want to do it?"

Eve rubbed her hands over her breasts, round and round before pinching her hardened nipples. Peter's face flushed, his heart beat faster and his mouth went dry as he watched her. He shifted in his chair.

"Does Eve hate you too, Bobbie? The way she hates me?"

"You know, I've done a lot to help her."

"For instance?" he said.

"I protect her from men."

"Including me?"

"Especially you."

"Were you there, when she met this Jordan guy?" Peter said.

"How'd you know about that?" she said, suspiciously.

"Eve told me about it. Were you there?"

"Of course I was there. That's why she got all confused. I had to get her away from him. I was doing it for you, just like you told me to."

"Good girl, Bobbie. What did I tell you?"

"Oh for Chrissakes. That we were made for you, and only you."

"And?"

"And that it's my job to keep it that way," she said, automatically.

"And Eve's okay with that?"

"We're not forcing her, she's just too tired. She just sits back and lets it happen."

"You mean, she's always there when we're together?"

"She's around."

"Does she see what we do? Does she watch us play our games?"

"No way. She's weak, no fun, wants to stay a little girl."

"How does she avoid seeing us?"

"She closes her eyes, covers her ears. She makes herself disappear."

Peter lifted his shoulders trying to release the grip on his muscles. He looked away from her.

"Okay, Bobbie, I have to say goodbye now—."

"What do you mean? I'm all ready."

She moved her fingertips rhythmically up and down between her legs, swiveling and raising her hips.

Pausing suddenly, she said, "you're not mad at me are you?"

"No, Bobbie, I'm not mad. I just wanted to talk to you for awhile, that's all."

"There's a first time for everything, I guess," she said, and relaxed back down onto the bed.

"Did I give you that name?" Peter said.

"You're Robert, I'm Roberta," she said. Then she whispered, "Bobbie, 'cause it's sexy."

Peter watched her squirm around on the table stroking herself some more. His chest heaved and tears started to form. He reached his thumb and forefinger under his glasses to quickly wipe them away.

"Sorry, I have to go. Please lay still and listen carefully."

She did as she was told.

"You will have no recollection of this conversation. All that has been spoken between us here will be gone from your memory when you awake, and the next time we're together you will behave just as always, as though this had never occurred. Do you understand?"

"Yes," she said, slowly nodding.

"One more thing. You must help Eve. Do not interfere in this thing with Jordan. It's confusing her, and if you continue it will cause discomfort for both of you. Eve must be allowed to function as a normal woman where he is concerned, and to complete her job of settling his father's estate. Is that clear?"

She nodded again.

"None of this has happened. You will not recall any of this conversation. Now sleep here for a while, until I'm ready to bring Eve back."

With that, her head fell slightly to one side, and he could tell from her slow, deep breathing that she was asleep. He had to help Eve get rid of Bobbie without the Judge finding out that he knew. Eventually, he would confront Robert with it, but not until he knew everything. This time he would have the leverage. So what if Robert threatened to sue him for malpractice? He would tape sessions with Bobbie as evidence... he would have to be extremely careful. If Robert found out too soon, it would destroy any chance of waking up Eve, and it would ruin Peter.

The last two hours had given him the possibility of an out. All he would focus on now was freeing Eve, and that meant freeing himself.

He scribbled a few notes onto a pad; she'd said something about the CIA. Whitman never belonged to the CIA, or any other governmental agency that Peter had known about. He needed to know how Robert had created Bobbie, and what triggered her to come out if he was going to find a way to eliminate or, even just for now, contain her.

Peter looked over at Eve as she lay sleeping. He had no choice. He tore the paper off the pad, folded it and slid it into his white lab coat. He moved toward the bed and gently brought her back.

"On ten you will wake up. Seven...eight...nine...ten. Open your eyes, now. Look at me."

She slowly opened her gorgeous green eyes and looked straight through his round metal glasses.

"How'd we do?" Eve said, in her own voice.

"We did fine. How do you feel?" Peter said, quietly smiling despite the pounding in his head.

"Mmm, a little queasy. I haven't eaten much today. What happened?"

"Let's go grab some dinner," Peter said.

PETER DROVE THEM TO A RESTAURANT far outside of town hoping to avoid seeing anyone they knew. As they walked toward the entrance, he reached over and rubbed Eve's back as if that would somehow bring comfort to the spirit inside. When she looked at him he looked away quickly trying to deaden the sting in his eyes.

They settled into a booth inside the restaurant and the waiter handed them each a menu.

"Okay, Peter, tell me why you're so serious," Eve said.

"You're meeting with this fellow again tomorrow, right?"

Eve nodded.

"I think you'll be able to get through your meeting without any difficulty."

"I hope so. But why did it happen in the first place?"

"It's difficult to say. Primarily, you're not used to the sensations brought about by...you know...by the male-female equation."

Eve laughed.

"The male-female equation? So clinical. Tell me doctor, do you suffer from this problem, as well?"

He grinned at her.

"I suppose, I do. I guess we all suffer that syndrome to some extent."

Peter pulled off his glasses and laid them on the table. He rubbed his eyes.

"Have you ever been in love, Peter?"

"Once," he said, "but that was a long time ago. Don't confuse love with what's happening here. After all, it sounds as though this guy — what's his name again?"

"Kyle," she said, as if he'd asked a hundred times before.

"This guy, Kyle, is the total opposite of your father. We both know how protective Robert has always been of you." Peter gulped some water. "It's natural, really, that you would be drawn to someone like Jordan. A sailor, no ties, a free-spirited type. See what I mean?"

"No. I don't see why I would want the total opposite of Father. Are you telling me that I'm overwhelmed with Kyle Jordan's *type,* and that these feelings aren't real?"

"I think we're getting carried away. You've only just met him. You've spent, what, twenty minutes in the same room with him? In a couple of days he'll be out of your life."

"I've never felt like this before."

Peter looked across the table at Eve. Her dark hair softly framed her delicate face and her large green eyes were opened wide with trust as she waited for his reply. Two strong hands reached inside and were twisting his heart like a cloth that needed wringing. Peter took in a deep breath.

"Let's eat. Our food is getting cold."

He lifted his fork to taste the first bite of pasta primavera. Peter wiped a drip of cream sauce from his chin and noticed that Eve was holding her breath. Her eyes were bulging.

"What?" Peter said.

"He's here," she said.

Peter turned around and peered over his shoulder at the blond-headed man sitting at the far end of the bar. He had that healthy look, like he hardly ever went inside, and he certainly wouldn't be caught dead in an office. Kyle raised a frothy beer glass at them and Eve smiled back, shyly.

"Of all the places...all the way out here...at the exact same time... ."

"Let's eat," Peter said. He shoveled in a few more bites of pasta while Eve gazed down the bar like a smitten teenager.

Peter threw some money down on the table and stood up abruptly.

"Ready?" he said, "We've got to get you home."

"I'm not finished."

"That's alright, you can take it with you."

Peter signaled to the waiter who collected the check, the money, and the unfinished pasta. He returned quickly with Peter's change and the wrapped package.

Eve was smiling broadly as they approached the bar.

"Hello, Mr. Jordan," she said.

"Well, if it isn't the pretty lady lawyer."

Peter shifted his weight from one foot to the other as he watched Eve's face flush.

"I'd like you to meet my friend, Peter. Peter, this is Kyle Jordan."

"Nice to meet you," Peter said, then turned to Eve. "Shall we?"

"Yes. I'll see you tomorrow," she said, still smiling. She seemed frozen in place.

"Right, one-thirty?" He smiled back at her. "You're not going to stand me up this time, are you?"

Peter hovered beside them. He took Eve's elbow.

"Really, Eve, we must go."

"Until tomorrow, then?" she said.

"Tomorrow," he said, raising his glass once more before spinning his stool back around to face the bar.

Eve stared at his back for a minute until Peter gently put his arm around her and guided her out the door.

As they walked through the dimly lit parking lot to the car, Peter said, "I want you to come to my office in the morning."

"Why?"

"What time can you be there?"

"Honestly, Peter, do you have to ruin it?"

"I'm a little worried, that's all. You don't have much experience in these matters, and I don't want to see you get hurt. Trust me, please."

"Fine. I'll be there at six-thirty, alright?"

"Yes, good. That's good."

CHAPTER FIVE

AFTER DROPPING EVE OFF at her car, Peter drove alone in the darkness. Eve could appear so normal. He'd done a remarkable job, and if not so surreptitious he could have been highly recognized. Genius, probably. Means nothing.

Maybe Robert was right...maybe Eve was better off never knowing the truth, her life might end up okay. The truth would destroy *him*, and his career. No, he had to help Eve, healing her now meant exposing the whole truth about her own life...and her father.

He drove out to the beach before going home to face the long night ahead. A strong breeze whipped off the ocean. Peter pulled a windbreaker from his trunk, the red one he wore on his daily run. He zipped it up and breathed the cool, salty air deep into his lungs before taking off suddenly toward the water. He sprinted across the cold, dense sand in his bare feet and pumped his arms angrily. The sand felt sharp like snow in winter.

Crashing waves helped to drown out the voices inside his head. Piercing voices penetrated his brain since the session when he met Bobbie. He ran along the water's edge faster and faster. He ran until he was breathless and his body was heaving and then collapsed down onto the sand. As he tried to slow his breathing the relentless sounds of the water rose up and engulfed him. Lifting crashing gliding, up, down, and back, lift, crash, glide. Something snapped inside him. He tried to push it away but could not escape this rising tide. A quiet tear slid down his cheek but then one followed after another, and another; he began to sob. He cried long and hard until he was completely spent. Sitting still, now the water soothed him.

Peter pulled himself up and trudged back to his car.

He drove into the parking garage of the most exclusive building in town (it was one of the infamous Innis expansion projects built by Robert Whitman), and stepped into the penthouse he called home. He poured himself a glass of brandy. He knew he had to focus on a strategy to help Eve but he was numb. He couldn't think clearly. He poured another brandy.

Halfway through his second glass he rose and climbed the circular staircase that led to his bedroom. Inside the room, he opened the closet door, reached to a back wall and unlocked a small door. Behind it was a safe where he kept all his important papers. He fumbled through the files growing more and more agitated; the brandy was coaxing all his buried rage to the surface rather than stuffing it as he had hoped.

Finally he grabbed hold of a video tape and yanked it from it's case. He stared at the black plastic casing. The longer he stood there staring, the louder the pounding became as it thrashed against the inner walls of his brain. He had not looked at this tape in twenty years. It had only crossed his mind once or twice in the very beginning, back during the initial sessions with Eve. After that, he had determined to forget it had ever existed. It was the only way he'd been able to carry on.

He stepped heavily back down the stairs, the tape in one hand, an empty snifter in the other. In the living room he threw the tape down onto the tan leather sofa. Suddenly, he was repulsed. He wiped his hand back and forth on his pant leg. He went to the liquor cabinet — another brandy to get through the tape. He poured, then gulped, his third glass. He poured another. He moved over in front of the sofa, grabbed the tape and jammed it into the VCR. *Don't do it*. He picked up the remote control and drained his fourth glass of brandy. He sunk into the sofa thinking how things had changed.

In another time, another place, back in the late fifties when he lived in New York City, he had been young and vital, brilliant, many people had said. Including his best friend, Robert Whitman. Peter's early research on the use of hypnosis and the healing process was being internationally recognized. Whitman was then a young attorney who had already managed to pull in a briefcase full of favors. He was sly and sharp, but not in a bad way. It was all kind of a joke to them, this ability they both had to manipulate people and situations in their favor. They had it all: money, prestige, women. Peter could never have imagined the plan Robert had in store for him back then. Even now, he couldn't quite believe it. But now he knew they had lived their lives as if engaged in a continuous contest. Always, one without a clear winner.

Until they had met Jennifer.

Peter remembered the first time they had seen her. They were at a cocktail party in honor of a famous French composer who was doing a guest appearance with the New York Philharmonic Orchestra. Peter and Robert were in a corner sizing up this one and that one, when she slipped through a cluster of people into the middle of the room. She was attractive, but her appeal went beyond looks. She wore glasses. Her shoulder length chestnut hair was parted in the middle and hung loosely around her face. She did not wear much make-up, except for a delicious shade of red lipstick which emphasized the fullness of her lips. She was petite with a nice shape, but her body did not compare with most of the others in the room. Her black evening dress was fitted but simple, and she wore matching gloves that climbed to meet her elbows.

When she had noticed them staring at her she walked towards them.

"Where does a lady get a drink around here," she asked, smiling.

"Allow me," Robert said, and left her there with Peter.

When he returned the two of them had their heads together laughing.

"What's the joke?" Robert said.

"Oh, Robert, please meet Miss Jennifer Swenson. She's new in town," Peter said.

"So she is," Robert said, raising his glass to toast her arrival, to which they all gestured in kind.

PETER PUSHED THE PLAY BUTTON on the remote. The tape began out of focus with Jennifer and Robert entering the door of Peter's old apartment in New York. They were dressed up, had obviously been out somewhere, and they had been drinking. They were laughing.

Peter wrapped his arms tightly around his body. He watched as they moved down the hallway, their voices were muffled. When Jennifer had disappeared into the living room, Robert stopped dramatically at the end of the hallway, turned around and looked up into a camera he had somehow managed to hide there. He puckered his lips, blew a kiss, and then waved.

"Bastard," Peter whispered.

The screen went black for a few seconds and then they were in the living room. Robert was popping a bottle of champagne and Jennifer was fidgeting with the stereo.

"Congratulations, Jenny," Robert said, holding up his glass, "I wish you and Peter all the best. Really, I do."

"I hope we'll always be friends. You mean so much to Peter." Jennifer said, her voice drifting.

"And he means a lot to me. I'm actually going to miss hanging around with the old boy. We go back a long way, you know. Had a lot of wild times. Has he told you?"

"Told me what?"

"There were a lot of women."

"Honestly, Robert, if I didn't know better I'd think you were trying to cause trouble." She laughed.

"Trouble is my middle name," he said, as he leaned in toward her face brushing her cheek with his.

She stepped back.

"Let's dance," he said, taking her hand.

"No, I don't want to dance."

"Aw, come on, Jen, what's a little dance? Besides you're going to be married in a couple days, this might be our only chance to tango."

"I don't know how to tango."

"I'll teach you. Here, have some more champagne."

Peter sat there like a voyeur, disgusted with himself for watching yet unable to move or take his eyes off the screen. He watched as his best friend and his fiancée began to move rhythmically around the floor of the apartment he'd once loved, where he had lived with such hope for the future.

He saw the shift in Jennifer — the exact moment when she had fallen under Robert's spell. Just then as Robert held Jennifer practically upside down, he took a moment to look up and wink at Peter through the hidden camera.

Peter moaned.

Knowing what happened next, and unable to watch as Robert seductively peeled off Jennifer's clothing, Peter sprang up and poured himself another brandy. He stayed beside the liquor cabinet to watch the next scene as if being farther away from the screen would make a difference. It did not. He watched as Robert and Jennifer made love.

Peter's back started to slide down the wall until his long legs finally folded to the floor. He crawled back to the sofa on all fours, tears were streaming down his face. He looked ahead at the screen again trying to focus through his tears. He gasped, then as if that sudden intake of oxygen had given him strength, he pulled himself up onto the sofa. Startled by his own crashing entrance onto the screen Peter watched this younger version of himself rush into the room. He remembered the pungent smell and the smack of betrayal that had overtaken him in that moment. He saw the horror in his own face through tear fogged glasses and wept while watching his own uncontrollable rage.

Through his sobs he heard Robert say to him on screen, "Hey, buddy. She's gonna make one hell of a wife."

That was it. That had been the precise moment which triggered the insanity when he had turned to attack Robert. Robert's laughter enraged him even further and so he had turned on Jennifer. He grabbed her by the neck, squeezing, strangling, and shaking her. In the final explosion of his fury he knocked her hard against the side of her head sending her body crashing into the glass table.

He had broken her neck.

It was all there, on the tape.

Peter took off his glasses to wipe away his tears, trying to escape the sounds of the hysterical scrambling coming from the television. On screen he was trying to bring Jennifer back to life, screaming and sobbing when he realized what he had done.

Peter took one last look then picked up the remote just as Robert was saying, "You've really gone and done it now buddy, but don't worry, I'm going to help you."

After that, Peter had followed Robert Whitman's instructions without question. And, as a result, he had saved himself. He was able to continue his work, but only with Robert's unyielding encouragement. It was Robert who had gotten him through the horror of what he had done. Robert was the reason why no one had ever asked him a single word about what had happened to Jennifer. Even though he knew that none of it would have happened if not for Robert, he could not help but feel indebted to him. He *had* saved his life.

And, of course, Robert was always there to remind him. Especially when he came to Peter with his first confession about his love for Eve. He had explained that his feelings were more than that of a father toward his daughter, he was so drawn to her that it was beyond his control. He needed Peter's help and he knew that Peter would understand. After all, Peter had been overcome with a force more powerful than himself before. Peter owed him but he had agreed only if Robert promised to stop.

Eve was seven then. It had taken Peter nearly two years to successfully repress Eve's trauma caused by the combination of her father's perverse attention and her mother's death.

He slumped further. He'd been afraid of his anger ever since it had taken Jennifer away. He'd managed to keep it buried until now. Now it would fuel him to do the right thing. This time he would be in control. Robert Whitman was finally going to learn what it was like to lose. Peter no longer cared about the consequences. Nothing mattered anymore, except that Eve survive this and they would both be free.

He walked straight to his study and pulled the stacks of duplicate files on Eve's case. He spent what was left of the night plowing through years and years of data, analysis and conclusions about her condition. He *had* been dedicated to her. Even though he was set up by Whitman, bound by the secrets they shared, Peter believed he'd been there for her.

Early morning sunlight was beginning to spill through the undraped windows of his study. He checked his watch, five-forty five had come fast. Peter took off his glasses and tossed them on top of the desk. He rubbed his eyes. He would call Sara, a colleague who specialized in trauma recovery. More importantly, she was his friend and confidante. When he realized it would be two-forty five in the morning in San Francisco he promised himself he'd phone later.

He arched back in his chair and gave his lean body a long stretch. He rose and headed upstairs for the shower. He was ready for the next step: a session with Bobbie at six-thirty. After that he would cancel his appointments for the day so he could figure out what to do next.

THE BRIGHTNESS OF THE EARLY MORNING LIGHT made Eve squint. She yanked the covers over her head and fell back onto her pillow still somewhere between sleep and wakefulness. She felt her eyelids closing, couldn't resist, they were being drawn down like tiny shades. Her mind told her to fight the temptation. Peter was expecting her. She threw back the covers and made herself sit up. Her long legs landed with a thud onto the floor. Mostly, she felt the same as when she was young, ready to rise and shine, except now her body was bigger. Lots of times she felt like a small girl trapped inside a big person's body.

When she was at work her mind took over and got the job done without her really knowing how. Even then sometimes she felt like a girl playing dress-up. Sitting on the side of her bed she looked outside at the promise of a lovely spring day. She delighted in the robins' return to her yard and she opened her window to listen more closely to their cheerful tunes.

That particular morning, though, the chirping began to disturb her. Strange emotions started to swirl at the center of her rib cage and upward. This sensation curled up through her heart, her throat, and into her eyes until tears were streaming down her face. She quickly closed the window tight and sat back down on the bed.

Eve vigorously rubbed the forefinger and thumb of her left hand together. A few minutes passed and then she got up and began to get ready for her visit to see Peter before a full day at the office.

When she remembered her appointment with Kyle Jordan, she hurried down the stairs, kissed her father on the cheek abruptly and raced out the front door without stopping for breakfast as usual.

WHEN EVE ARRIVED at the clinic precisely at six-thirty her eyes glittered. She had more grace and composure than Peter had ever seen in her.

"You're looking well, this morning," he said.

"Me, really? I slept well."

Peter was tempted to call off the session. Obviously, Bobbie was following his command to back off. Would it be better for Eve to let things go? To let her move through this in her own way? He thought of what Robert was doing to her, what he would continue to do.

Peter directed Eve into the sterile room; he needed to rely on the sodium amytal until he learned how to awaken Bobbie without the drug.

Eve did not question him, she only said, "I really don't need this today you know. I'm only doing it for you."

Peter smiled and nodded.

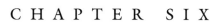

CHAPTER SIX

THE SESSION WAS MUCH BRIEFER than usual but Eve was glad to have an early start to the day. Most of Innis was still sleeping and she'd never felt more awake.

Something about the prospect of seeing Kyle again brought a whole new quality to her day. She felt as if someone had flipped a switch and turned a light on inside. She swung into an empty space in front of the Bread and Roses Café. Her stomach was tickling her, she needed to put something in it to quiet it down.

"Two chocolate croissants, please," she sang to the round lady with the rosy cheeks and the bun on top of her head.

That's funny, she thought, smiling even bigger. Eve bought a treat for Doris as well. She knew Doris was on a diet. Doris was always on a diet but she got one for her anyway. When she got to her office, she wrapped one of the croissants inside a napkin for Doris and left it on her desk.

After stepping into her office, she was pulled to the window by the golden strokes of early morning light. She sighed and watched the sailboats already skating across the harbor. They look so free, she thought. Suddenly she wanted to be somewhere else, someplace she'd never been. The happiness she'd been feeling slipped a notch...and then another. She let the friction between her thumb and forefinger ease the unproductive thoughts from her mind. She turned to her desk and sat down to face the business of the day.

An hour later, she heard the loud clopping of high heels in the outer office and then a squeal of delight. Doris must have found her surprise. Eve smiled, and looked up when she entered the room.

"Good morning. I made coffee," Eve said.

"Well, well. Coffee, croissants, a smiling lady on a pretty spring day," said Doris. "What have we here?"

Doris scratched her head and crunched up her face. She dropped her arm abruptly which caused her armful of bracelets to jingle. Moving closer to Eve, she tilted her head of long red curls and squinted at her.

Eve laughed.

"Doris Stanley, what has gotten into you? You know, you should be an actress."

"Are you feeling alright honey? I mean you look gorgeous, but do you feel okay?" Doris said, leaning onto the edge of the desk with both hands and frowning.

Ignoring her, Eve fumbled through her paperwork without looking up and said, "I'm fine. Don't I look fine? I've got a lot of work to do."

Then she looked up at Doris and smiled a little.

Doris put one hand on her hip, and waved the other one rapidly through the air as if she were swatting a bug.

"Oh, sweetie. Do I understand. He's in at one-thirty, you know. Make sure you eat some lunch," she said, pointing at Eve. "Thanks for my surprise," she said as she passed through the doorway.

Eve smiled again. Doris was barely out of sight when Eve's phone buzzed.

"Yes, Doris?"

"About this fine looking pastry, I mean, why don't I just tape it to my thighs? It's going to end up there anyway."

Doris let out a bright, lyrical laugh which penetrated Eve's heart like a beautiful sonata.

The morning passed quickly and at noontime Doris ordered them both chicken salad sandwiches on whole wheat bread. Doris always said how important it was to eat, and Eve went along with her this time.

At one o'clock Eve began to carefully prepare for her meeting with Kyle Jordan. She was looking forward to seeing him but this time she did not feel undone. She wanted to help him, and felt ready to do so: she knew it wouldn't be easy for him.

The documents were lined up on her desk in order of priority. Eve's mind wandered. She stared at the letter on her desk from Paul Jordan. How many times had she wished for such a letter from her mother? Something written just for her. Something that would have explained her death. She never talked to her father about it; he had always made it quite plain that she was never to bring it up.

The buzzing phone startled her. She reached for the intercom button and asked Doris to send Kyle in. She stayed in her chair and watched him walk toward her. He looked great in his navy blue, double-breasted blazer. He wore jeans and a crisp white t-shirt underneath, she liked that. She smiled as he moved closer.

Kyle grinned.

"Shall we get started?" Eve said.

"Please," Kyle said.

He cleared his throat and crossed his foot over his knee. He seemed relaxed; Eve knew she'd be all tied up inside. She picked up the envelope and carefully slid the silver letter opener into its corner. Kyle sat motionless as he watched her open the envelope. She pulled the letter carefully out and unfolded it. Her hands shook slightly. Leaning with both elbows on her desk she began to read.

"Dear Son,"

Eve glanced quickly up at Kyle who was already looking away. His eyes were glassy and hard. She continued:

> *"This is one of the most difficult things I've ever done, given the fact you've lived practically your whole life without a father. I'm not sure I can explain why or even if I want to. Instead, I'd just like to tell you a little about myself. I would've said these things to you myself if I'd had the courage. I suppose with death staring you down, you tend to get a little more clear. More certain about what's right and how to pull it off."*

Eve paused again to look at Kyle. When he did not acknowledge her she resumed reading.

> *"The first thing is, the day you were born was one of the best days of my life. You were screaming until your face was purple then when the nurse handed you over to me you went completely silent. We all thought something was wrong. But you just laid there in my arms, looking up at me like an old friend from long ago. I knew then the true meaning of love.*
> *"I cared about your mother. I would've liked nothing*

better than for the three of us to travel the world together. But she had her own ideas about what family meant and was too concerned about what people would think. She was a good woman, and she wanted what she thought was best for you. I thought she knew best. I stayed for as long as I could. Eleven years is a long time for a man to have his heart wrapped up in a place where it doesn't belong. I realized one day on my way home from work at the insurance company, that I was ready to explode. I knew I was no good to either of you if I was going to turn into a cranky old brute who blamed everyone else for my misery. I knew I had to go, that you'd both be better off without me. I hope I wasn't wrong. I hope I didn't fill you both up with hatred as I filled myself with peace."

Even though Eve was riveted to the page she was compelled to check on Kyle. He was staring off into a distant space. He waved his hand for her to continue.

"While you were young I tried to go back often to see how you were. Over the years I watched you grow. You just didn't know, it seemed better that way, less complicated and confusing for you as a boy. I saw you score the winning touchdown in the fall of your junior year, I was there when you beat the school record at the regional swim meet in your freshman year, I saw the way you looked at that little red-haired girl when you played the role of Puck in "A Midsummer Night's Dream." I think you were in eighth grade then. I've always had a subscription to the Greenfield Gazette, so I could keep up on the things

happening in your life.

"I'm proud of you Kyle. You've probably turned into a fine man. I lost track of you shortly after your mother died, I would have come then, to help you but I was in Morocco when it happened. I didn't find out until I was stateside again, almost two months later. Nobody knew where you'd gone. I was proud of the way you took care of your mother. I know I must have broken her heart especially as the years wore on. I guess she always thought I'd come back. But she made a choice, too. And if there's one thing I've learned about life, it's that everyone has their own choices to make. We're given opportunities along the way and whatever we choose determines our next possibilities.

"Your mother could have rebuilt her life. She chose not to. I hope if nothing else, you will forgive me for her choices. I hope you'll be able to let go of the anger you must feel toward me because of how your mother ended up.

"Life is full of possibilities, Kyle. It's all in how you look at it. I never did remarry but I was very much in love for a long time. She was an exquisite Tahitian woman named Jari. She understood me before we'd even said hello. She allowed me my freedom, and I always came back to her—."

"Why is he telling me all this bullshit? What gives him the right?"

Eve flinched. She cleared her throat and looked up gently.

Kyle sat back down.

"Shall I continue?" she said.

After a minute, he nodded.

"Once, upon my return from a longer than usual expedition through Tanzania, Jari greeted me with a tiny wiggling daughter. We named her Leia, after the island flowers. As Leia began to grow up, she and Jari started asking me to stay longer — which I did. My stays at home between trips grew longer and my excursions became shorter. Then one day, I joined a crew who were sailing north of the Society Islands, toward the Hawaiian Islands on a pearl expedition. It was such a successful journey that on the sail homeward I decided to settle down in Tahiti for good. I had planned to contact you, as you were finishing college that year, and ask you to come and meet your seven year-old sister.

"Things don't always work out the way we want, though. When we returned home, we found tremendous damage from a terrible wind storm which had set the isle on fire for three days and two nights. The village where Jari, Leia and I were living had burnt to oblivion. They were both dead. It took me six days of searching through charred remains of many people I had come to love before I finally found their bodies. I found out later that they had tried to save themselves but got trapped in the crossfire several miles from the village.

"I've always believed they were taken from me to repay a sort of karmic debt for leaving you. It can not be undone, not any of it. I learned to accept it with time, but I couldn't stay there. I wandered aimlessly for many years, until a sailboat delivery brought me here to Innis. I felt at peace here, so I stayed.

"Since you're reading this now, I'm gone. I have lived

well. I have been true to my own heart's longing and I believe that's the point of living. I hope you'll do the same with your own life, that you will listen carefully to your soul's urging and follow the path it beckons to you.

"Life is full of wonder, rich in possibility. I have always loved you, Kyle, in my own way I've walked beside you all the days of your life."

Eve looked up at him once more. Kyle held his head in his hand and when he looked back at her there were tears behind his eyes. She quickly returned to the letter.

"I do have one request," Eve read.

"For the past six years I have lived in a small apartment which overlooks the harbor. From there I've been with the sea even when I could no longer be on it. Miss Whitman has the address. I've collected artifacts from around the world but I've kept just a few. Aside from those, which are mostly of sentimental value, I haven't accumulated many possessions. My legacy to you comes in the shape of an eighty-foot schooner. You'll find it moored at the Windward Yacht Club, and again, Miss Whitman has all the details. The last time I tried to find you there was a rumor around Greenfield that you'd become 'just like your old man.' That you were drifting through life on a sailboat somewhere in the Caribbean. I hope it's true, that you not only know how to sail but that you love it as much as I have. The schooner is yours, it has a spirit that belongs to you.

"I would like you to sail my cremated remains back to Tahiti and scatter my ashes with Jari and Leia. I've left

*you navigational instructions and the information you'll
need once you reach Papeete. After that, you'll be on your
own. But if you listen closely, you'll always hear the whispers
of my smile surrounding you in love.*

"*Until we meet again, my son, live well and true.*

"*Signed Your Father,*

Paul Jason Jordan

February 29, 1996"

Eve had been so affected by the letter that when she looked up at Kyle and saw him buckle, something let go inside her, too. When he dropped his head into his hands and his shoulders shook she swallowed back her own tears. She stood up slowly watching the strength of his back heaving up and down. Seeing him cry so close to her made her heart full and heavy. She had never seen anyone cry like this. She knelt down beside his chair. She wanted to touch him. She gazed up at him, trying to see into his eyes. They were squeezed shut like a small boy might do. She placed her hand gently on his knee.

"That was a beautiful letter," she said.

He did not move but his breathing began to slow. Gradually he grew calmer. He looked down at her. When he saw the tears in her eyes, the gentle expression on her face, he let out a small sigh. He shifted in his chair and straightened his back.

Eve reached up and stroked his face. She felt plugged in, like all of her circuits were running for the first time in her life. Waves of energy pulsed through her. She trembled as if the years of Kyle's disappointment, anger and fear were her own.

Kyle lowered his cheek into her palm and brought his own hand on top of hers. When they looked into each other's eyes everything was changed. Something had happened between them, something sent and received, something electrical, instinctual and telepathic.

"I have to get out of here," Kyle said.

"Where are you going?" Eve said, her voice was tight.

"I don't know, anywhere. It doesn't matter," he said.

Eve glanced at her watch. It was three-thirty, the middle of a work day.

"Can I come with you," she said, moving back to her desk. "Do you want me to bring your father's keys?"

Kyle stared blankly at her.

"Listen, Eve, this is complicated." He swallowed.

She looked down at her desk.

"I'm engaged, I have commitments."

"How about tomorrow?" she said.

Kyle stood up without taking his eyes off her.

"I've got to go. Can I have the letter?"

"Of course," she said, lifting it as though it weighed a hundred pounds.

Kyle took the letter from her and turned to leave.

"I'll give you a buzz about the details," she said, as he began to walk away.

Eve was clearing her desk when he turned back to look at her. Feeling his eyes on her she felt submerged into a place too deep, like she didn't have the necessary breathing apparatus for such an abyss. Her movements were muffled and slow.

As he stood there staring at her, the pressure inside her head rose. She thought she would implode from a lack of oxygen.

He walked toward her and around the desk. He turned her to face him and held her close. She let out a small cry and a tear rolled down her cheek.

Eve thought she would die if he let go.

"You want to take a walk?" he said.

She nodded, sniffling.

They quietly said goodbye to Doris and stepped out of the office onto the peaceful streets of Innis. They walked toward the waterfront without speaking. Kyle reached his arm around Eve and pulled her tightly to his side. She looped her arm around his back and they walked together as if they had done this forever.

Eve thought the gallery and boutique owners were glaring at them through their windows. She saw expressions of surprise, and even shock, from the corner of her eye. It occurred to her that all those people had never seen her with any man other than her father. The thought worried her and the more she focused on it the more invasive the townspeople's gazes became.

Heads with huge eyes were surrounding her, floating in midair without bodies. They were closing in on her, filling up the space around her, taking away the very air she breathed. Her pulse began tapping inside her head. She tried to push the pesky noises away. She made tiny rapid circles with her thumb and forefinger.

Kyle stopped her. He took hold of her shoulders and turned her towards him. Eve felt all the eyes of Innis attach themselves to her. Panic washed across her face; her eyes darted left and right whenever someone passed by.

She felt Kyle squeeze her arms gently.

"Eve," he said, "what is it? Are you alright?"

Her green eyes stared up at him. She was rubbing her thumb and forefinger together frantically.

Kyle took her hand and pulled her away from the direction of the waterfront. He brought her to the parking lot of the small nearby Inn where he was staying. Standing beside the blue Ford rental car he unlocked the door and gestured for her to get in.

Eve gasped.

"I am so sorry. I don't know what came over me. This has been such an emotional day, the letter from your father, you and me, all those people staring at us like we're criminals. Maybe I should just go home. You have a lot to think about, you don't need me around making everything —."

"No," he interrupted.

Eve looked at him and tilted her head.

"No," he said. "Whatever it is, I'll help you."

Eve could not argue. She did not want to argue. The magnetic pull toward him was stronger than she was; she looked away.

Kyle leaned down and kissed her lips lightly.

Eve was lifted to a higher place, an exhilarating safe place, a place she'd never been before. She said nothing.

"Come on, get in," Kyle said.

They drove out of town and headed toward the beach. As they rode along the coastal route they passed by a blue and white sign that read: Windward Yacht Club. When Eve noticed Kyle's jaw flicker, she reached her hand over, timidly, and placed it on top of his. He slowed the car and looked at Eve.

"That's where his boat is?" he said.

"It's yours now," Eve said. "Do you want to see it? It's beautiful."

"No," he decided out loud. "I'm not ready for that."

They drove in silence until they reached the same stretch of beach that Peter had been on the night before. Kyle parked the car. They listened to the sounds of rolling waves and seagull's calls. The air between them was thin and jittery.

Kyle reached over and pulled her close.

"What was my father like?"

"I didn't have the chance to get to know him very well," she said.

"I would have liked to have known him."

Eve looked up at Kyle a little too quickly which broke something in him. Tears fell down his face.

Eve understood what it was like to long for something you could never have, and of the huge void created by that final, lost possibility. She turned his face to her so that their lips were almost touching.

"Kyle," she whispered.

Their lips collided and in that single kiss they each gave to the other the missing piece. They exchanged something so familiar it was like coming home. Eventually they dozed off, their limbs entangled like the twisted roots of an ancient sequoia tree.

The next morning when Eve opened her eyes there was a thin veil of early light, hovering misty white just above the beach. It moved and began rolling across the vast expanse of water. Her eyes traveled over the surface of the stillness of the sea until her gaze reached the horizon. She watched as a thin, dark line was drawn at the edge of the world where the water met the sky. It seemed to have appeared just for her, that line, as if to show her that there was indeed a separation between heaven and earth.

She did not move. She kept her head very still safely resting on Kyle's chest. For now, she thought, there is no separation and I will not move from here.

CHAPTER SEVEN

KYLE STARTLED EVE from her sacred moment when he awoke. He looked at her through sleepy eyes, then smiled and stretched.

"Let's take a walk," he said, after kissing her on the cheek.

They jumped out of the car and raced down to the water. The air was crisp and cut straight through their clothes. They ran together, farther down the beach to take the edge off the chill until Eve stopped suddenly. She turned to Kyle breathlessly and he wrapped his arms around her. They walked back to the car, arm in arm, pushing their bodies through the force of the swirling wind.

They slammed the doors shut and stared straight ahead with watery eyes and dripping noses.

"We should probably go," Kyle said.

Eve continued to look straight ahead, watching the churning of the sea.

"I know you don't want to. Something's bothering you that you don't want to face," he said.

Eve's chin protruded as she pursed her lips and a single tear rolled down her cheek. It stung. The wind had made her delicate skin raw.

She shrugged.

"I'm here," he said, and reached over to take her hand.

Eve grabbed his hand, lifting it to her face. She kissed his palm and held it tightly to her cheek.

"Come on," he said, "let's go find some breakfast."

Eve let his hand go slowly, hesitantly, as if sending a dove into flight for the first time after a mended wound. She sunk into the back of her seat, saddened by the release.

As they approached the entrance to the Windward Yacht Club, Kyle asked if there was a café inside, a place to grab a cup of coffee and a donut. Eve nodded and Kyle turned into the entrance. He cast a silly grin toward Eve which made her laugh. Instantly, she felt lifted. She slid closer to him.

"It's a brand new day, Ms. Whitman," he said, smiling. "And the good thing is, it's the weekend."

Eve had not considered what day or even what time it was. She had lost all sense of routine and its inherent restrictions. When Kyle reminded her, she was struck by the realization that she was always expected to be in a certain place at a certain time. Her father was waiting for her to join him in the breakfast room at that precise moment. A vise grip took hold, grabbing the back of her neck. She rubbed her finger together with her thumb slowly and rhythmically.

Kyle reached over and placed his hand on hers.

"Why do you do this?"

No one had ever asked her that question. And no one had ever given her the answer either. She looked at him blankly, her eyes blinking erratically.

Kyle pulled the car over to a full stop at the side of the road. He turned off the engine. He put his arm around her shoulder.

"You seem upset," he said.

She jerked her head back to escape his gaze.

"It's just that my father is expecting me for breakfast." She turned to look out the side window. "I haven't been home all night, he must be worried sick."

She turned back to Kyle with guilt rising in her throat. Her face must have shouted blame because he withdrew from her. She knew it wasn't his fault but her stomach twisted and she pulled farther away from him, leaning into the car door.

"Eve, you're a grown woman. Surely your father wants you to have your own life," Kyle said.

"Oh, no," she said, "not at all. Father wants me to be in his life. That's all he's ever wanted."

"Do you want me to take you home?"

"I think that would be best," Eve said.

"Alright. But I want you with me when I see the schooner for the first time. Can we meet later?"

Eve nodded quickly and looked away again.

Kyle pulled the car around. As they drove toward town he watched Eve inspecting herself in the passenger visor mirror. She fumbled through her purse for her brush and raked it through her hair. She carefully applied a thick layer of soft pink lipstick.

"You're beautiful," he said.

Eve ignored him and continued straightening herself and fidgeting with things inside her purse until they reached her office where her car had been left the night before. When Kyle stopped, she clapped her hands together.

"I'll see you later, then?" she said.

"How's two o'clock?" he said.

"Fine," Eve said, and quickly let herself out of the car. She bent down, flicked a glance across the front seat where they had just spent the last fourteen hours together and said, "Bye, now."

The car door slammed shut. Kyle was stunned for a moment. When he realized that Eve was standing by her car waving, he waved back and slowly pulled away. He circled around; on his way back he saw that Eve's car was still there. He drove around again, once, twice, three times until he saw Eve come out of her office wearing a complete change of clothing. He watched her hurry toward her car hanging back just far enough to be out of sight. He would follow her home to make sure she got there safely.

This is the good part of town, Kyle thought passing the lavish entrances to numerous estates as they wound around the immaculate tree lined road. Ahead, Eve's red brake lights shone. Slowing down, he watched her swerve into a driveway and disappear through two tall stone pillars. Kyle's heart fell. He knew her father's house was off limits. He also knew that Eve was a kind of prisoner to that place. He was uneasy, and felt he was being lured into dangerous territory.

He drove slowly past the iron gate. A faint, familiar voice said, *make a run for it, this thing's got disaster written all over it.* But he knew he could not leave her. He might be the only person who could save her. But, from what?

EVE SNUCK INTO THE FRONT DOOR. She crept up the spiral staircase and slipped into her bedroom. She was trying to take off her suit in a hurry even though it was fresh, the spare one she kept at the office, she knew she had to put on something more appropriate for a Saturday morning. Her hands shook so much that she had trouble with the buttons. She managed to get her skirt off and her blouse was half undone when her father came barging through the door. She gasped, yanking the sides of her blouse together.

"Eve," he said, firmly. "Where have you been? I've been waiting all night. You know I worry, couldn't you have phoned?"

Strangely, his voice sounded like a whining child. She lowered her head to keep from laughing then looked back at him, smirking. It was as if she was seeing her father through someone else's eyes. She felt giddy.

"You think this is funny?" he said. "I am at a total loss, Eve. I thought we had an understanding."

Eve felt uncontrollably high.

"I don't know what you're so upset about, Daddy. You'd think I'd just committed a murder or something."

She held his gaze with one hand on her hip. Her blouse had fallen loose revealing her white lace bra beneath. She watched as her father's good looks contorted, his face twitched. He shifted his weight, reached for the door knob for support and cleared his throat.

"Why don't you finish getting dressed, and come down to breakfast. We'll discuss this further then."

Eve marveled at the way he seemed helpless and flustered in her presence. As she undressed, she felt heat prickling her skin. She turned, gazing curiously at her body in the mirror. Strange fluids rushed through her veins; her heart was beating faster. Slowly she slid her hands up and over the surface of her thighs swaying her hips like a dancer. She touched the skin across her stomach and around her breasts with her fingertips. She tingled everywhere; tiny beads of moisture surfaced. How mysterious and delicious this strange sensation! She brought her eyes forward and even though she did not recognize the woman looking back at her, she liked her. She liked her very much.

Eve pulled on a pair of jeans and a tee shirt and bounced down the stairs to join her father. She smiled at him when she entered the sunny room and strode gracefully over to kiss his cheek.

Several minutes passed before her father spoke. When he did, his voice was shaking.

"Haven't I always been there for you?"

Eve nodded casually as she sipped her coffee.

"All through grade school, high school, college, even law school?"

"Yes, Father. What's your point?"

He looked at Eve abruptly.

"What has come over you? The Eve Whitman I know would never speak to me like that."

"Like what, exactly?"

"That — attitude... ."

"I'm just being honest, Daddy. Didn't you always tell me to be honest with you?"

"Where have you been?"

She swallowed hard. Eve looked at her father and then away again. With her head tilted slightly downward, she said, "I was with Kyle Jordan —."

"You spent the night with a man — My God, Eve, how could you —." He glared at Eve and when she looked back at him she saw his eyes fill with tears.

Eve dropped her fork with a clang onto her plate and fell back into her chair.

"I think I'm falling in love, Father. You need to face it. Did you really think I was going to live here with you, my whole life?"

Now the tears broke through her weak barrier. She sat crying silently for a moment and then got up and left the room.

All the air had escaped Robert Whitman's lungs. His chest had fallen, pulling his shoulders down. Suddenly, he lifted his chest and marched stiffly up the stairs. He headed straight for the secret cabinet where he kept his illegal supply of sodium amytal. He still had friends in Washington who owed him, they kept him supplied no questions asked. He removed a needle from its sterile packaging and inserted the tip into the plastic ampule. He clicked the liquid with the flat of his fingernail, smiling. He could not live without Eve, he had always known that.

He walked toward her door and knocked quietly. He put his ear to the door. She was sobbing. Her whimpering melted his heart. He knocked louder.

"Eve? I'm sorry I upset you. Can I come in?"

He opened the door and walked through. Eve was lying face down on her bed. He turned and locked the door before she could notice. He stepped carefully toward her like a lion going in for the kill. He sat down on the edge of her bed and began to rub her back. When Eve felt him apply the cool alcohol to her arm she rolled away quickly.

"It's just a shot of B-twelve, Eve. I thought you could use it. After all, you must be tired. Come, sit down over here."

"No, Father. I don't need that. Besides, I don't think Peter wants you to give it to me anymore."

"Peter?" he said, his voice rising. "What the hell has he got to do with this?"

"I just don't think he would, if he knew," she said. "He's my doctor, and it seems like he should know about any —."

"You are my daughter and you will do as I say," he said.

Eve's entire body went lax. Her face dropped and her eyelids closed halfway. She moved automatically over to her father and sat down beside him.

"That's my girl," he said, as he reapplied the alcohol with the cotton ball.

Eve flinched slightly as he inserted the sharp point of the needle into her vein. Almost immediately, she slouched backwards. Whitman caught her and laid her gently down upon the bed. He stood over her. Looking her body up and down, he trembled with anticipation. He rubbed his hands over his face several times before he spoke.

"Oh, Bobbie," he sang, "come out, come out, wherever you are."

Eve's body stirred, then stretched.

"Okay, Bobbie, open your eyes now. It's safe to come out."

She opened her eyes and moaned softly. She looked up at him with the cool detachment he loved.

"How hungry are we today?" she said, in her distinctive, throaty voice.

"We are very, very hungry today," Whitman said.

She extended her arms toward her father. He jumped onto the bed like an excited puppy.

Afterwards, he laid his head on Eve's breast and began to weep. She stroked his thick brown hair as she was supposed to.

He told her that he was deeply in love with her and that he could not exist without her.

"I guess that makes two of us," she said, blandly. "Without you, I'd be history, too."

IT WAS PRACTICALLY NOON when the constant chirping outside her window penetrated Eve's brain. The repetition of the cheerful robins calls grew louder and faster, faster and piercing, until the sounds became pesky like flies all around her. She tossed from side to side feeling irritated but unable to pull herself away from the dense sleep still holding her.

When Eve remembered her date with Kyle she jolted upright and reached for her alarm clock with a jerk.

Why was she sleeping half the day away? She began a fuzzy reconstruction of the earlier exchange with her father. Must have cried myself to sleep, she thought. She massaged her temples trying to erase the dull ache she felt there. She stood up feeling off balance but moved slowly into her bathroom. A shower would help her wake up.

She rubbed her hair dry with the towel then paused to listen to the robins' song. She sat down, very still, listening closely. A smile spread across her lips and she had the oddest sensation that her mother was sitting there beside her.

She thought of Kyle. She began rushing around her room. She needed to get out of this house. Without a word to anyone she fled down the stairs, jumped into her small white sports car and took off. Her breathing was hard and fast as though someone, or something, was chasing her. She was filled with fear, or was it excitement?

Once out of the gate, she felt high. She yanked on the top of her convertible — wanting more air, more space, more wind whipping through her hair. Once the top was down she laughed out loud. She laughed all the way into town not even caring that her hair would be a mess.

She brought the car to a sudden halt and leapt out. She cast a huge, brilliant smile at Kyle who stood leaning against his car. Her whole body was smiling. She plunged herself at him and he caught her firmly, his strength calming her slightly.

She pulled away, looked up at him and shoved the hair out of her face.

"I love you," she said. "I cannot exist without you."

Kyle gently took her face in his hands. The gesture had a kindness that lacked the passion she sought. She tried to pull free. When she could not she frowned at him. She squinted at him angrily. When he would not let her go, when he insisted that she quiet herself, she felt a surge of confusion and sadness envelope her. The more he held her in that manner, gently gazing into her eyes, the sadder she became until she began to cry.

Once Eve had released all that she could, Kyle lifted her chin and looked into her eyes.

"Somehow, it seems like you and I belong together," he said. "I know the feelings you have, I have them too. But we need to take things slowly. It's complicated. We need to get to know each other. I have a partner I've committed to and I'm not sure I want to give up all my plans. Things have been going pretty well for me lately... ."

Eve felt like he'd punched her in the stomach.

"All I'm saying is, let's take some time to think this through."

Eve nodded.

He took her by the hand and led her to the deli across the park. She held tightly to his hand, and didn't speak. Kyle bought some things for a picnic and from there they went into a grocery store for some other supplies to last a few days. While they shopped, Eve held onto his hand. They brought the bags to the car and drove to the Yacht Club in silence.

As they approached the marina, Kyle asked Eve for some help, where was his father's schooner moored?

"You can't miss it, it's called the *Kyle Jordan*," she said softly, then turned to smile at him.

"Hmm?" he said, raising his eyebrows.

"It's called the *Kyle Jordan* and it's one of the biggest boats here. Turn here, and head over to parking lot E."

Eve fished through her purse for the key.

"Your father brought me here once, in late winter, just a few weeks before he died," she said. "For some reason he wanted me to see the boat. I had to help him just to make it through the wind. He stopped when she was in sight, pointed and said, 'There's the mighty *Kyle Jordan*.'"

Kyle gave her a sad smile.

As they walked out onto the pier, Eve pointed. "Look, isn't it beautiful?"

"My God," he said.

They stood staring until the harbor master came out to find out who they were and what they were doing.

"I'm Kyle Jordan," Kyle said, as if he didn't really believe it himself.

"Are you now? Can I see some ID?" said the man with the thick white beard.

Kyle pulled out his wallet and showed him his driver's license. The harbor master held out a strong, friendly hand.

"Your father was a fine man. I'm sorry to hear of your loss," he said, shaking his head slowly. "They don't come any better than Paul Jordan. You're a lucky boy to have had a father like him and to have a ship like her." He nodded in the schooner's direction. "Name's Conner. Frank Conner. You just let me know if you need anything. Anything at all." He raised his furry eyebrows at Kyle and patted his shoulder firmly before turning to walk back down the pier.

"There is one thing, Mr. Conner," Kyle shouted after him, "who's been taking care of the boat?"

"Stop in my office after you've had a look around, I'll answer all your questions," he yelled back.

Eve tugged on Kyle's elbow and they walked closer to the schooner. Kyle's eyes grew wider with every step. When they reached the boat, he stopped then walked the full length to the bow. He studied the *Kyle Jordan*, the elegant line from bow to stern and up the tall wooden masts. She was built in the tradition of a New England clipper, he explained to Eve, rigged for speed. Eve stood patiently at his side. After a while he turned to her, his eyes were still and clear, and so blue.

Eve reached up to stroke his face.

Kyle took her arm and pulled her close to him.

"I'm not ready to go aboard. I'd like to see the paperwork first. Do you have that?"

"Everything's at your father's apartment, along with the instructions for Tahiti."

Kyle stepped back quickly wiping tears from his face.

"Want to go there instead?" Eve asked.

"Yeah," he said. "I need to get past this thing. Let's go and we'll fix some lunch. I'm starving."

They wrapped their arms around each other and slowly walked down the pier. When they were at the end, Kyle looked back at the schooner once more. He turned to Eve with a boyish grin and she lifted herself up onto her toes and met his lips with a kiss.

EVE DIRECTED KYLE to his father's apartment. She explained to him that the rent was paid through the end of the month so that he might consider staying there until then. It would give him three weeks, she said, time enough to solidify his plans. Kyle shrugged, as they pulled into the small resident parking lot of a large white Victorian mansion with wrapping porches and several doors.

Eve searched for the keys to Apartment #6.

"Park here," she said, pointing to the spot labeled #6, "he's around back."

Kyle frowned at her.

"No, he's not," he said. There was a sharp edge to his voice. "He's dead. My father's dead."

Eve looked at him, her eyes searching.

"I'm sorry —," she said.

"No, don't apologize. I'm sorry. I guess I just needed to say it out loud. I keep expecting to meet him face-to-face, you know?"

Eve looked at him blankly.

"Forget it," he said, "let's go up."

They each grabbed a bag of groceries and Eve led the way up the back stairway to the second floor apartment with the wrought iron number six on the door. She placed the key inside the lock and pushed the door open. They stepped into a clean, charming kitchen. It had white cabinets with glass doors and an antique oak pedestal table with four ladder back chairs around it.

Kyle walked into the room slowly and set the groceries down onto the counter. Turning around in a circle, he tried to take in the simple comfort of what had been his father's home. He breathed in the smell of spiced tobacco and saw the blackened pipe tipped up in an ashtray on the counter by the sink. He hadn't known his father smoked a pipe. He felt like an intruder in a stranger's home, like a thief who had no right to be there.

"Why don't you have a look around, while I put these things away?" Eve said.

Kyle stepped out of the kitchen which brought him into another room, out of Eve's sight. How similar their tastes were. The room, the furniture and artwork was familiar and comfortable. He moved to the darkened windows and pulled the drapes opened to reveal french glass doors leading out onto a small deck overlooking the harbor.

He imagined his father sitting in this room, night after night, alone, watching the sun disappear below the horizon. What would he think of as he watched the ripple of the water, the shifting of the sky? Would he think of him? Of the Tahitian woman he had loved? Of his daughter who had died much too young? Would he be sad, as he looked back on his life? He must have been lonely in his final days.

Kyle sat down at his father's writing table. It was a fine old table with two small drawers and strong, sturdy legs. This table must reflect him, Kyle thought. Simple, strong, scarred. He looked out at the boats in the harbor; a strange quiet came over him, the way water washes everything clean. Yes, he decided, it will be good to stay here.

Eve brushed his shoulder and handed him a glass of wine.

"Perfect," he said, and smiled up at her.

He pulled her onto his lap and they sat at his father's desk talking quietly and sipping wine until the sun had hidden all its rays and they were alone, together, in the darkness.

C H A P T E R   E I G H T

PETER WAS GOING to tell Sara everything. The problem with Eve was too big to handle alone and Sara Daniels was the only person on earth he trusted. He'd met her at a conference in Zurich fifteen years ago; they had been close friends ever since.

Peter had always thought that Sara shared an uncanny resemblance to Eve's mother, Carolyn. Same build, same dark eyes and pouty mouth. He had never told her though, always careful not to expose his own role in the Whitman family tragedy. Things were different now, though.

He waited on the balcony of his penthouse staring at the harbor while someone at the *Sexual Trauma Center of San Francisco* paged Dr. Sara Daniels. It was Saturday but Peter knew where to find her. For Sara, work was life.

"Dr. Daniels, here," Sara said.

"Yes, Doctor. This is Dr. Peter Weiss calling from Innis, Connecticut —."

"Peter! What a nice surprise. How are you?"

"I'm okay. How're you?"

"Crazy, as usual. What's up?"

"I need your help."

"Wait a minute, let me get to my office, okay?"

"Sure."

"Peter?"

"Sara, it's good to hear your voice."

"Why don't I like the sound of yours?" Sara said. Peter pictured her dark eyes scowling.

"Have you got some time? It's a long story," Peter said, hopefully.

"I can give you about twenty minutes, how's that?"

"It's a start. I'll try to condense things," he said.

Peter rubbed his forehead as he decided where to begin. He had discussed Eve's case with Sara over the years, but only peripherally.

"Do you recall a long-term case of mine about an incest survivor whose mother died when she was a child?"

"Yes, vaguely."

"I believe she's headed for a breakdown. I've just discovered she's coping with a pretty dramatic dissociative disorder."

"How long have you been treating her?"

"Since her mother died. Twenty-two years."

"Jesus, Peter. And you just found out?"

"It's complicated," Peter said, clearing his throat. "Her father created a sort of alter ego using hypnosis, I suspect he relies on sodium amytal to keep this other self hidden and that he can call her out at will."

"Wait a minute, that's not dissociative, that's criminal. Wasn't he a friend of yours?"

"A long time ago."

"So, he's still abusing his daughter. Is that what you're telling me?"

"Yes—." Peter's breath quickened, his jaw clenched. Speaking of this aloud made his heart beat out of control.

"Okay, Peter. I'm coming out there," Sara said, firmly. "I'll have to clear my schedule, it might take a few days. Can you hang in there?"

"Are you sure?"

"You're kidding. In all the years we've known each other, how many times have you been there for me? The one time you ask for my help, you think I'm going to wish you good luck and have a nice day? I'm coming. I'll let you know when, as soon as I can."

"Thanks."

"No you don't. Hey, by the way, I've been meaning to call you. I went to this amazing lecture a couple of weeks ago on using music in the healing process. The man was a genius, and guess what? He lives in your town. Can you believe that? I went up to speak with him afterward and he said he'd just moved out east about a month earlier. When I asked him where, he said, Innis. It blew my mind."

"What's his name?"

"Justin Templeten, with three e's. Maybe you should look him up. His theory is fascinating and he's had phenomenal results with trauma victims. It's borderline new age stuff but, hey, if it works, right?"

Peter smiled. He had always admired Sara's endless energy for healing. They agreed to talk again the next day. When Peter hung up the phone he felt an unbearable weight had been lifted. Sara was known for her success with incest recovery and he thought Eve would relate to her well. *Why did that man's name sound so familiar?*

He went inside to change. He would take a long run and try to chase away the constant jitters that were keeping him from eating lately. Then it would be time to get ready for the annual "Whitman's Way" dinner. He did not want to go but Peter knew if he wasn't there the Judge would be on his case immediately. He needed to keep things stable between them. At least, for a while longer.

ROBERT WHITMAN WAS YANKING on his black tuxedo jacket. *It's the annual country club gala, goddamn it. Where the hell is Eve?* He paced back and forth in front of his bedroom windows. This was the most important event of the year, she knew that. Without it, much of the funds raised to clean up Innis would never have been there. Ten years ago he started this, not once had he ever attended without Eve.

He had paced for over an hour waiting for the shining of her headlights up the drive. As each minute passed and she did not appear his posture fell forward from the gravity of his heart. He glimpsed himself in the mirror, he looked shorter.

He stiffened upright as his thoughts landed on Peter Weiss. After all, he thought, this is not Eve's fault. Not at all. Peter was to blame for the fact that something was wrong. He hadn't been paying the proper attention. Robert rubbed his hands together as his pace quickened and his steps widened. He felt better now that he had a target. He tossed the unwanted feelings aside. Instead, he tapped the well of anger deep within him. He could always rely on that. He let the familiar fury simmer and brew and thicken. This was the potion that gave him his courage and strength.

Robert glanced at his watch one last time and knew he had to leave. He had to keep up appearances for the community. After all, they depended on his leadership and his money. He picked up the phone near his bed and told his driver to bring the car around. He checked his image in the mirror. He clicked his tongue inside his mouth and pointed a finger at his reflection as if drawing a gun. Still handsome and charming; he was in the mood to flirt tonight. Perhaps he'd even remind Peter of Jennifer, his long lost love. He laughed aloud as he walked through the door.

"You're looking well tonight, Judge," said the tall, lanky driver. He held open the rear passenger door to the black sedan.

"Thank you, Stevens. I feel good, too. Not bad for an old guy, not bad at all."

The Judge laughed and Stevens laughed along with him. They rode in silence until the driver looked into his rear view mirror.

"Another Whitman's Way dinner, sir? Expect to raise a lot of money again this year?"

"Oh, I suspect so, Stevens. It gets better every year. You know how it works with this crowd, it's a contest to see who can be the greatest philanthropist. All they really care about is getting their names on a plaque, nailed to a wall somewhere."

The Judge looked out the side window as he spoke. He studied a faint reflection of himself. Robert had always thought of himself as immortal, like nothing could touch him. Nothing ever had. Tonight a hint of doubt clouded his face. Something about the way his mouth went soft, his eyes distant.

He was a self-made billionaire. He had created his world by controlling the people around him and going after everything he had ever wanted. He ground his teeth together and felt his chest tighten. He would find Peter Weiss immediately after the required social pleasantries and hold him accountable for Eve's conspicuous absence.

"Here we are Judge," Stevens announced as they pulled up to the elaborate entrance of the Innis Country Club Ballroom.

Robert waited for the driver to open his door. He stepped out of the car like a celebrity. This was his show, he was always the center of attention with the members of the upper class of Innis. He bowed his head to several lovely ladies and shook hands with many of the town's fathers, smiling broadly. They all asked for Eve.

Smiling still, he climbed the grand entrance to the ballroom glancing briefly at the small plaque on the wall by the door which read, "The Whitman Ballroom ~ Generously donated by Judge Robert Whitman in honor of his beloved daughter Eve." There was a strange, metallic taste in his mouth.

When he finally spotted Peter, Robert noted that little had changed from the old days. They were still the most sought after bachelors in town. He mused over the fun they used to have together, the women, the power. He snuck up behind Peter holding his finger to his lips so that the circle of elegantly dressed social climbers would not let on that he was encroaching.

Peter shivered from the sudden whispering in his ear from behind him. He whiffed Robert's cologne.

"You son of a bitch. You owe me one hell of an explanation. Eve is out — God only knows where right now — and you'd better know why. You'd best have a plan to put a stop to this. Now which one of these beauties is mine?"

Peter grinned at the admiring women as though the Judge were telling him a joke. Of course, they did not know the real Robert Whitman and chances were, they never would. Sometimes, he knew, the power of public image could become so ensconced in people's minds that when faced with the truth they simply refused to see. It might reflect them, somehow. They might be viewed by others as guilty by association. It was far easier, far less risky to look the other way.

Peter played along.

"Ahh," he said, "if it isn't the esteemed Judge Whitman."

He bowed down to Whitman like a servant to a king. The small circle of women giggled. Each of them nervously touched their hair and fixed their dresses, hoping to be noticed by the wealthy and still handsome — not to mention, available — Judge Robert Whitman.

Whitman returned a dignified bow to Peter then turned to face the ladies.

"Mmm. What have we here, Doctor?" Robert said. "I do believe this is the finest collection of Innis ladies I have ever had the pleasure to be near."

"Indeed," said Peter, who knew this game well. "Do you know everyone?"

He began to make the introductions clockwise around the small circle until the Judge became fixated on a young girl with a striking resemblance to the one woman Peter had ever loved.

"Jennifer?" Robert said, rather loudly. "How delightful."

Peter's skin ignited. The similarities to the past were excruciating. Peter, himself, had been basking in the young woman's presence who reminded him of his lost love. But hearing Robert say her name made his knees go weak. His eyes stung from standing too close to the flame. He politely excused himself saying there was someone with whom he must have a word. The woman named Jennifer was smiling at the Judge's blatant flirtation but Peter could feel her eyes follow him as he walked away.

"Don't worry sweetheart, he'll be back," Robert said, loud enough for Peter to hear.

"PETER, MY FRIEND," Robert said, boisterously, "what brings you out here, all alone, when such loveliness awaits you within?"

The people on the balcony turned and smiled. They cooed with adoration for the Judge. Peter smiled enough for everyone to see there was nothing wrong. Pulled by the beauty of the star-filled sky, he had wanted to appreciate its wonder, to enjoy a breath of fresh air, that was all. Satisfied, the others on the balcony returned to their discussions of local politics and the latest research on anti-aging remedies.

Peter and Robert kept their voices low. They covered the content of their words with an occasional grin or an affectionate gesture. It was a technique they'd both mastered long ago. Never let them see you nervous or agitated in any way. That had been their credo. Words to live by, tools for modern living they used to joke.

"What the hell is going on? What's happening to Eve?" Robert said, breathlessly.

Seeing this lack of control gave Peter a sense of being on top, he decided to play his advantage. He knew that Robert would never allow a confrontation to occur openly between them, especially not on this night.

"You would know, Robert. I mean, about being out of control." Peter smirked.

"What the hell is that supposed to mean?"

Peter eyed Robert, watching as he carefully and methodically regained his composure.

"I need to know what's happening to Eve, Peter. Haven't you sensed that the treatments are losing their effectiveness? I'm afraid she's heading for some kind of breakdown."

Peter leaned casually against the rail.

"Are you aware that she's spending a considerable amount of time with this Jordan guy? He's a fucking sailor, Peter. We don't know a thing about him. He's probably just after her money." Robert smiled, turning to face the others on the balcony.

Peter sipped his wine slowly as he considered his response. He couldn't let Robert suspect that he knew about Bobbie.

"I understand your concerns," Peter said, finally. "But perhaps it's time to let Eve make some of her own choices, her own mistakes."

"That's not your decision," Robert said. "If and when I think Eve is capable of making her own choices without risk, I will say so. Until then, you will do as I say. Or, have you forgotten —."

Peter held up his hand.

"This is your night, Robert," he said, raising his chin to the festivities inside. "Why don't you go in there and step into that spotlight you love so well. Put on your charming mask and have some fun. We'll find a more appropriate time to discuss this. Besides, people are beginning to stare."

Peter knew those last words would pull the Judge away from his attempted interrogation. Whitman turned to see several clusters of people looking their way. He smiled at them again and turned back to Peter.

"Fine. But I want to hear what you're going to do about this situation *tonight*. I'll meet you at the clinic later. One o'clock."

The Judge let out a noisy laugh and clapped Peter on the back. Holding his arm there, he turned Peter around and forced him back into the ballroom.

"I wonder if that cute little Jennifer with the nice round tits is as hot as your Jenny was." Whitman said. They smiled and nodded at the crowd as they walked in. "What do you think, Peter? Shall we find out? You and me — two on one."

"Fuck you, Robert," Peter said, smiling, then turned away from him to find his way to the bar.

Peter stayed as long as he had to and not a moment longer. He watched the Judge from a distance. He knew Robert was on edge, even though the others didn't. Robert Whitman would be attractive to a group like the CIA, he thought, he was a master at concealing himself.

It was time to turn the tables on the Honorable Judge Robert Whitman. Adrenaline pumped forcefully through his veins while Peter waited for the valet to bring his car around. He felt twenty years younger.

When he reached the clinic, he called the chief orderly. The large black man loped into his office.

"Good evening, Caldecott, I've got a serious situation that must be handled tonight. Who's on staff in the men's ward?"

Dr. Weiss nodded with a small frown as the chief orderly listed the on-duty staff. All good, strong men, he thought, which is what he would need to hold down the venerable Robert Whitman.

"Here's the situation," Peter said. "Are you familiar with my business partner, Judge Robert Whitman?"

The orderly nodded affirmatively.

"Good. Apparently, he was involved with a top secret governmental operation and is suffering some strain as a result. The government has contacted me and asked that he be detained for observation. I am expecting him here this evening — at one o'clock."

He paused for confirmation from the orderly.

"I'll need you and your men to detain the Judge, in the usual way, the moment he steps through the door. It will be a shock to him, so you must be fully prepared. And keep in mind, he's had professional training in the martial arts."

The orderly nodded again, this time more slowly.

"Please understand that Judge Whitman has done nothing wrong. In fact, he's considered a hero by the Central Intelligence Agency. This action is being taken for his own good, for his health and sanity. Do you understand?"

"Yes sir," Caldecott said.

"Good, prepare your staff. Report back to me at exactly twelve-thirty." When the orderly was half-way out the door, he said, "Oh, and Caldecott?"

Caldecott turned back.

"Yes, Doctor?"

"I don't need to tell you that this must be kept confidential. If any of this leaks out of this clinic, you will all be dismissed immediately."

"Yes, sir."

As Peter watched the orderly pass by his hall window he was confident that he would be able to pull this off. He glanced at his watch. Eleven o'clock. He had enough time to prepare mentally for the hypnosis session he planned to do with Robert. He had done considerable research on patients who were resistant to hypnosis as he suspected Robert would be.

Over the years he had achieved a one-hundred percent success ratio in overcoming such resistance. His technique had never been published, he'd been afraid it would be used by the wrong people, someone like Robert Whitman.

Peter had stumbled onto the key to unlocking the subconscious mind accidentally. His discovery had involved a teenage boy who had been sexually abused by his grandfather between the ages of four and ten. The damage this abuse had caused the boy seemed irreparable; he alternated between extreme aggression and total withdrawal. He was a deeply wounded soul who had lost all ability to connect with anyone or anything outside of himself.

The boy was in Peter's office for a regular session one day when he noticed the portable recording device that Peter used for quick annotations on patient therapy. Peter also used the device to listen to lectures and classical music while on his daily run. That day, the headphones were still attached and the boy was intrigued. Since Peter had made no inroads with him, he was willing to try anything. Peter showed him how the headphones went around his head and covered his ears. He pushed the button to start the music. It was Brahms that day, the orchestrated version of one of the *Haydn Variations,* known as *The Tragic.*

Within minutes every muscle in the boy's body had gone limp. He fell back into his chair. At first his eyes glazed over and then he slowly closed them. Peter watched as waves of emotion swept through the boy. Single tears came down at first, then a steady stream of tears washed over his face. The whole time his eyes were gently closed. Eventually the boy was sobbing uncontrollably.

It was a turning point for Peter and for his patient. Brahms' masterful chords had succeeded in unlocking a world of pent-up emotion within the boy where Peter had failed. For the young boy it was the beginning of his recovery. For Peter it was the beginning of a whole new area of research.

He conducted a series of experiments regarding the effects of various musical tones upon the human psyche. The real breakthrough had come when Peter began to experiment with combining the force of music with the power of hypnosis. Through these experiments Peter had learned that blocks to wholeness required a simultaneous healing of mind and spirit, that the two needed to be unified in order for a person to cope successfully with the physical demands of living. And that for people who had suffered the trauma of abuse a mending of the spirit could be significantly enhanced through music.

The specific kind of music was unique to the individual — no single piece of music had the same effect on any two people. Peter theorized that each person carried their own vibrational frequency and that musical chords could be either in harmony or disharmony with that individual's own rhythms. Finding a method to determine a person's frequency had tremendous healing potential but it was also potentially dangerous.

Peter had worked secretly with a musician and an inventor to devise a piece of equipment which translated a person's frequency into a somewhat crude piece of music. Through the study of this output Peter had been successful in matching certain styles of music with a specific patient's vibrational makeup. By accessing the unknown metaphysical self, and by simultaneously guiding the patient's mind to verbally release painful traumatic memories during hypnosis, he had achieved some stunning results.

Peter thought of the man Sara had mentioned on the phone but that would have to wait. He needed to stay focused.

He suspected that Robert had suffered some type of emotional childhood trauma which he had succeeded in repressing. Robert's drive for public approval was so strong, Peter theorized that it had taken on a separate identity that overrode his internal, injured one.

As the time drew nearer, Peter's conviction to unleash Robert's need to control his daughter grew absolute. He knew it was only half the equation required to heal Eve — her response to the truth about her father was a wild card — but this was an important piece of the solution, nonetheless.

The sound of footsteps resonated down the hallway. He put away his files leaving out only a single pad of paper with encoded notes. The clop of hard-soled shoes making contact with the linoleum ceased and there was a knock at the door.

"Yes, come in," he said.

The door swung open and standing there, a half-hour early, was Robert Whitman.

"Robert. You're early."

"Don't look so surprised. Am I interrupting something?" he said, looking around.

"No, not really. I was just reviewing some patient files. You know me, always the work to keep me going."

"Yes, that's true about you, Peter," he said, taking both hands and slowly rubbing them repeatedly through his hair. Still standing, he shifted his weight from one foot to the other. He paced back and forth in front of Peter's desk. Now he rubbed his eyes continuously with one hand while the other hand was buried deeply inside the pocket of his tuxedo trousers.

Peter glimpsed his old friend from long ago.

"What is it Robert? Did something happen?" he said.

Robert stood still. His back was turned slightly away from Peter. His shoulders, slumped downward. He moved slowly toward the chair and collapsed into it then looked up at Peter through clouded eyes.

"What did happen, Peter?" Robert said, slurring. "I was hoping you could tell me. I feel like I can't —." He dropped his head into his hands.

Another knock upon the door.

Peter stood up quickly and went to the door.

"Yes, Caldecott? What is it? I'm with Judge Whitman right now...is this urgent?"

"Yes, Doctor, sorry to disturb you but we have an extremely agitated patient in twenty-four."

Peter paused.

"Right," he said. "Robert? Can you excuse me? I'll be back as soon as I can."

"That's fine, Peter, go. Take care of your patient. I'll be here."

As Peter went out of the office and closed the door he felt a blow to his stomach. His resolve had weakened. But the wheels had been set in motion. He had no choice now but to follow through. Besides, he reassured himself, he was doing the right thing.

When they were far enough down the hallway, Peter turned to face the orderly.

"Doctor, I apologize," Caldecott was saying, "he must have come in the side door and we weren't prepared for him until one."

"I know, Caldecott. It's not your fault," Peter said. "We have to move quickly. Follow me into the lab where I'll give you the injection solution. Alert your staff and go immediately to my office. Judge Whitman has been drinking. I'm sure he'll put up a fight but he may not be able to sustain it. You'll need to inject him as soon as possible, whether you do it before the straitjacket has been secured or after — I'll leave that to your good judgement. Once he's fully sedated set him up in my private session room. Be sure to lock the door when you leave. I'll be back in forty-five minutes."

They walked briskly down another hallway toward the laboratory.

"You mean you won't be here?"

"Nothing will go wrong, Caldecott. I have complete faith in you. Just view it as another detainment procedure."

"But, sir, it's Judge Whitman...what if he remembers who did this to him?"

Peter turned toward the orderly outside the laboratory door.

"Joe," he said, calmly, "the government is relying on our help. That's all you need to know. Make sure your men understand the importance of this procedure. Focus, Joe. There's no room for doubt here."

The orderly did as he was instructed without another word. He took the injection solution from Peter and moved quickly to gather the others.

Once he had left the room, Peter felt ripples of nausea wave through him. What he was doing was illegal, unethical. Whitman could easily pull strings. Peter's license could be revoked. Worse, he might spend the rest of his life in prison.

Peter walked past the front desk guard.

"Need some air, be back shortly," he said.

He passed through the outer glass doors feeling time slow. Outside, he breathed deeply. Keep walking, keep moving, one foot in front of the other. He couldn't feel his feet hit the ground.

Twenty minutes later the fog created by his own fear began to lift. He reconstructed the steps of the plan he had so carefully and thoughtfully prepared. He turned to retrace his steps to the clinic, back to the softly-lit room where Robert lay helpless on a rust velvet couch. It was a chance to set things right, he told himself. An opportunity to replace pathology with wholeness. A way to finally help Eve wake up.

CHAPTER NINE

AS PETER WALKED down the long corridor toward his office he glanced nervously at his watch. One-thirty A.M. The clinic was quiet, surreal. He felt the slow, heavy breath of sleep all around him. He stopped, took off his glasses and was rubbing his eyes when Caldecott startled him.

"Dr. Weiss. Everything alright?"

Peter straightened. "Mmm, fine. How's our patient?"

"Smooth as silk sir. When we got in there, the Judge was passed right out in the chair. We slipped him the injection, before he even knew what hit him, he was out again. He's in your anteroom."

"He didn't put up a struggle?" Peter said, wanting to linger in the hall rather than face the next two hours.

"Doc, there were four of us. He was pretty out of it, kept calling out for someone named Evelyn."

"Evelyn? Are you sure?"

"Absolutely. He was practically shouting it."

"Did he say anything else?"

"No, that's it: Evelyn."

"Thank you," he said, frowning. "Good work."

Peter unlocked the door to his office. He walked slowly through and then into the session room. He pinned his eyes on Robert who lay flat and still. The straitjacket was wrapped tightly around his torso. Peter winced. How many times had he worked with patients in jackets? It was for their own good but he'd never been struck so hard by the humiliation, the degradation of being trapped inside your own body. The jacket on Robert was pathetic; Peter inhaled deeply.

He cleared his throat.

The Judge's foot flinched.

"Now, Robert," he said, in his most soothing tone of voice, "we're going to take a little trip together. Can you hear me?"

Robert nodded.

"Let's go back to a time when you were a child, tell me where you are. What do you see around you as a boy of ten years old?" Peter leaned in, resting his elbows on his knees.

"Oh, boy," Robert said, in a young boy's voice. "She's at it again." His head wagged back and forth.

"Who's at it? And what's she doing?" Peter said, his heart was beating too fast.

"That woman who calls herself my mother. I don't know how I ever got stuck with a mother like her. She's disgusting. Sex, sex, sex. That's all she ever thinks about, and she doesn't even try to hide it. I'm getting out of here soon as I can."

"Who's your mother with?"

"Who knows? I can't keep track. Makes me want to puke."

"Why do you think she does it?"

"Says she has to do it. Says she has no choice. Times are tough, Dad died in the war, gotta put food on the table. A person always has a choice, that's what my Dad used to say. She's no good. Just a whore."

"What's your mother's name?"

"Eva."

Peter paused. Eve, Eva, Evelyn.

"Let's move forward in time now Robert. You're older now, you've gotten out, away from your mother. Where are you?"

"This place sucks," Robert said. His face grimaced in disgust; he was spitting out his words. "I swear, some day I'm going to own these bastards. They think they can control me my whole life, they've got another thing coming."

"Where are you?"

"I'm in hell, is where. They keep us in the basement like fucking rats."

"Who does?"

"Top secret. We're being trained to do the government's dirty work."

This is it, Peter thought. "Why you? How did you get there?"

"Because I'm smart, for one."

There was a long pause while Peter thought about how to get at this.
"How did you end up there?"

"I had an accident, alright? Nobody's goddamned perfect."

"What did you do wrong?"

"I didn't say it was wrong — it just happened is all. I couldn't take it. Got so mad, I killed her."

Robert's tone of voice was matter-of-fact. Not a trace of remorse.

"You killed your mother?" Peter said, falling back into his chair.

"That's right."

"And then what happened? Didn't you have to go to jail?"

"No," Robert laughed, amused by Peter's naiveté, "doesn't matter what you do, as long as you're smart — and you know people. You gotta know people who'll get you off the hook."

"Who got you off the hook?"

"After it happened, these men showed up. Nice suits, slick hair, the whole bit. They asked me if I wanted a second chance. I ask, what's it gonna cost? They think this is funny, they tell me they like me, ask if I'll take some tests. I shrug, ask if I got a choice. They say sure, take the test or spend four years in a juvenile home and ten-to-twenty in prison."

"So you had a choice, and you chose the tests?"

"Right, a person's always got a choice."

"You chose to kill your mother."

"I like to think I set her free. I'm sure she's a lot happier now."

Move on quickly, Peter thought. Don't let this sink in too deep.

"Tell me about the tests. What were they about?"

"Different things, IQ, physical fitness, emotional stability."

"So you passed these tests... ."

"Beat out everybody."

"Now what? What are you doing now?"

"I'm going bananas, is what. If I don't get outta here soon, I'll lose it."

"What do you do there?" Peter said, leaning in again, studying Robert's face.

"We learn things. All day, practically all night. The food's real good, that's one good thing."

"What are you learning?"

"I'm learning Korean, and martial arts. I've already finished college and I'm not even eighteen."

"How long have you been there?"

"Three years, but my time's coming. I can feel it."

"Then what will you do?"

Robert shrugged casually.

"You don't know?"

"They don't tell you, but obviously I'm headed for Korea."

"Are you afraid?"

"What's there to be scared of? I can do anything."

"How old are you?"

"Seventeen."

Peter sat back heavily in his chair. His body was dense, weight had filled his limbs and heart making it hard for him to breathe. The only part of him that felt alive were his eyes which drifted from the lamp over to Robert, from the drapes to Robert, the carpet, Robert. His mouth was getting dry. He was sinking too deep when Robert's leg jerked. The drug was wearing off; he would be awake soon. Robert coughed and Peter quickly left the room. He called Caldecott telling him to sedate the Judge and move him into a private, maximum security room.

He made notes about the session, he wrote Eve, Eva, Evelyn...over and over. He planned to take things slowly. Peter had to cover his tracks; people would be suspicious about Robert's disappearance. It was Sunday — that would buy a little time.

Once Robert was safely locked away and sleeping soundly, Peter left the clinic and went home to get some sleep of his own. Two hours later he was jolted awake by the telephone.

"Peter, is that you?"

"Yes, Eve, what is it?"

"It's Father, he didn't come home last night. Did you see him?"

Peter cleared his throat and raised his torso onto his elbow for support.

"Last night was the Whitman's Way Gala," he said. "He was having a pretty good time, maybe he met someone."

"Oh, no," she heaved. "I completely forgot. Oh my God, Father must have been devastated. What did he say?"

"Calm down, everything's fine. He mentioned he was worried about you but he's fine. What about you? You alright?"

Peter waited.

"Eve? Are you there?"

"Yes, I'm here," she said. "I'm sorry to bother you. Go back to sleep."

"Are you okay? Do you want to talk about it? Come for coffee, I'll—."

"No, Peter. I'm fine, really. I have to go now."

Peter moaned as he lay in bed still propped up by his elbow with the dial tone buzzing in his ear.

EVE SLOWLY PLACED THE PHONE DOWN; tears flooded her eyes. The water was rising so fast that she began to choke and gasp for air between deep sounds rising from her gut. She wailed until she felt a hand patting her back. She turned quickly. It was the housekeeper. Eve looked up at the matronly woman who stood there firmly like a mountain. She peered at Eve with a cool, detached downward cast of her tiny blue eyes. Eve turned her head away and looked at the floor.

"Is everything alright, Miss Eve?" Mrs. Bristol said.

Eve understood how inappropriate it was to display overwrought emotion, especially in this particular section of the house. She mumbled something. The housekeeper sighed with her hands on her hips and Eve brushed past her on the way upstairs.

Trudging up the stairs, she was barely able to hold her body upright. She used the polished cherry hand rail to help her climb. If only her mother were still alive, she would help her. Eve thought she loved Kyle but she was frightened. Like a captured bird, she was afraid to fly away from the safety and confinement of her cage.

She wished she'd never met him. That everything would go back, the way it was before, back to normal. At least then she would have Father. But now she didn't even have him. She had forced him to turn away.

Eve crawled onto her bed and cried herself to sleep.

She dreamed she saw a woman far, far away, hovering in midair. Pale golden streaks of light surrounded her. She beckoned to Eve from the edge of a deep, thick wood. There was a clearing behind her, a beautiful meadow dotted with tiny wild flowers, buttercups, daisies and Indian paintbrushes. And there were animals, deer and squirrels, rabbits and fat black bears. They were all still, as if waiting to see what Eve would do. Robins spun a halo around the woman's head. She was waving for Eve to come closer, her arms outstretched. Eve was running, trying to reach the woman. But no matter how hard or how fast she ran, she could not get any closer.

From behind, a man softly called her name. Eve flung around; it was Kyle. Relieved, she rushed toward him. As she reached out to embrace him he instantly became her father. Jumping back, away from her, he let out a horrible, prodding laugh. His laughter grew louder, piercing Eve's heart like poisonous darts as she tried frantically to grab him.

Exhausted, she fell to the ground in the darkness of the forest and breathed in the earthly essence of rich dark soil. The sweet musk satiated her heart, calming her until she drifted away, into a long deep sleep.

PETER KNEW HE'D NEVER get back to sleep. Eve had sounded so confused; he had to go see her. He showered and dressed thinking of what to say to the Whitman household staff.

He rang the front door bell. Mrs. Bristol answered.

"Dr. Weiss. Please, come in."

"Hello Mrs. Bristol."

The stout woman smiled broadly which made her eyes almost disappear.

"Have you got a moment?" Peter said.

"Me?" she said, placing her fingertips to her bosom. Her cheeks flushed a dark shade of pink.

"If you don't mind. Is there somewhere we can speak privately?"

"Of course," she said. "We'll go into the study."

"Very good," said Peter, amused that she would choose the master's inner most sanctum.

Peter followed her and closed the door behind himself. He gestured for her to take a seat which she did, but just on the very edge of the dark chocolate brown leather sofa. Peter remained standing.

"I've just got word from the Judge, Mrs. Bristol. It seems he's decided to take a much needed rest to Bermuda."

"You don't say? Well, he does work terribly hard, it's true. But doesn't it seem odd?"

"What's that?"

"He never goes anywhere without his precious Eve," she said. "And such short notice, too."

"Well, he says he's just plain tired," Peter said, smiling, trying to be nonchalant.

"That explains it, then," she said.

"Explains what?"

"Earlier, Eve was down here slobbering all over herself like a spoilt child. That girl could not take care of herself if her life depended on it." She stopped suddenly, checking to see if the Doctor disapproved.

"I'm depending on you, Mrs. Bristol," Peter said, looking directly into her small blue eyes, "to take responsibility over the house in the Judge's absence. You'll need to explain this to the rest of the staff and run interference with anyone who calls. He doesn't want anyone to know where he is."

"And Eve," she said, "what do I tell her?"

"I'll explain it all to her."

Peter sat down on the sofa beside her, so close, their knees were almost touching. He leaned in slightly. Mrs. Bristol flushed again and smoothed her uniform across her thighs.

"Can I count on you?" he said.

"Absolutely, Dr. Weiss."

He took her hand in his, layering his other hand on top.

"The Judge is right, you are a peach. I'm going to tell him to be sure to hang onto you for just as long as you'll have him."

"He said that? About me?"

"Indeed, he did. Now then, may I see Eve?"

Mrs. Bristol's mouth turned down at the mention of Eve's name. She stood up, straightening her uniform over her round hips with chubby hands.

"I'll go and get her. You just sit here and relax. Can I bring you something?"

"Some tea would be nice, thank you."

She returned fifteen minutes later with a tray of tea and scones and informed Peter that Eve would be down shortly.

Peter was sipping his tea when Eve appeared at the doorway to the study. She stood very still, fervently rubbing a clump of wet tissues with both hands. Tiny spears of rolled paper fell to her feet like white rain. Her hair was tangled, her face drawn. Dark half moons loomed, shadowy beneath her dull green eyes.

"Eve," Peter said.

She stood in the doorway with her head down. She was mute and still.

Peter stood up and stepped toward her. Eve looked up with a gasp and ran to him, grabbing hold, clinging desperately.

Peter hummed low, shhh, warming her cool skin. He held her close swaying gently, shh, okay, shhh. He stroked her hair, smoothed her back, held her tightly. Twenty minutes later they were still fastened together in the middle of the study. They didn't notice Kyle Jordan standing at the door with Mrs. Bristol gaping by his side.

"What's going on?" Kyle said.

CHAPTER TEN

DORIS SCRAPED THE LARGE white plate with her fork, trying to scoop every drop of hollandaise sauce onto her tongue. She smiled at her friend and mentor, Justin Templeten, who sat across the table from her at The Bread and Roses Café. He had first come into her life twenty years ago, at a time when she had felt completely alone.

Justin had worked in the hospital where she had been rushed after the attack. She was a senior in high school and no one had believed her about what happened. They asked questions like, "What were you wearing? Did you have on something low cut? And, what exactly were you doing walking alone at seven o'clock at night?"

The man who had raped and beaten her had just walked away.

Justin believed her though; he had helped her through. Meeting him had changed her life.

"God, I love Eggs Benedict," she said, and the man across the table laughed. "I'm so glad you're here. I still can't believe it," Doris said, shaking her long red curls.

She stared into Justin's eyes, they were the color of rich black coffee. When he smiled at her, his eyes shone.

"I'm really worried about Eve," she said.

Doris knew first hand of Justin's abilities to see events, past, present and future. She had seen him bring peace to people who were facing death. He would talk to them about the lessons they'd learned, the good they had done. He made them feel special by recounting little things they'd done to help others, or to somehow make a difference. He would gently prompt the grandfather to remember the helicopter ride he'd given his seven year old grandson, and how the little boy would always remember the joy he'd given him that day. With a touch of his hand he had sent relief to AIDS victims who were in terrible pain. He would remind them of their courage in illuminating the world's oppressive attitude toward diversity. He said they were changing the world with their pain, making it a more compassionate, humane planet.

There were countless examples of Justin Templeten's kindness and Doris was amazed how he always seemed to show up where he was needed most at just the right time.

Justin nodded.

"It's difficult," he said.

"She's falling apart," Doris said, "you should have seen her on Thursday, she ran right by me, didn't even know I was there."

"Chances are, it will get worse before it gets better. Remember when we first met?" Justin said, leaning both elbows on the table, which emphasized his muscular physique.

"How could I forget? You saved my life back then."

"No I didn't. You decided how to handle that, I just coached you a bit. You're the one who saved yourself, not me."

"Oh. So, what you're telling me is that I'm just supposed to sit around patiently waiting until Eve is about to go off the deep end and then offer my help, is that it?"

"It won't do any good to offer help if it's not wanted. A person has to be open, ready to receive. Timing is very important. Besides, she has plenty of help right now," Justin said, fiddling with his spoon.

"What do you mean?"

"Many are being drawn to help her, and to help themselves in the process. These people are living out their karmic destiny. We need to honor that and try not to get in their way."

"Who exactly?" Doris said, crunching up her nose.

"Eve and her father of course—."

Doris put down her coffee cup and rolled her eyes. "That creep," she said.

"And now there is Kyle Jordan, who's very connected to her," he said, ignoring her comment and lowering his eyelids. "Peter, he's coming around, starting to see things more clearly. And another important person is on her way. Her influence will be the most profound in this whole process and unfolding. And let's not forget that very special person, Doris Stanley who's always willing to lend a helping hand."

"Oh stop," Doris said, trying to cover her embarrassment with a flick of her hands. She frowned. "Who's this other person and where is she coming from?"

Justin smiled and leaned back in his chair. "Let's just say that she's the one person on this earth who can knock Robert Whitman off balance," he said.

Doris smiled. She knew that Justin understood more than she did so she didn't push any further. She was relieved that he had confidence in this stranger. And the fact that Justin, himself, was here and involved, however remotely, was enough to put her heart and her anxiety about Eve to rest. At least for now.

"KYLE," PETER SAID, moving across the Whitman's study and leaving Eve to stand alone. He extended his arm. "I'm Dr. Peter Weiss, Eve's psychiatrist, and a long-time friend of the family."

Kyle nodded. He kept his arms folded across his chest.

"We need to get Eve to the clinic so we can run some tests," Peter said, quietly. "I'll be able to keep a close watch on her there."

"What makes you think I want you watching her?" Kyle said.

"I'm afraid that's not up to you, Mr. Jordan."

Peter looked over at Eve who stood awkwardly in the middle of the room. She was fidgeting with her hands and her gaze was aimed at the floor. She peeked up at them and then quickly looked back down again.

"I'll take her to your clinic," Kyle said, observing her strange behavior. "But I want an explanation. I've known from day one that something was not right with Eve. I want to know what's happened to her."

"I have issues of doctor-patient confidentiality to consider but I'll tell you what I can. Once Eve is back to herself, she'll have to decide how much she wants you to know."

Kyle nodded and began to move toward Eve.

"She'll be alright," he said, wrapping his arms around her and kissing her forehead lightly.

THE THREE OF THEM moved down a brightly lit hallway at the clinic; Kyle supported Eve as they walked.

"I've taken the liberty of having a cot set up in Eve's room," Peter said. "That way you can rest when she does. You'll be no good to her if you're exhausted."

"Thank you," Kyle said, "but when can we talk?"

"I've got an emergency to attend to right away. Keep Eve company for a couple of hours, try to keep her awake, and when I'm through with my other patient, I'll give her something to help her sleep through the night. We can get to know each other over dinner."

"Fine," Kyle said. "You'll come and get me then?"

Peter nodded and opened the door to a bright, sunny room decorated in pastels. There was a white dressing gown with tiny pink flowers laid out on the end of the bed.

"There, now," Peter said. "Why don't you get changed and settle in? I'll be back to check on you later."

Eve kept looking around the room. Her arms hung limply by her sides.

Peter left the room and Kyle stepped toward her but she moved away. She went to the window which looked out over a field of tall grass, surrounded on three sides by New England pines and edged with slender, white birch trees.

"Why do men talk about women as though they're not there?" Eve said.

Eve watched Kyle move toward her; she couldn't escape him.

"Please, don't push me away," he said. He was holding her chin, looking into her eyes, invading her.

She lowered her eyelids.

Kyle continued to hold her chin as if he were trying to see inside her soul. Her lip quivered and tears dripped down her cheeks. One by one, Kyle kissed them away. Eve stood very still. Inside, her chest was growing tight, her throat squeezed together so that the sides almost touched, there was no air, she could not breathe, and yet she didn't move. She watched him from a distant place as he pecked at her cheeks. Each kiss felt like another puncture to her skin. And still she did not move. She thought she must be bleeding all over but she barely felt the pain.

"You were so quiet, Eve. I thought you didn't feel like talking," Kyle said.

"I didn't. No one ever asks me what I want."

PETER'S NERVES WERE RAW as he approached the door to the room where Robert was being held. He pulled the master key from his pocket and turned it slowly inside the lock. His hand shook. As he pushed the sound proofed door open, Robert's enraged voice blasted his ears.

"You bastard," Robert said.

Peter's heart pounded hard, his stomach leapt to his chest, his breakfast was starting to make its way up his throat. He forced it back down. He had the leverage, he told himself. He looked at Robert still wrapped in a crisp white straitjacket, and now strapped to the bed. He spewed expletives but Peter did not hear the words. He encircled the room to keep from collapsing. Finally he stopped at the foot of the bed and stared deeply into Robert's eyes.

"You're a sick man, Robert," he said, as if it had just occurred to him for the first time. "I'm going to find out what I need to know to help Eve. She's all broken, and I've helped you. Now, it's up to me to try to put the pieces back together. But I found out recently that I don't know the whole story, right?"

Robert was silent, his eyes darted left to right.

"It happened quite by accident really," Peter said, breathing heavily. "I was worried about Eve. As you know, my technique didn't seem to be holding up under her attraction to Kyle Jordan."

Robert grunted. He jerked his shoulders and chest, trying to free himself.

"I decided to put her under with sodium amytal."

Robert's eyes grew large. He laid still waiting to hear what Peter would say next.

"That's when I met Bobbie. She's really something, quite a piece of work." Peter moved around to the side of the bed. He bent down, directly over Robert's face. "You're the bastard," he said, "and this time you're going to pay."

Robert spit forcefully into Peter's face.

Peter straightened his torso, wiped his face, turned and left the room. He stopped off at the nurse's station in preparation for his treatment with Robert, whom he had labeled as Patient W, room 360. Of course, they all knew by now that it was Robert Whitman in there. But this was Peter's turf and they respected him; he had counted on that. At least he'd done something right, his staff didn't question his professional judgment. Peter told the nurses on duty that the patient had wet the bed and instructed them to change his dressing and bed sheets as soon as he was fully sedated.

Peter planned the session while waiting for the effects of the drug to take hold, then reentered room 360. He brought Robert under hypnosis while still strapped to the bed (he wasn't taking any chances), and brought him back to the days when he had served in Korea.

"My name is Lieutenant Robert S. Whitman, serial number 701319." His voice resonated from his gut.

"And what is your mission there?" Peter said.

"I can't tell you."

"How long have you been in Korea?"

"Fifty-three days, twelve hours."

"How long is your tour?" Peter said, and moved his chair closer.

"Until it's over."

"What do you hope to accomplish?"

"You'll kill me before I'll tell you."

"We'll place you under torture," Peter said calmly, trying to sound threatening.

"Go ahead. I'm not talking," said Robert.

Peter would have to break through Robert's security training from another angle.

"Let's move up to the recent past. Let's talk about the last time you were with Bobbie."

A smile spread across Robert's face.

"Where are you now?"

"I'm in her room." Robert said, and his shoulders relaxed.

"Whose room? Eve's?"

"It's hers some of the time but now it's ours."

"Tell me what happened that day," Peter said, firmly.

"Eve had been out all night, screwing that Jordan guy."

"Did she tell you that?"

"No, but she didn't come home," Robert whined. "She said she was with him. She had this stupid grin, and shitty attitude — very disrespectful, the little slut."

"What happened when she got home?" Peter said, standing up to get a full breath.

"I told her to come down to breakfast where we could talk, when she came down she was all happy, really sexy — I could hardly speak."

"What did you say?" Peter said, moving around the bed.

"I asked her, haven't I always been there for you? Haven't I taken care of you?" Robert's face began to twitch.

"And?"

"She said, 'Yeah, so? What's your point?'" Robert said, his face was contorted and his voice trembled. Then his voice hardened. "Ungrateful little bitch."

"So Eve hurt your feelings, Robert? She made you feel bad?" Peter said, stopping at the head of the bed. He watched as Robert began to whimper, he spoke through clenched teeth.

"She doesn't know how much I love her, I don't know what I'd do if she left me."

"What happened next?" Peter said.

"She said she was in love, that I had to face up to it. Then she left the room crying."

"And then?" Peter said, refusing to let up.

"I won't let her go. I went up to be near her."

"What did you do?"

"I brought an injection with me."

Bingo, Peter thought. "Sodium amytal?"

Robert nodded.

"Where do you get it?"

"From a guy who owes me."

It's not important, Peter decided. "How did she respond?"

"She didn't want the shot. She seems suspicious ever since this Jordan came around. He's fucking everything up."

"How did you make her do what you wanted?" Peter said, trying to conceal his own agitation.

"Same as always. I said, 'Eve, I'm your father and you will do as I say.' Works like a charm, a little trick I learned in Korea. Post-hypnotic suggestion."

Now we're getting somewhere. "And did you learn how to create Bobbie there, too?"

"Yeah," Robert said, then laughed. "We used to turn those gooks into our guys. They'd go out there and kill each other, just because we told them to. The power is incredible."

Peter dropped his arms and turned away from Robert. He knew he had to keep going. "And you feel powerful with Eve?" he said.

"I would never hurt Eve, but she's got to understand that she belongs to me," Robert said, plainly.

"Why do you think that?"

"It's just the way it is. She lives for me."

"Then how do you explain the feelings she has for Kyle Jordan?"

"Trying to make me jealous, is all."

"You're hurting her now, Robert," Peter said, raising his voice slightly.

"She's beginning to have a breakdown, she will never be the same once she knows the truth."

"She'll never know. I've got the power to keep her safe. That's why I created Bobbie."

"And how do you get Bobbie to come out?" Peter said, moving back to his chair.

"I say, 'come out, come out, wherever you are!' It's a game we play."

"Is it fun for Eve?"

"No," Robert said, sadly. "She doesn't usually play."

"Did she used to play?"

"When she was younger. She used to really like it."

Peter turned away. "How do you know that?" he said.

"She always giggled, and she never told her mother."

"Why didn't she tell her mother?" Peter asked, already knowing the answer.

"Because I told her we wouldn't be able to play together anymore if she did, and that our family would be destroyed."

"Maybe she didn't want to upset you—."

"Of course she didn't want to upset me. Her mother's the one who always upset me."

"What happened to Carolyn?"

"Her own damned fault. If she hadn't made such a scene and scared poor Eve like she did, I wouldn't have gotten so mad."

"Did Carolyn see you and Eve together?"

"She walked right in on us, didn't even knock."

"What did she see?"

Robert rolled his head away from Peter.

"Tell me what she saw, Robert," Peter said.

"I was letting Eve touch me," he said, without turning his head back. "She was curious about the difference between boys and girls, I was helping her to understand." He turned his head back now and his speech quickened. "Carolyn made that ridiculous face and Eve thought she was going to get into big trouble. Everyone started screaming, Carolyn said she would never let me see Eve again. I had no choice."

"You told me that a person always has a choice."

Robert thought about this for a moment and then said, "I chose Eve."

Peter paused. He took off his glasses and rubbed his eyes.

"What happened to Carolyn?"

"I put her out of her misery."

Peter froze. He had finally heard what he had always suspected and it ate him up inside to think how he never had the courage to confront Robert or to use it against him to protect Eve. What had he been thinking all these years? Why had he been so afraid? Noticing the time, he realized he couldn't linger. Eve and Kyle were waiting.

"Our time is up now," he said wearily, "I'm going to count backwards and on 'one' you will come out of hypnosis, you will remember everything that we've talked about here today. Do you understand?"

Robert nodded.

"On 'one' you will wake up and remember everything. Three... two...one. Now open your eyes, Robert."

Robert Whitman opened his eyes very slowly. He stared straight up at the ceiling, refusing to look at Peter, who remained sitting in the chair beside his bed. Robert turned his head away when Peter stood up and quietly left the room carrying a tape recorder.

CHAPTER ELEVEN

PETER TOOK THE STAIRS just to keep his legs moving. Standing still meant sinking further into the quicksand. Just a while longer, he told himself, keep moving.

He knocked on Eve's door, Room 432.

He opened the door and stepped through to a complete shift in atmosphere like he'd just flown in and landed on another continent. Five minutes ago he was perspiring from the volcanic heat generated by Robert's truth. Now a cutting chill was present in the air.

Eve and Kyle were huddled on the bed with their backs to him. Kyle stood up quickly. There was betrayal and blame in his eyes; Peter recoiled from his glare. Truth sliced him again, sharp, jagged and clear.

Peter looked at Eve and when he saw the way she clung to her unbuttoned blouse, he understood what must have happened. Eve's buried memories were rising from a long, dormant sleep. They were hovering over her, pressing down on her, demanding some attention. Her perceptions were clouded. She hadn't distinguished Kyle from her father.

Peter tried to speak.

Kyle frowned and shifted his weight. He was wringing the dressing gown intended for Eve in his hands. He moved around the end of the bed toward Peter.

"I tried to help her undress," he croaked. "She got really agitated like she was afraid of me. What the hell is going on?"

Explaining was the last thing Peter wanted to do but he moved quickly and efficiently. A nurse with a kind face came into the room. She was there to help Eve change and give her a sedative.

Peter finally convinced Eve that all this was for her own good. He told her that he was going to step out into the hall with Kyle for a little while, and she calmed down enough for them to leave.

KYLE AND PETER SAT FACE-TO-FACE at a table in a nearby pizza parlor called Father John's Pub. The only other customers on that Sunday night in March were a few sturdy men all wearing plaid shirts scattered around the bar, silently drinking beer.

Peter took off his glasses and laid them on the table. He rubbed his tired, pink eyes.

"When's the last time you got any sleep?" Kyle said.

"Got a couple hours this morning."

"You can't do that to yourself, man, you'll be no good to anyone if you're exhausted," Kyle said, grinning.

Peter relaxed slightly. "There's a lot going on right now."

They both leaned back while the waitress plunked two frosty white mugs and a clear plastic pitcher of beer down on the table. Kyle poured them each a glass.

"Do you believe in destiny?" Kyle said.

"I'm a psychiatrist, I've seen too much to believe in some grand scheme."

"Ever been in love?"

Peter swallowed the last of his beer.

"Once," he said, "only once."

"What happened?"

"I don't want to go into that. We came here to talk about Eve."

"Right. I just wondered if you believe that people come into our lives for a reason."

"I guess there are some relationships which seem preordained...but, if both people don't feel the same way, that's when you can get into all sorts of pathological behaviors."

"You mean like incest?" Kyle said, flatly.

Peter's heart raced. He nodded and looked directly into Kyle's blue eyes. He saw intelligence and compassion in them.

"Incest is one form of behavior manifested by that type of imbalance. Obsession, depression, and delusion are others."

"How long has this been going on between Eve and her father?"

"Eve's case is very —."

Kyle leaned forcefully across the table bringing himself as close to Peter as he could get.

"Cut the bullshit. I'm falling in love with her for reasons I don't even understand and I've got a fiancée back in the islands. I'm risking a lot being here. I don't even know what I'm doing." He sat back in his chair and ran his hand through his hair. "Are you going to level with me, or not?"

"Look," Peter said, leaning onto the sticky table, "I want to help Eve as much as you do, believe me. But patients have to be ready to help themselves before any real progress can be made."

Kyle grabbed the pitcher and emptied the last bit of beer into his glass. He held it high to cue the waitress to bring a refill.

"What kind of crap is that? All you have to do is take one look at her and you can see she's in trouble."

"But," Peter said, "does *she* know she's in trouble?"

"What the hell are you talking about?" Kyle said.

"Alright," Peter said. He liked Kyle, maybe it was the beer and lack of sleep, but he liked him. "Let me start from the beginning. But you have to realize that by telling you this I am in breach of patient-client confidentiality. After what I've done the last couple days, the last twenty years for that matter, my professional ethics are shit anyway. Much of what I'm about to say, I've only just uncovered in the last three days. And to my knowledge at this point, Eve is completely unaware of the abuse."

"How can she be unaware? The way she's acting—she's traumatized," Kyle said.

"Trauma is an opportunity for healing. Awareness and acceptance are necessary components in order for the recovery process to begin."

"So are you telling me that we've only just begun?"

"We haven't even scratched the surface yet," Peter said.

As Peter told him Eve's story he watched the horror on Kyle's face. Occasionally, he blurted out 'shit', 'oh God', and 'fuck.' Peter explained the weekly treatments which had allowed Eve to live productively. He explained Whitman's history and expertise in coercion through the military. He told it all except for the real story behind the death of Eve's mother, Robert's creation of Bobbie, and the blackmail Whitman had used against him.

For a long time, neither one spoke.

"It's amazing she's survived this long. Where the hell is that creep? And what about you? How could you have done this?" Kyle said.

Peter squinted. He'd brought Kyle into the cage with him which had done little to ease his own isolation.

"I had my reasons," Peter said, clearing his throat. "Robert Whitman has a way of getting what he wants. He's strapped to a bed in the maximum security ward of the clinic right now, though. He can't hurt her anymore."

"You put him there?" Kyle said.

Peter nodded.

"How long are you planning to keep him there?"

"I don't know. I'm still working that out."

Kyle shook his head. He leaned in slowly and looked into Peter's eyes.

"What's he got on you?"

"I'd rather not go into that right now."

"Yeah well whatever it is, it must be pretty ugly for a guy like you to turn your back on someone like Eve. Fuck." Kyle paused. "Is she going to make it through this?"

"She's got you, that helps," Peter said. "Having you around will remind her that there's something better waiting on the other side. Something worth living for."

"I don't know," Kyle said.

"Get some sleep. Tomorrow I'll begin the process of helping Eve to remember. We'll take it one step at a time, that's all we can do."

Kyle cupped his hand over his mouth and then rubbed his lower lip back and forth.

"She is beautiful," he said, raising his eyebrows at Peter. "But, that's not it. I've known a lot of beautiful women. No one has ever affected me like this. I can't explain it. When I'm with her I feel whole, something went off the minute we met. It's like I look inside her, and I see myself. I don't even feel this way about my fiancée. Does any of this make sense to you?"

"More than you know," Peter said.

Kyle nodded, signaled to the waitress to bring their check, they drove back to the clinic in silence.

CHAPTER TWELVE

T HE NEXT MORNING while Eve hid behind the pages of a magazine Kyle shifted and paced around the room.

"I'm going to find Peter," he said, abruptly.

He stepped up to the nurses' station asking where he could find Dr. Weiss. The nurses mumbled. No one had seen or heard from the Doctor yet. Kyle said he had a nine o'clock appointment with him; the nurses shrugged. Dr. Weiss was never late, they said; an emergency must have come up. They smiled brightly. Kyle scowled, then smiled at the pretty one with the perfect teeth. Was there some way to contact the Doctor? Could they call him at home? She blushed slightly and said she would see what she could do.

Kyle returned to the room and Eve looked up inquisitively.

"He's not in yet. Some kind of emergency."

Eve smiled sympathetically at Kyle, as if he was the one who needed help.

"Kyle," she said, "you don't have to hang around here. Why don't you go out for awhile, get some fresh air. Peter will be here soon."

She sounded so normal, so confident. Just hearing her sweet voice put Kyle at ease. He moved toward her, wanting to touch her, to hold her. But as he moved closer to the bed, her expression shifted. She pulled away, squashing her back deeper into the pillows behind her. The chords in her neck popped out slightly. Kyle went past her and walked over to the windows instead.

"Would you do me a favor?" she said, timidly.

He turned.

"I need to take care of things at my office. I'm not sure how to handle it." Her voice cracked. "I know Doris is probably wondering... ."

Kyle sat down on the bed and lifted his hands to her shoulders, rubbing them tenderly; he gazed into her eyes.

"It's alright," he said. "I'll take care of it. Maybe you're right, I should get out for a little while." He lifted her chin and said, "I'm sorry if I seem restless, I just don't know what to do for you."

"Being here is enough."

Eve fell into the curve of his neck and his arms folded around her. He pulled back slowly and kissed her on the cheek before getting up to leave.

WHEN KYLE STEPPED INTO the reception area of Eve's office, Doris jumped up from behind her desk.

"Mr. Jordan. Good morning, how are you? Where's Eve, have you seen her? It's not like her to just—."

"Hi," he said, raising his hand. "Yes, I've seen her, she asked me to stop by and check on things for her."

"Check on things?" Doris said, scowling and then placed one hand on her hip.

"Yes, you know, to make sure everything is under control."

"Well, it's pretty tough to run a law office without a lawyer," she said. "Where is she?"

"I can't go into it right now. Eve and I are trying to work through some things. We need you to kind of hold down the fort for awhile."

The phone rang. "Whitman Law Office," Doris said, without taking her eyes off Kyle. "Yes, Mr. Cunningham...right...hmm...well, I know Eve would want to handle that for you, but she's been called out of town unexpectedly. Is it urgent, or may I have her call you when she returns? Fine...I will. Thank you, goodbye."

Doris placed the phone down, still looking up at Kyle. She stood up and marched over to him in her purple high-heeled shoes, grabbed his hand and pulled him over to the sofa. They sat down together and she turned her shoulders to face him. Her eyes grew narrow.

"Look," she said, "I've been working with Eve for over a year. She's like a kid sister to me. You roll into town, barely a week ago, and suddenly everything's upside down. What gives?"

Kyle shifted in his seat, not really knowing whether he could trust her.

"She's in some kind of trouble, isn't she?"

"Oh, no," Kyle said, "nothing like that."

"She's in trouble. I can feel it. Where is she?"

Doris softened her eyes and took Kyle's hand; she lowered her eyelids and sighed heavily.

"You need to talk about it, maybe I can help."

"In what way?" he said, pulling his hand away.

"You tell me. What happened?"

Kyle looked down at the floor.

"Oh, I get it," she said. "You're afraid I'm some nosey Nelly, just looking for some juicy news to spread around town. Well let me tell you, there's nothing I could say about Eve and Judge Robert Whitman that hasn't already been said."

"What do you mean?"

"The story goes like this," Doris said, waving her hands as she spoke. "Eve's mother died mysteriously when she was just a girl. No one ever really knew what happened, there was no investigation, no stories in the paper — nothing. After that, Eve had some emotional problems, and Judge Whitman used his connections to establish what is now called the Weiss-Whitman Psychiatric Clinic."

She gasped and brought her palm to her chest.

"That's where she is, isn't it? She's strapped to a bed in that clinic."

"No, Doris, she is not strapped to a bed —."

"Is she okay? Is she having some kind of breakdown?"

Kyle fell back into the the sofa. "I don't know, something is wrong but I don't know what to call it."

"And where's the Judge?" she said.

"I had no idea that you and Eve were so close," Kyle said, sitting up and turning to face her more directly.

"Yeah, neither did she probably," Doris said, pensively.

"So what happened, after Eve's mother died?"

Doris explained how no one saw Eve for a long time after her mother died. How she never attended public school again and how she was chauffeured back and forth to private school during her high school years. She told about the bodyguard who followed her everywhere as she got older, even through college.

"Why, for God's sake?"

"That's what the people of Innis have always wanted to know. The public view is that her father loved her so much that he wanted to keep her safe from harm's way every second of every day."

Kyle nodded with a frown. "And, the private view?"

"The private view," she said, "is that there's always been more to their relationship than what meets the eye."

"People were that suspicious and nobody ever did anything?" Kyle said.

"Like what?"

"Like report it to the authorities."

Doris let out a snort. "Around here, honey, Judge Robert Whitman is the authority. He's got it all wrapped up — and besides, there's never been a whole lot of sympathy for Eve."

"Why not?"

"Oh, you know how people can be, they like to talk, they say she's partly responsible, you know, like Lolita." Doris flopped her hands into her lap.

"Anyway," she said, "Eve has everything anyone could ever want from all outward appearances and because of the way he's always kept her so sheltered, people think she's a snob."

"What about you?"

"I know better."

"I don't know what to do." Kyle said, slouching into the sofa again. He ran his hands through his wavy blond hair.

"Let me help you. I think there's a way to get at this. Can you come to my place tonight? I'll cook you dinner."

Feeling like this was someone he could talk to, Kyle welcomed the invitation. He smiled sadly at her, thanked her for helping with the office and said he had to get back to Eve.

KYLE WALKED INTO THE CLINIC and went directly up to Eve's room. When he walked in, she rolled over and opened her sleepy eyes. Seeing him brought a sweet smile to her lips.

He smiled back and walked over to the bed, sitting down beside her, he gently rubbed her back.

"Did you see Doris?" Eve said.

"She's kind of a character," he said.

Eve giggled. "Isn't she great? She always knows how to make me laugh."

"So she's a good friend, then."

"Mmm, I guess she is. I've never thought of her that way but she's always been there for me — she's kind of spiritual. She's into some weird stuff."

"Like what?"

"Oh, I don't know, like reincarnation, karma, astrology. She always says there are no coincidences in life, that everything happens for a reason."

"Do you think that's true?" Kyle said. He brushed a strand of hair away from Eve's face.

"I don't really understand it," Eve said, rolling over on the bed. "A lot of people are in pain, I don't know what reasons there could be for starvation and poverty...all the suffering in the world."

Eve frowned and her eyes watered.

"You okay?" Kyle said.

She nodded, turning to hide her face in the pillow.

"Eve?" he said. "Talk to me."

She turned to look at him. Kyle lifted her to his chest and began rocking her in his arms like a child. Eve pulled away.

"I'm so confused," she said. "I don't know what's happening to me — I feel so out of place, like I don't really belong anywhere."

"You belong with me."

Eve wiped her eyes and fell back down onto her pillows.

"Where's Peter?" she said.

"I don't know. Apparently, he's still tied up."

"I hope he gets here soon. I really need a treatment."

"Treatment?"

"It's part of my regular therapy, it's kind of like a guided meditation. It's wonderful, always makes me feel more relaxed."

"Eve?"

She looked up at him.

"Where's your father?"

Eve looked down again, she was fidgeting with the pink blanket.

"Eve?"

She shrugged, still looking down and fidgeting.

"I'd like to meet him; seems he should be here with you."

"He's in Bermuda," she said, flatly.

"Are you angry with him for being away?"

She looked up quickly, staring right through him.

"It's my fault he's gone away," she said.

"What makes you say that?"

Eve's shoulders began to shake.

"I forgot all about the gala," she sniffled. "It's a very important night for him and we've always gone together. I made him go all alone and the next day Peter told me he was gone."

"Is that such a terrible thing?"

"He didn't take me," she whined.

"Where were you when this dinner took place?"

"I was with you."

"And you think that was wrong?"

"It was terribly selfish and that makes it wrong."

"What's wrong with following your heart," Kyle said standing up. "You've spent your whole life trying to please your father and look at yourself, you don't even know who you really are." Kyle looked down at her. "You're a mess. You can't even decide how you feel."

Eve put her hands over her ears.

"Stop it," she said, "just stop it!"

Kyle brought his hands to his face. When he tried to comfort her, she hid from him, burying her face into her knees. He was in way over his head. He had no right to be there. Besides, he could still follow through with his plans, go back to his real life.

The nurse rushed in, having heard the commotion and flashed a questioning look at Kyle.

He shrugged his shoulders, stood up and ran his hands through his hair.

"What happened?" the nurse said.

"We were talking about her father, she got upset."

"Okay, shh, it's all right Eve, shh," the nurse said, softly. Looking up at Kyle, she whispered, "Perhaps you could leave us alone?"

"Fine," he said, and left the room.

Kyle moved quickly down the hallway toward the elevator. He was suffocating, he had to get out of there. He stepped off the elevator and nearly ran into Peter.

"Thank God you're finally here. Where've you been, man?"

"I had some business. What's going on?"

"Eve's losing it and I'm not much help."

"What happened?"

Kyle told Peter how he'd lost his patience. Things were building up, his anger was surfacing. He wasn't sure he should stay but he'd be back later.

A couple of hours passed and Kyle returned to the clinic but before he entered Eve's room, a nurse hurried over to explain that Peter had given her a sedative to help her sleep, and that he had gone into Hartford to pick up an associate at the airport.

Kyle frowned, he searched his mind for any mention of an associate.

He smiled weakly at the nurse and went through the door. He brushed Eve's cheek softly then went over and collapsed onto the cot. Maybe Eve had the right idea, sleep was a better state to be in right now. He took several deep breaths, trying to release the tension and after staring out the window at the late afternoon clouds he forced himself to close his eyes.

WHILE KYLE WAS SUSPENDED somewhere between wakefulness and sleep, the third floor staff doctor passed by room 360 in the maximum security ward. Robert turned away from the peering face of Dr. Phillip Ross. Then, thinking twice, Robert looked over at the window and did his best to shoot a playful smile back at him.

Dr. Ross turned the key and opened the door; he stepped through tentatively.

"Hello, Judge, I'm Dr. Phillip Ross —."

"I know who you are, Phillip. For chrissakes, I'm not a lunatic. What the hell are you doing here? Where's Peter?"

"Peter's not in, I'm filling in for him."

"Well good. Then you can get me the hell out of these confinements."

"Perhaps you can tell me why you're in these restraints, Judge?"

Robert thought and turned confidently toward Dr. Ross.

"Listen Phillip, I have no intention of telling you all the sordid details of my history with Peter. Let's just say it's something like sibling rivalry. I came in to see him after the Gala, I was a little gone, I'll admit and Peter took advantage of the situation. This was his idea of some kind of practical joke — he wanted to see if I was tough enough to take it. Now let me out of here, I've had enough. Where is he anyway? I'm surprised he'd want anyone else to know about his little charade."

"Have you ever been an agent for the CIA?" Ross said.

"The what? The government? Me?" Robert laughed. "Now, where would you get a crazy — oh, that's the story Peter concocted to get his staff to drug me up, eh?" He laughed again, shaking his head. "He's really got one up on me this time!"

Ross smiled feebly and then moved toward the bed and began releasing the restraints.

"Where's Peter?"

"He's gone to the airport to pick up a consulting psychiatrist —."

Robert frowned, thinking immediately of Eve. He pulled himself up into a sitting position, his body ached.

"Get my things," he said.

Robert was in the bathroom cleaning up when Dr. Ross returned.

"And what about Eve, Judge? Is she part of the joke, too?"

Robert turned off the water and looked up at himself in the mirror. What could he mean by that? What would Eve have to do with this? She must be here in the clinic. Why else would this idiot bring her up?

"She's not still here, is she?" he said.

"Why, yes, she is, as a matter of fact."

The Judge opened the door. "What room is she in?"

"She's upstairs, in 432. There's a young man staying with her."

Robert spun around and threw the towel to the floor.

"If I find out there's anything wrong with Eve because of this clinic's lack of discretion, I'm holding you personally responsible." He grabbed his tuxedo jacket and left.

A SHADOW CROSSED HIS FACE and Kyle opened his eyes. When he saw the man standing there, bending over him, he knew it was Eve's father. He tried to sit up.

The Judge leaned down and placed his hands expertly around Kyle's throat. Kyle was losing air, his face was filling up with pressure. Can't breathe, everything's going black. Just then, he heard Eve's father speak in a low, muffled whisper.

"Get the fuck out of here, and don't ever come back. You stay away from my daughter or I swear, next time, I will kill you."

He released his grip leaving Kyle coughing and gasping for air. The Judge yanked him up by his shirt and shoved him toward the door. He opened it and slid Kyle through smoothly. The door clicked behind him and Kyle glanced, red-faced, at the nurse, who was moving quickly towards him.

"Are you alright? What happened in there?"

"I think she's really in trouble. Can I call you at home to check up on her?" Kyle said, still trying to take in a full breath.

She nodded without hesitation and pulled a pad from her pocket to write down her name and phone number.

Kyle walked out of the clinic in a white hot daze. Voices circled inside his head. *Don't give up on her. Get the fuck out. You've got plans. Make a run for it. One step at a time. Get the fuck out. I'll kill you. Follow your heart.*

He managed to find his way back to the pizza place where he and Peter had been the night before; this time he joined the other men at the bar.

CHAPTER THIRTEEN

P ETER PACED BACK AND FORTH in front of the windows as he waited for Sara's flight to land. It's been almost a year, he thought. He reached up to smooth his thinning hair across the bald spot on the back of his head.

He eyed the stream of passengers as they spilled out into the gate area. Each time someone new appeared at the entrance he hoped it would be Sara. There she was, she looked even more like Eve's mother as she got older. She was about the same age now as Carolyn was when she died. When Robert killed her.

Sara spotted Peter standing off to the side, away from the crowd. She stood still, taking him in carefully while moving bodies passed between them. Peter dodged through the frenzy until he was in front of her and gave her a warm hug.

"It's good to see you," he said.

"You've looked better," Sara said, "but I'm glad to be here."

They chatted about baggage, flight comfort and turbulence, about how difficult it was for Sara to get away until they were finally in Peter's BMW and driving toward Innis.

Peter began to lay the foundation for Sara as they drove. Staring straight ahead, he told her how Robert had blackmailed him over thirty years ago, how he had established the clinic using Robert's money and connections, and how Robert had used it against him to bring Eve out of a catatonic state after her mother had died.

"He killed her didn't he?" Sara said.

"How did you know that?" Peter said, almost swerving off the highway.

"Just a hunch."

Peter told Sara about his recent discovery of Eve's alter, Bobbie, and how Robert's past played into it all. He ended by saying that both Eve and her father were at the clinic; things were pretty bleak.

"You left Eve, alone?" Sara said. "You know, I could've found another way in —."

"No, she's not alone. Kyle Jordan was going to stay with her."

Peter had forgotten to mention Kyle. He did the best he could to describe their instant connection. As strange as it sounded, he said he believed in it.

Sara was staring out the window.

Peter used the dead air between them to call the clinic on his car phone. After a brief and stilted conversation, Peter hung up.

"Shit," he said.

"What?"

"Robert took Eve out of the clinic."

"Here we go," Sara said, as if she knew that was going to happen.

"I never liked Philip Ross, I should have known I couldn't count on him to keep his nose out of this. I thought I had the bases covered with the CIA thing —.”

"Really Peter. It's pretty far fetched, even for our business. I think you just enjoyed pretending to be a spy or something. Is that a long term fantasy of yours?"

Peter ignored her. "We'll go straight to my place. We need to make a plan."

"That's an understatement."

"Why are you acting like this?" Peter said.

"What? Excuse me if I happen to be questioning your professional judgement, Peter. But don't you think after what you've just told me, I have the right to a little adjustment time?"

Peter apologized. He needed Sara and besides, he really did appreciate her honesty. They drove silently the rest of the way to his penthouse.

ONCE KYLE HAD FINALLY silenced the voices inside his head he went to Eve's office to meet Doris. She looked up when he walked in.

"Oh God, what happened?"

"He tried to kill me, Doris. He really tried to kill me."

"Eve's father?"

Kyle nodded.

"Leave your car here. We'll go back to my place, you can take a nice hot shower, I'll fix dinner and you can tell me all about it."

Doris led him out the door, down the street to her car and drove to her house.

She kicked the door open to her apartment. It was an old building, she chattered, and the sudden warm weather had caused the doors to stick, or swell, or both. She flitted around the small space, doing the things Kyle imagined she did every day when she came home from work. As he watched her, he looked around the room.

It felt like a beach house, light and airy. The small couch was natural textured cotton and there were two big white wicker chairs with blue and white striped cushions. An oversized treasure chest sat in the center with a thick piece of green glass on top. Several white candles, different sizes and heights spired upward from the glass top along with an incense burner that was shaped like a toboggan. Victorian prints of angels and Maxfield Parrish prints of dreamy, faraway places adorned her walls. Rich shades of blue, purple and gold draped the room in comfort. Her book shelves were packed with new age books on increasing psychic powers, understanding auras, interpreting the Tarot and using astrology to live out your full potential.

"Has Eve ever been here?" Kyle said.

"Just once. She brought me home from work when my car was in the shop; she said it was like a doll house."

Doris waved Kyle through the door and into a big, bright kitchen with a picture window that framed the harbor below. Her fridge was covered with children's artwork.

"Nice view," Kyle said.

"Here," she said, shoving a beer towards him. "Let me show you where the shower is. Have you taken your new boat out yet?"

Kyle turned to Doris.

"I really appreciate this," he said, slowly. "I'm kind of freaking out, though. Suppose we could slow down a bit?"

"I am so sorry," Doris said, raising her palm to her forehead. "I do tend to ramble and rush. I'll start dinner, you take a shower and, I'll see you when you come out. Okay?"

"Okay," Kyle said.

He leaned against the wall of the shower stall, letting the hot steam seep into his pores. He closed his eyes and saw the evil look in Eve's father's eyes as he had loomed over him, calmly cutting off the blood supply to his brain. He quickly opened his eyes again. *Make a run for it. Forget about her. Go to Tahiti. I'll kill you. Don't give up on her. Get the fuck out.* Kyle slammed his clenched fist into the side wall of the shower sending out a clap of thunder.

"Kyle?" Doris said, through the door. "You alright in there?"

"Dropped the shampoo," he said.

Kyle finished his shower and got dressed. He was looking across the kitchen at Doris from the doorway. His eyes were like saucers, his breathing shallow.

"Did I tell you that Eve has a split personality?"

She moved toward him and coaxed him into sitting down.

"No, you didn't tell me," Doris said, with one hand on his shoulder, "but I already knew."

"How did you know," he asked, looking up at her, "did it hit the papers already?"

"I just know things," she said, gently.

He squinted at her and blurted out an uncertain laugh.

"You're kidding, right?"

Doris turned toward the oven.

"What are you telling me? That you're psychic or something?" Kyle said, leaning back.

"I'm something, that's for sure."

He laughed holding up his empty beer bottle. "Got anything stronger?"

"It's not a good idea to drink a lot. It'll just take longer to sort through the confusion you're feeling."

He stared blankly at her not really wanting to be mothered.

"Vodka, or wine?" she said.

"Vodka."

She threw some ice into two glasses and poured a generous amount in each. She slid his glass across the table and plopped herself down into the chair opposite him.

She took in a deep breath and let it out with a long, noisy sigh.

"Look. Just look at the way the light is playing down there on the water."

Kyle followed a sailboat slip across the harbor.

"I can't have kids," Doris said. "I was raped as a teenager and while I was in the hospital — I was banged up pretty good — they found a little cyst on my ovary. My step-father insisted that I have a complete hysterectomy. He thought I'd asked for it, and not having children of my own would be a good punishment."

"Jesus. Where was your mother?"

"She was afraid of him by then, had no strength to stand up against him. Besides, I knew she thought I'd be better off without kids. I'd be saved from living her hell of putting up with some horrible man, in a horrible marriage. She meant well."

Kyle was stunned. Thrown by the way Doris was so open, even casual, about her tragedy.

"Why do women stay in relationships like that, anyway?" he said.

"Fear. They're afraid if they leave, the assholes will track them down and hurt them, maybe even kill them — or worse, hurt their children. No money, no way of getting any. They're trapped, always believing that if they just try harder and love the guy a little more, he'll be nice, he'll eventually realize what he's got."

"You don't think that happens?"

"Ha! Once in a blue moon, maybe, and not without a lot of help."

"Eve told me that you believe everything happens for a reason. Why were you raped? How can you make sense of that?"

Doris took a sip of her drink then swirled it around, the ice tinkled against the edge of the glass. "It was my loudest moment of truth," she said, looking straight into Kyle's eyes. "While it was happening I understood something so profound. Well, maybe not *while* it was happening but afterwards, when I met this amazing man. Anyway, it changed my life."

"I don't understand," Kyle said.

"I knew that no matter what anyone did to my body, my spirit would overcome it. I found a place, deep inside that connects me to God — it's untouchable, impossible to scar. I've been able to let that penetrate me so I can be happy."

"What about the man who raped you? Where's his spirit?"

"It's there, it's just really buried. Besides, that man didn't set out to hurt me. It didn't have anything to do with me, really. He was punishing himself for something, for feeling unlovable and all he accomplished that day was to make sure he hated himself so much that no one could ever love him, even if they wanted to."

"I don't know if I buy that. Maybe some men just loathe women, and that drives them to do hateful things."

"But before a person can hate they must first hate themselves," Doris said arching her eyebrows and gazing at Kyle with a long pause. "It's the same with love. Eve doesn't know how to love you because she hasn't the slightest idea how to love herself."

The timer on the oven blared. Kyle flinched. Doris smiled and said, "Vegetable lasagne."

She asked Kyle to grab the salads and the wine from the refrigerator. She pulled the bread and lasagne from the oven.

"Smells great," Kyle said.

"You're feeling better. That's good. There is hope, you know, even when it doesn't feel like it."

Doris smiled brightly up at Kyle, her ivory skin was flushed from the heat of the oven, almost matching the scarlet of her hair. Kyle thought she looked angelic and he went over to her.

"There," she said, breaking free from his hug, "consider that a pact, we're like blood brother and sister now."

They stepped away from each other and Kyle felt lighter than he had in days. They shared the evening together easily, sweetly. But when Doris had gone to bed and he was crunched up on her couch, feelings of paralysis and doom haunted him once more.

Get the fuck out. Don't give up. He was unable to turn it off and he tossed and turned all through the night while his heart pounded heavily for Eve.

He'd been awake two hours before Doris finally began to stir in the next room. He didn't get up off the couch; he just stared at the early morning shadows on the wall. Whatever lightness he'd felt the night before had disappeared.

Doris flew into the room buckling a wide blue belt around her bright yellow dress. She walked over to Kyle, took his hand and yanked him into the kitchen. The sun was streaming in so brilliantly that Kyle squinted and covered his eyes.

"Coffee?" she said. "I also have tea, herbal or regular. Hot chocolate?"

"Coffee's good," he mumbled, still trying to open his eyes.

Doris tossed a business card down onto the table. Kyle picked it up and read it aloud.

"Justin Templeten, psychic advisor. Channeled sessions, auric readings, past life consultations, soul alignment — what is this, a joke?"

"Hardly, my young pale-faced brother. Him medicine man."

After Doris finished swishing around the kitchen with coffee and muffins she sat down and looked into Kyle's bloodshot eyes.

"There's a lot to this thing with Eve," she said. "I think it would help you to do a little spiritual detective work before deciding how to handle it. If you understood the past life connections between you, Eve, and her father it might make more sense to you."

"I know I told you last night that I believe in reincarnation, but this is a bit much...don't you think?"

"Trust me. Justin is an authentic clairvoyant. He sees auras, consults with the akashic records for information on your past lives, he's an amazing healer, really. Go and see him."

"I don't know," Kyle said, looking at her from the corner of his eye. "What makes you think I'll be able to see him today, anyway?"

"I've already talked to him. Ten o'clock. He's blocked out two hours for you, which believe me, will be more than enough for your first session," Doris said. She wiped her mouth and stood up to brush the crumbs off her dress.

In a flash, Doris was gone and he was standing alone in her kitchen. Kyle reached into the pocket of his faded jeans and his fingertips rustled an unfamiliar piece of paper. He pulled it out, uncrumpled it and read the name and phone number of the nurse with the perfect teeth. He stood there staring at the wrinkled paper, he saw Eve's father's eyes, felt the push that had sent him away from her. He wondered if she was all right, if she was still at the clinic. Where the hell was Peter? He picked up the phone and dialed the number on the paper.

Kyle wasn't surprised to find out that Eve had gone home with her father soon after he had been sent away. He thought about packing his things and heading for Tahiti that morning. He imagined Eve bound and gagged while her father pranced around her lecherously. His body flushed with heat and his legs wobbled. He knew that what he had to do was nothing short of kidnapping Eve if he was ever going to save her. But then, would he be able to bring her back, to help her remember who she was?

A breeze burst through a slightly opened window and pushed the clairvoyant's card to the edge of the table in front of him. He picked it up, wondering how to get to 17 Ocean Drive.

CHAPTER FOURTEEN

THE ROBINS' SONG DRIFTED in on the soft spring breezes that blew through Eve's window. She turned to check the time. 9:45. She jolted upright. Should she be at work? Was she late for breakfast? What day was it?

She sat stiffly, yanking the covers up to her chin. Her eyes darted around the room as she searched for the invisible intruder whose eery presence she felt against her skin. It was her room, the same room she had always known. But she felt she did not belong there anymore. She was afraid, something horrible was lurking in the shadows.

Robert popped his head around the edge of the door.

"Good morning, puppet," he said. "How are you feeling?"

"What did you just call me?" Eve said, scowling, still squeezing the covers.

Robert stepped into the room and closed the door.

"Don't you come near me," she said.

"Eve," he said, "stop that."

"You can't tell me what to do."

"You are my daughter and you will do as I say," he said.

With these words, the stiffness in her body went lax. Her head dropped forward causing strands of black hair to sweep across her face. Her hands went limp in her lap. She looked like a rag doll that had been dragged around day after day for years, the tattered, worn-out companion of a child.

There was a flickering across the Judge's forehead as he saw the sorry sight before him. She wasn't as much fun to play with as she used to be. Maybe it was time to discard her, throw her into a heap with other abandoned toys and find a new doll, one with a little more enthusiasm. Bobbie!, he thought. He went out of the room and headed for his secret cabinet. He returned quickly with the syringe in hand, a sneaky grin across his lips.

Eve had barely moved an inch. He sat down beside her, pealing the blankets off her body until her bare legs were exposed. She wore white cotton panties and a loose fitting white tee shirt without a bra.

Robert rubbed a white cotton ball drenched in alcohol back and forth across her leg, above her knee. A few drops of the clear liquid squeezed out and rolled lazily around the curve of her inner thigh. Intrigued by the wandering drips on her slender leg, he lifted the cotton ball and filled it once more with alcohol. His tongue slid out of his mouth, wagging slowly left and right between the corners of his mouth. He reached up to her belly, pinching the bottom seam of her shirt. Slowly, he lifted the shirt to reveal her breasts, covering her detached face from his view. He reached forward with the other hand he rubbed the drenched cotton ball around and around her nipple. He was delighted as the contact and the coldness drew her nipple out. It grew tall and hard. As he rubbed the cotton ball around the fullness of her breast, he squeezed lightly to release the liquid. He watched closely as tiny drops fell down off the hardened tip onto her stomach like a little stream of tears. He had the urge to lean forward and lick them up but then remembered it was alcohol and not the pleasing salty taste of Eve's real tears.

Robert sat up and injected the sodium amytal into her leg. Eve's body flinched. He waited a minute, then went to get her hairbrush and makeup case. He turned her body to an angle and began to stroke her hair with the brush until it lay smooth and shiny. He leaned his nose into the curve of her neck and inhaled her scent deeply. He laid her down, flat upon the bed. Her eyes were still closed. He did his best to apply some makeup to her face. He was not very good at it but he wanted her to look beautiful for him the moment she opened her eyes. He managed to paint on the bright red lipstick fairly well. There were a couple of places where he'd gone outside her lips but for the most part he was pleased. The green eye shadow was a little blotchy and the black eye liner too thick but he liked the way it transformed her.

He stood over her, trembling slightly. She belongs in black, he decided. He rummaged through her bureau drawers until he found some black stockings still attached to a garter belt. He looked for a bra to match. He hurried to her closet for the highest pair of heels he could find.

As he slid her white panties down, over her hips, his hands shook. He put on the black panties and then the stockings. They twisted and frustrated him. He was losing precious time. He tore a hole in one of the stockings causing a run to slide down the entire length of her leg. He smiled at the way it looked on her leg. He took off her white shirt in a hurry which smeared the red lipstick. He held her upright while he clasped her lacy black bra into place.

There. He laid her back down.

His mouth was dry. He ran down the stairs almost bumping into Mrs. Bristol on his way to the liquor cabinet. He tried to slow down. He found a chilled bottle of Dom Perignon and grabbed it along with two glasses.

He saw Mrs. Bristol scowling at him from the corner of his eye so he forced himself to walk back calmly. Once he reached the stairs, though, he ran up, taking them three at a time.

He entered Eve's room and locked the door.

"Come out, come out wherever you are!"

Bobbie let out a big cat yawn.

"Mmm" she said, "champagne? How yummy."

He popped the cork loudly, letting it fly up and slap against the ceiling. They both burst into laughter and he poured them each a glass.

KYLE PULLED INTO THE crushed stone driveway of a quaint cottage with a large number 17 on the mailbox. Tiny flowers spread bursts of vibrant pinks and blues in patches that crawled and hung delicately over a small stonewall of gray-speckled granite.

As he stepped tentatively out of his rental car, a tall, striking, dark-haired man appeared at the door of the small white cottage. As he walked closer, Kyle could see the man's eyes were as black as coffee. They seemed to drink him in. The man smiled and his eyes shone. He had a powerful presence, like an honorable, dignified knight from another era.

"You're surprised," the man said.

"No, well, yes — a little."

The man extended his hand which showed the strength in his arm. "I'm Justin Templeten."

Kyle took his hand and was somewhat reassured by the firmness of his grip.

"Kyle Jordan."

"It's nice to meet a friend of Doris Stanley's," he said. "She's a special lady."

Justin gripped Kyle's hand a little longer than usual. He gazed steadily into Kyle's eyes.

"Yes," Kyle said, taking back his hand. "I'm finding that out."

"Please come in, I'm all ready for you," he said, with a graceful wave of his arm.

"I wish I could say the same," Kyle said.

The mysterious man let out a musical laugh. Kyle followed him through a charming living room and down a hallway into a sunny room lined on three sides with book shelves. There was a round wooden table in the corner with a tape recorder on top and two chairs facing one another. A small sofa sat below a picture window with a brightly colored throw of purple and green tossed over the back.

"Let's sit here," Justin said, motioning to the table. "Can I get you something? Some tea, or juice?"

"Water would be good," Kyle said, clearing his throat.

After Justin left the room, Kyle looked over the books. Plato, Aristotle, Camus, Dante, Emerson, Sappho and Poe. Kyle had a strange, vivid, childhood memory of his father telling him that you can learn a lot about a person by what they read.

Templeten was back.

"Do you like to read?" he said.

"Hmm? Oh, yes. It's a good escape, I guess."

"From what were you escaping?"

Kyle shifted in his seat.

"Oh, you know...just regular life," he said, feeling dumb.

"I see," said Justin, lowering his gaze.

As Justin Templeten closed his eyes and breathed deeply, Kyle felt a dark shadow had been cast over the room. He fidgeted with his hands as he waited for him to say something. Kyle felt his throat pulsing in and out as if his heart had risen and settled there.

Justin finally opened his eyes and looked gently at Kyle.

Kyle realized he was holding his breath. He exhaled and shifted in his seat.

"Our lives are like stories within stories," Justin said. "If we understand some of the stories of the past, it may help us to understand the story of our present, and perhaps, to let us glimpse the stories awaiting us in the future."

Kyle nodded.

"For you, there is much to be accomplished in this life. Self-acceptance, self-love will bring happiness to you and to those around you. You have been drawn here to once again cross paths with Eve, and for the chance to heal old wounds."

"What old wounds?" Kyle said, frowning.

"There was a time, back in the late 1800's when you and Eve fell in love. It was not without misfortune and it caused pain for others, as well. Eve was then married to the one who is now her father, they had a family, a daughter. Eve's father at that time was a well-known ship builder in Boston and you came there from England to be his apprentice as your own work and vision showed much promise.

"Your meeting with Eve was very strong for both of you. You were drawn to one another from many other soul connections which had remained incomplete. The two of you had an affair which caused you both much grief and heartache. Those were days in which these things were not as accepted as they are in these times, particularly for women.

"Eve was unable to follow her heart, which would have meant leaving her husband and perhaps her daughter. She stayed with her family but it was not a happy life for her. Her husband had discovered her infidelity and so he turned away from her and toward the daughter for his required affection, and also to punish Eve. She was unable to forgive herself during her remaining years. She blamed herself for the wrongful attentions her husband gave their daughter and for the regular beatings she withstood. But she was unselfish in her suffering."

"Whoa, wait a minute — you're moving a little too fast for me. Are you telling me that Robert Whitman also abused his daughter in that life?"

"Yes."

"And, who's that person now?" Kyle said. His heart still stuck inside his throat.

"That would be Eve's mother," Justin said, softly.

There was silence. Justin Templeten waited as Kyle tried to make sense of these words.

"Eve's mother is dead," Kyle said, matter-of-factly.

"Things are not always as they appear," Justin said.

"Are you saying that Eve's mother is not dead?"

"The woman that was once in the role of Eve's mother was, in fact, killed. But she has returned."

Kyle let out a laugh that turned into a moan.

"Where is she then? And, who is she now?"

"You have not crossed paths with her yet but you will very soon."

Kyle sat back in his chair, the information buzzed through his mind. This is crazy, he thought.

"Who was Eve's father at that time? The man that I came to work with?" he said, sliding to the edge of his chair.

"That would be your own father of this time."

Kyle shook his head. "Were we close?"

"Quite. He taught you much, not just about shipbuilding but about life. He loved you as a son and did not turn away from you when the news about you and Eve was exposed."

"And I suppose he's not really dead either?" Kyle said, sitting back.

"It was his time," Justin said, calmly. "He has chosen to remain where he is for a while, that he may reflect on his life and the lessons he learned. He does watch after you during this time, however."

Kyle shook his head and then stood up. He needed to move around for a minute. He combed his hand through his hair and turned back to Justin.

"Was he actually conscious of bringing Eve and me together in this life?" He turned away quickly. "That's absurd," he said, "what am I even talking about."

"You're right," Justin said. He stood up and placed his hand on Kyle's shoulder. "Please, sit down."

Kyle moved back toward his chair. He swore he had felt heat emanating from Justin's hand, he felt it still. He looked at him curiously.

"You're right in the sense that your father's higher-self instructed him to bring you and Eve back together. It wasn't a coincidence, did you think it was?"

"Well, yes. I mean, no, it felt familiar, completely natural, like we'd known each other a long time. But I have other obligations and commitments — meeting her is throwing my life into a tailspin. All my plans—."

Justin nodded.

"Are you telling me that Eve has deliberately placed herself in her previous daughter's role — that she has asked to be abused, as some kind of penance?" Kyle said.

"No. She did not ask for the abuse, but yes, she placed herself there with faith that the chain might be broken. She has great courage."

"What chain?"

"The chain that links her soul to that of her father's, the chain that will continue to destroy their love, by twisting it into a relationship of power and control until one of them has the strength to break it."

"How can it be broken?"

"Forgiveness is the key. Acceptance. They must forgive themselves, and each other."

"That's easier said than done. Especially since Eve doesn't even know what's going on...what do I have to do with it?"

"Your own heart is heavy. You haven't forgiven yourself for not rescuing her from that other life, which for Eve was filled with both emotional and physical pain. You have come together once more for the chance to heal and to complete the drawing together of your souls."

"What am I supposed to do?" Kyle said, softly.

"That is a question you must answer for yourself."

Kyle smiled but felt his eyes filling up with tears. "Is she going to be alright?"

"Over time, there is that probability. But she must be given the necessary room and time to heal," Justin said.

"What about her father?"

"He has accumulated many karmic debts. His healing will begin only once he's able to see his own mistakes and the pain he has caused others."

"But there can be healing for me and Eve because we've already acknowledged ours somehow?" Kyle said, tentatively.

"That's correct. And because your love for one another is pure and true — that gives a powerful antidote to pain."

Kyle fell back in his chair. His heart felt truth in what this man was saying but his mind told him to get back to reality.

"What happened to Eve's mother?" Kyle said.

"Her father killed her."

"What? How could he have gotten away with that?"

"He did it to protect his relationship with Eve and to defend his position within the community. He has learned over time to use power against others, and so he has accumulated a long list of favors by taking advantage of other people's weaknesses. In times of crisis, he's able to draw upon his knowledge of other's poor choices in order to cover up his own," Justin said. He reached across the table, picked up a mug of some strange smelling tea, raised it to his mouth and took a sip.

"What will happen to him?" Kyle said.

"That remains to be seen," Justin said, replacing the tea to the table.

"Do I really have the power to help Eve?"

"That's up to you. If you choose not to, there will be other opportunities. There is a risk however, given the depth of trauma to both their souls, that Eve and her father would continue on a downward path of self-destruction."

"I don't really have a choice then, do I?" Kyle said, timidly.

"Choice is a matter of the heart. Fear, that is a matter of the mind," Justin said. He sat back in his chair and crossed his foot over his knee.

"Are you saying that I'm afraid?" Kyle said, studying every movement Justin made.

"If you learn to trust your heart, and not your logical mind, you will not be led astray."

Kyle took in a deep breath. He stared out the window, seeing nothing but the many shades of spring green.

"Green is the color of the heart," Justin said, smiling. "It is the promise of nature that all things begin anew, bringing fresh hope and lightness to our souls."

Kyle turned back to face this remarkable man. His eyes were filling with tears again.

Justin leaned in toward him, taking a firm hold on his shoulders. He pulled his chair closer to Kyle's looking deeply into his eyes, inside his heart.

Tears spilled out as Kyle stared into Justin's dark gaze. He felt he was receiving a transfusion. He was immersed in something powerful, elusive and strange. The room, the chair, even his body seemed to have slipped away as though he was sliding down a waterfall of energy. He had no desire to break the connection because it brought relief. Kyle felt something shift deep within him just as water washes everything clean.

Justin released his hold and the gateway closed.

"You are being given the opportunity to have faith in what cannot be seen but nevertheless exists. Listen to your heart," he said, "all you need to know will be found there."

Kyle felt a floodgate open deep within and he understood. He looked up at Justin who smiled radiantly.

Kyle could not help but smile back. He's not human, he thought and stood up to leave.

Justin rose to join him. "Remember, you are not alone. There are silent forces at work to guide you, and help you. All you need to do is listen. And there is someone else on the way, as well."

"What? Who?" Kyle said.

"Someone who will be able to assist in negotiating Eve away from the Judge. She possesses the energetics which will nullify the hold Eve's father currently has over her. And that will help Eve to begin to tap into her own strength."

"Energetics? Can't you just tell me so I can put a stop to this? This is insane."

"All things in their own time, and it is Eve who must ultimately do the severing."

Kyle sat back down. New questions had entered his mind.

Justin remained standing.

As he looked up at Justin, Kyle was reminded of the Indian totem pole in the town square where he had grown up. Templeten had a similar mystique.

"It's time for you to go now," Justin said.

"I just wanted to ask you a couple more questions," Kyle said.

"Our time is up and you have enough to mull over. Besides, Doris is waiting for you."

"Right. How does she fit into all this?"

Justin reached down and lifted Kyle up by the elbow. They walked together to the door.

"Doris has a special kind of hearing which directs her to the place where she can be the most helpful," Justin said.

"You make her sound like some kind of angel or something."

Justin was silent.

Kyle looked at him and when he saw Justin's expression, his smile turned into a frown.

"Another time," Templeten said. He patted Kyle on the back.

"Just one more question?" Kyle said.

Justin nodded.

"This may sound strange, but what were our names in the other life?"

Justin inhaled deeply. "You were Jason, known as Jake. And Eve was known as Evelyn."

"Hmm," Kyle said, nodding. "I was just curious. And what about my father?"

"Clyde," Justin said, softly. "Now enjoy this beautiful day, and remember to trust."

Kyle got into his car, turned the key, placed the gears into reverse and began to back away. When he looked up to wave goodbye, Justin was already gone. He backed out and drove slowly along the waterfront toward Eve's office.

When he opened the door to Eve's office, Doris was standing there waiting. He smiled when he saw her.

She grabbed his hand and jerked him over to the guest couch.

"Tell me everything," she said.

Kyle laughed.

"No, really. What did he say? Isn't he amazing?"

Kyle found himself staring at Doris. He was looking for a halo of light, hovering just above her head.

"Cut that out," Doris said, prodding him with her fingertips.

Kyle took in a deep breath and shook his head slowly. Staring down at the Oriental rug, he began to lose himself in the intricate designs there.

Doris poked him again.

He looked up at her.

"I'm losing it, Doris," he said, slowly. "None of this feels real. I feel like I'm in the fucking twilight zone."

"Welcome to life on earth," she said.

He looked into her shiny, chestnut eyes, they were glimmering like a horse's coat in the sun. They looked like regular, human eyes to him.

"Would you quit it," Doris said. "We've got work to do and you're sitting here like you're in a coma or something."

Nothing made sense. Kyle looked over at her again to see if she was really angry, or just playing around.

She gave him a sweet and gentle smile.

"Hungry?" she said.

Kyle frowned.

"Okay," she said. "Let's go. I'll put on the answering machine and we'll go back to my place. You can relax while I fix lunch."

Kyle nodded.

They rode in silence for a while. Kyle thought about everything Eve had endured and tears began to well up in his eyes.

"Hey," Doris said, "it's going to be alright. Really, it is."

She reached over and patted his back then returned her hand to the steering wheel but not before Kyle saw her wipe away a tear of her own.

Over lunch, Kyle told Doris what he had learned from Justin Templeten.

"It's natural for you to have doubts," she said. "It's a matter of sitting with it and deciding for yourself whether you believe it, or not. Sometimes it takes time."

"Did it take time for you?"

"Not really," she said.

"Why not? Why is it different for you? If this is the way the universe operates, that we are reincarnated again and again to conquer and complete other lives, then why isn't it common knowledge for everyone?"

"Save that thought," Doris said, raising a finger, "and we'll talk about it tonight. Right now, I have to get back to the office."

"Why bother? It's going to be a while before Eve practices law again, if ever," Kyle said.

"Maybe. But it's important that I keep up appearances, for Eve's sake. I have a nagging feeling that word is going to spread quickly."

"What word? What do you mean?" Kyle said, turning to Doris.

"I mean, I think something happened. Something at the house that might give people the impression that Eve is at fault."

"What?" Kyle said, raising his voice.

"Calm down," Doris said.

"Don't tell me to calm down. If you know something, tell me," Kyle said, loudly.

"Are you sure? You know your presence here is a miracle. You need to have faith —."

"Oh Christ, Doris," Kyle said. "I'm sick of all the sweetness and light and bullshit platitudes. What happened?"

She slid back in her chair and took in a breath while gazing down at the harbor.

"This morning while I was working, I began to have a sharp pain in my temple." She turned to face him and pointed to the indent beside her right eye. "I get that sometimes right before I have a vision."

"A vision?" he said, his voice softer.

"Sometimes I see things that have happened in the past, sometimes I get a glimpse of something happening as it occurs and sometimes I get messages from the future."

"What are you saying, Doris?"

"Well, today, this morning, I had a simultaneous vision."

She hesitated.

"What did you see?" Kyle said, his voice rising again.

Doris waved a hand at him and told him to sit down.

"I saw Eve and her father in her bedroom but it wasn't really Eve, it was just Eve's body. Mrs. Bristol was spying on them outside, in the hallway, and so she thinks that what she heard was Eve enjoying herself but she doesn't even realize that it wasn't Eve at all, it just seemed like it was her."

"What the hell are you talking about?"

Doris sighed. She moved over to the cupboard and pulled out the vodka and two glasses. She poured them both a drink.

"Oh shit," Kyle said, "it's bad. I don't know how much more I can handle... ."

Kyle looked up at Doris with desperation.

"You'll be alright," she said. "You're a tough guy."

Kyle rubbed his hands over his face and back and forth over his head.

Doris sat down across from him and leaned in after sipping her drink.

"I've been trying to figure this thing out for a long time," she said slowly. "I've always known that something was really wrong, that it went beyond father-daughter incest. Today when I saw them together...I realized that when she's with him...she's actually a different person."

"You mean like a split personality? We already knew that."

"Yes, but this is different," Doris said.

"How?" Kyle said.

Doris took another drink. "I saw an empty syringe by the bed."

She swallowed; her hand shook slightly as she raised the glass once more to her lips.

Kyle sat motionless, his eyes glaring. He made a steeple with his hands as if he were about to say a prayer. Then, without a word, he motioned for Doris to pass the vodka. He filled his glass, swallowed the whole of it in one long gulp and slammed it back onto the table.

Doris shuddered.

Kyle pushed his chair away and headed toward the door.

"Take my car. I'll walk back to the office," she said.

CHAPTER FIFTEEN

THE STEERING WHEEL WAS SLIPPERY under Kyle's tight grip. His chest pounded as he focused on his plan to punish Robert Whitman. The car was shaking but Kyle didn't notice. He didn't realize he was pushing the little Subaru to eighty miles an hour. He followed the curvy, tree-lined road clenching his teeth as he got closer to the Whitman's driveway.

The flicker of blue lights flashed in his rear view mirror. Wailing sirens blared louder as the police car drew closer.

"Shit," he said.

He pulled the car to the side of the road slowing to a full stop.

The police car pulled up rapidly behind him. Two cops jumped out and marched toward him.

Kyle squinted at them in the mirror.

They halted on either side of the car, standing back just enough so that Kyle could not see them without having to twist his body to the left or to the right. Both men leaned down and pushed their noses and chins forward, just to the edge of the windows.

"License and registration," said the officer to his left.

"Ah, well, this isn't my car," Kyle said.

The two cops eyed each other.

"License and registration, please," the cop repeated.

"Okay. Here's my license, let me see if I can find the registration."

As he began to reach toward the glove compartment, the officer he had passed his license to, drew his gun.

"Hold it right there," he said.

Kyle stiffened. He looked up at the police officer who had the gun pointed at him.

"Wait a minute. I think you've made a mistake." Kyle said, stopping when he saw the determination in the cop's face. He leaned back into the sticky, black bucket seat and brought his hand to his forehead to rub away the pounding.

"Okay, Jordan," the cop said, "out of the car."

Kyle stared up at him.

The other cop drew his gun, and said, "Now."

Kyle reached for the door handle. He slowly pulled it toward himself, opened the door and stepped out. When he tried to close the door, the handle had jammed and he began to fidget with it so it would close.

"Quit stalling, Jordan. Over here, hands above your head."

Kyle turned around, arms at his sides, and squinted at the two cops.

"You mind telling me what the hell is going on here?" he said.

The silent officer grabbed his arm, pulled him over to the front of the car and pushed his torso down onto the hood. The car was hot against his cheek. He heard steam hissing out of the engine. His hands were cuffed behind him and one of them was spreading his feet apart with a club.

"Hey, hey," Kyle said, "what is going on?"

"We'll tell you what's going on, pal, Judge Whitman tells us that you've got plans to run drugs into our quiet little town."

Kyle tried to stand up, to protest, to explain they had it all wrong but the quiet one shoved him down hard, back onto the hood.

"Listen here, sailor boy," the talkative cop said. "You've got exactly forty-eight hours to take your fancy boat and get the hell out of Innis. If we see you around here after that, we're going to throw your ass in the slammer."

Kyle didn't move.

"You got it?"

Kyle didn't answer.

The quiet one grabbed his wrists and yanked them hard causing Kyle's back to arch. He moaned. The cop took a tuft of Kyle's blond hair and pulled his head up further.

"Answer him," he whispered, through clenched teeth.

"I get it," Kyle said.

"Good," the other one said. "Forty-eight hours. After that, we'll come looking for you."

The quiet one released Kyle and let his body slam down onto the hood of the car. He unlocked the cuffs and Kyle stood up slowly, rubbing his wrists as they backed away from him. They returned their weapons, reentered the police car and drove away.

Several minutes passed before Kyle could move. Then he began fiddling with the door handle of Doris' car. It was still stuck and he became engrossed in his attempt to free it. The more he fidgeted with it, the more rattled he became at his inability to return it to a normal, functioning state. His pulse quickened. He hit the door with his fist. He hit it again. And again. The latch remained frozen.

Kyle let out a deep, angry cry. He raised his hands high above his head. He squeezed his eyes together tightly. After the release, his body was still as he tried to let go of the tension around his eyes. Slowly, he opened his eyes and looked up into the sky. He watched as wispy threads of white mist passed overhead like fragments of an angel's hair. He lowered his arms onto the roof of the car. *What's happening to me?*

He closed his eyes again and laid his head down on the roof of the car letting the warmth of the sun on his face soothe him. There was a voice inside him, one that was not his own, which said, get going. There isn't much time. He got into the Subaru, turned the key and drove off.

He drove in a daze to his father's old apartment. He trudged up the stairs, and unlocked the door. Stepping inside, he threw the keys onto the counter. He walked through the kitchen and over to the writing table which contained all the instructions for his journey to Tahiti. He tried to review the maps and information his father had prepared but he couldn't concentrate. He couldn't make sense of the words. He stood up and walked aimlessly from room to room.

In the bedroom, he pulled out some bags and began packing up the things of his father's that he wanted near him. He threw the instructions for Tahiti into one of the bags and sat back down at the table. He pulled some paper and a pen from the top drawer, and began to write.

> *Dear Eve,*
>
> *There are forces keeping us apart that I can't explain. I don't know how to save you, how to help you. It seems that, at least for now, the choice has been made for me — I must leave Innis. Your father has seen to that.*
>
> *I'm going to Tahiti to carry out my father's wishes. I wish you could be with me to feel the wind on your face, to let the power of the sea nurture you, restore you, and bring you back to health. I promised never to leave you—*

Then why are you? Fuck this, he thought, and threw the pen down on the table.

Kyle pulled an envelope from the drawer and shoved the unfinished letter inside. There was a gnawing in his gut. He was not sure if Eve would be alright. He did not have faith that good would prevail. His hand trembled as he sat there holding the letter. He was losing her. She was slipping away before he'd really had the chance to hold her.

He tossed the envelope into the bag with the other things and moved quickly, out the door, down the stairs and into the car. He pulled out of the parking lot and drove toward the marina.

When he reached the marina, Kyle went to see Frank Conner, the harbor master. He needed to put together a crew of six men and to thoroughly acquaint himself with the *Kyle Jordan* in just a few hours. He did this with the type of familiar detachment that he'd relied on throughout his life. Something had been ignited since he'd met Eve but now he had to put that out, to let the blaze die down and slowly turn to embers, maybe even to ash. This would not be that difficult, he'd done this before. But still, he knew he had to try to help Eve — even if it meant losing her. Getting her away from her father was what mattered most.

Once everything was prepared, he left the marina to go see Doris. When he got there she was camped out on the lawn.

"Hi," he said, getting out of the car.

Doris stood up and walked toward him in her bare feet. She held out her arms and wrapped him up in a warm, caring hug.

He pulled back and looked at her.

"Are you alright?" she asked.

"I'm fine. But we have a lot to do."

"When are you leaving?" she said.

"As far as anyone else but you is concerned, seven-thirty tomorrow morning."

"Are you sure you want to —."

"Doris," he said, "I have no choice. The Judge sent his dogs after me."

She gazed up at him. "I was afraid something like this would happen. I should never have told you about that needle."

"It's not your fault. It would have happened anyway. They pulled me over because I was speeding but when they saw my license they let me have it. They were looking for me anyway."

"You never made it to the house?"

Kyle shook his head. "Come on. What are we doing standing out here, anyway?"

"I couldn't get in, brat. You had my keys."

"Oh, yeah. By the way, your car door needs to be fixed."

"Thanks a lot," she said.

Doris and Kyle ordered pizza and went over the details of Kyle's plan. Thoughts of the unknown lingered just above their heads, like tiny particles of dust spinning all around. Unspoken concerns rested between their lips and on the tips of their tongues but they did not bring these concerns into reality by giving them voice.

Instead, they let them hover, suspended in midair, floating, drifting, and somehow connecting them to something bigger than themselves.

PETER LOOKED AT SARA. She had tears in her eyes and he realized he'd never seen her cry. Sara had always managed to keep herself emotionally removed from Peter. She was absorbed in her work, as he was. That's what had drawn them together. Whatever pain they each may have had in the past had never entered into their friendship, until now.

"I'm sorry to bring you into all this," Peter said, "I know it's —."

"That's alright," Sara said, sniffling. "I've been through so many cases like this, I don't know why this one is hitting me so hard. I guess part of it has to do with you, how difficult it's been for you all these years."

She began to cry harder and Peter held her for a while.

"I never told you," she said, "my sister committed suicide when I was a kid. My father had been sexually abusing her for years. I never spoke to him again, after Sabrina died. I was only six —."

Sara's shoulders shook as she fell into Peter's chest.

"Shh," he said, holding her.

Now Peter understood. Sara had been devoted to the study of psychological abuse of all kinds but had always been especially concerned with incest survival. In all her years of working with survivors she still hadn't been able to answer the one question she sought: Why? Understanding that had been her singular quest in life. He remembered many of their discussions about the importance of forgiveness in the process of healing incest related pain. Sara had always had trouble with that. Instead, she focused on helping her patients to forgive themselves. Maybe she needed help forgiving her own father, he thought.

Sara's body was crumpled in a heap of heaving bones and muscles, her tears were wetting Peter's shirt. Strands of hair were glued to her cheeks. Her stomach contracted again as another wave of emotion stirred through her body. She began to heave so hard she was gasping. Muffled sounds from a deep untapped reservoir found their way up through her lungs and out her mouth.

Peter stayed with her, rubbing her back, trying to comfort her.

"I'm so sorry," she said. "I don't know what's wrong with me. Why is this case throwing me so much? I feel so vulnerable."

"It's okay, Sara," Peter said. "You just needed to let go. You've been holding onto so much, for so long."

Sara nodded and stood up. She stared out the window for a while.

"Okay," she said, "how are we going to approach this thing?"

Peter smiled. "I have this theory," he said. "It has to do with combining music and hypnosis to harmonize with an individual's energy frequency.

I've experimented and found that the two tools work together to unlock hidden memories, blocked memories."

Sara moved toward him and sat down on the couch beside him. She raised her eyebrows and widened her eyes.

"Why haven't you ever told me? How long have you been working on this?"

"I stumbled onto it with a patient about four years ago. Since then I've been progressing with technique and results. I never told you, or anyone, because I feel it's very powerful. I didn't want it falling into the wrong hands."

"You mean Robert Whitman."

Peter nodded.

"I've been working with an inventor on a prototype machine that actually let's me record a person's energy field. Each person has their own unique energy pattern which surrounds them like a bubble — it's like a huge set of finger prints. The fields contain a lot more than just a person's individual material identity. They contain hundreds of memories and life experiences that are stored there. At least, until a person decides to release them."

"So," Sara said, "the patterns contained within the energy field affect a person's perspective. If they have a lot of painful trapped memories, chances are they won't be able to live a healthy and balanced life."

"That's right," Peter said. "So how it works is, once the frequency patterns have been recorded, I apply them to a computer program I've created. The program matches the frequency vibrations to certain, specific pieces of music. When we get a good match, one that resonates the same or harmonic frequencies, I use those selections of music during the sessions with the patient. Sometimes the results are instantaneous. I've been able to unlock pools of repressed memories, allowing patients the first step toward recovery which, as you know, is grief."

"It's brilliant," Sara said. "Remember the man I told you about on the phone, Justin Templeten?"

Peter nodded.

"Let's go see him. He was talking about the same kind of thing except his theory includes the concept of reincarnation so that the memories tap into many different lifetimes. It's more about being held captive in a way, to our past pain, like we're kind of stuck to certain individuals, sometimes the very people we're here to break free of."

"Oh, please —."

"No, really Peter. This guy makes sense and he's right here in Innis. If you ask me, that's a little spooky right there. Of all the places in the world, he's here. And you're working on something which he might be able to help advance. Let's go see him."

"Desperate times require desperate measures, I suppose. But if he turns out to be a weirdo I'm not staying and I'm really only doing this for Eve...and you. In the meantime, though, I think it's time to find out what happened when Eve's mother died. We need to get a session with her, away from Robert."

"Agreed," Sara said, and she stood up to search her bag for Justin Templeten's phone number and address.

CHAPTER SIXTEEN

D ORIS AND KYLE WERE up at first light as they had planned. They moved in silence around her apartment until it was time to leave.

Kyle glanced nervously at his watch.

"All set?" Doris said.

"One last thing," Kyle said. He took hold of her hand and gently drew her into the bright, sunlit kitchen he'd grown to love. He looked down at the harbor and pulled out the letter he'd written to Eve. He dropped his chin and stared down at the envelope.

Doris held out her hand to take the letter. "Enough, already," she said.

He looked over at her. She snatched the envelope from his hand and brought her eyes up to meet his.

"Will you take care of her, if anything happens to me?" Kyle said.

"Of course."

"No, I mean, do you really think you can help her?"

"I'll do what I can," she said.

They didn't say another word until they were at the marina and all his gear had been unloaded from the rental car.

"Want to come over and see the boat?"

Doris shook her head and pointed with her eyes to a man whose back was to them; he was standing beside a phone booth.

Kyle looked at her and frowned.

She winked and lifted her arms to embrace him when the man at the phone booth turned their way. She went through the motions of wishing Kyle a safe trip and assured him once more that she would look after Eve.

Doris backed out of the parking space in the dark blue rental, glancing briefly at the man who was now watching them sideways. She waved casually at Kyle and left him standing there alone, surrounded by the bags at his feet.

Just as she was about to turn the corner, Kyle shot his arm high into the air grinning after her, then bent down to hoist his gear. As he moved toward the pier where the *Kyle Jordan* waited, he felt the man's eyes follow him. He drew in a long breath of clean, salty air. Climbing on deck reminded him of how good it felt to be free.

"Permission to come aboard," shouted Frank Conner.

Kyle turned. The weathered man with the full white beard stood on the pier looking like a kid on Christmas morning. There was a group of five young men behind him, all anxious to sail the schooner bearing Kyle's name.

"Good morning," Kyle said, waving them on board. He glanced toward the phone booth. The man had moved over to a bench, sipping from a white styrofoam cup. Kyle turned back to his crew and began instructing them for their journey. When they were all in place Kyle took his position behind the ship's wheel.

There were good, strong winds that day and after the mainsail had been hoisted they picked up speed rapidly, reaching across the harbor toward the open sea.

Kyle turned to Frank Conner. "I really appreciate this," he said. "I couldn't have done it without your help."

"Don't mention it," Conner said. His bright eyes flashed at Kyle. "Your father was a friend of mine. Glad to help. Besides, Judge Whitman is not exactly one of my favorite people." He smiled, looking straight out to the sea.

AFTER HE HAD RECEIVED the phone call, Robert went out to the edge of his patio with his binoculars. He smirked with satisfaction as he watched the schooner sail out of the harbor. *Finally, Jordan is out of the picture. Maybe now things can get back to normal.* He watched through the lens until Kyle and his boat were out of sight then turned to get ready for work.

MRS. BRISTOL STOOD TIGHT-LIPPED at the front door of the Whitman mansion.

"Good morning, may I see Eve, please?" Doris said.

The housekeeper tried to stand up taller and raised an eyebrow. "And you are?"

"I'm her executive assistant," Doris said, with authority.

Mrs. Bristol cast her eyes downward as the sound of quick footsteps echoed across the marble foyer.

"Who's there?"

The plump woman looked at Doris. "What did you say your name was?"

"I didn't."

The two women stared at each other.

"Mrs. Bristol?" he called.

Doris waited.

"Your name," Mrs. Bristol said, looking up and not at Doris.

"Doris Stanley, Eve's executive assistant."

"Wait here," she said, and closed the door, leaving Doris standing outside on the doorstep.

The door swung open quickly; an attractive man was smiling at her. Doris recognized Eve's father from the Gala last year and like all the people of Innis, had seen frequent pictures of him in the newspaper. She was struck by his healthy good looks, and the brightness that shone out from behind his hazel eyes.

She smiled back.

"Hello," he said, robustly, tucking the morning paper under his arm. Stepping aside he waved her in. "So, I finally have the chance to meet Eve's secretary in person."

Doris stepped into the foyer still smiling.

He brought his hand forward. "I'm Judge Robert Whitman."

"It's nice to meet you. How's Eve? Do you suppose it would be possible for me to speak with her?"

Doris brought her fingers to her lips and tilted her head to one side. She watched as the Judge studied her. His eyes narrowed as he looked her over.

Doris leaned in toward him slightly, laughing softly.

"I'm sorry." She winked. "Sometimes I just talk too fast."

"Why don't you take a seat," he said, clearing his throat. "I'll go up and see if Eve is up to it."

"Thank you so much," Doris said, raising her right hand to rest lightly on her chest.

"My pleasure," he said.

Doris turned away and walked evenly over to the sitting room. From where she sat she was able to watch him as he walked smoothly up the elegant staircase. He looked down at her with a gaze that brought a chill to the surface of her skin. She fumbled through her briefcase full of paper work.

After he was out of sight Doris looked around the beautiful room, so perfectly decorated, everything in its place, so neat, so tidy. She heard his footsteps and pulled a file from her briefcase. She scowled at the papers until the Judge was standing directly in front of her.

"Well then, Miss Stanley," he said.

"Oh," she said, looking up. "I'm sorry, I didn't hear you."

"It is Miss, isn't it?"

"Miss," she said as she stood up. "How is she? Can I see her?"

"Yes, yes, of course. Did Mrs. Bristol offer you some coffee? A muffin, perhaps?"

"No, she didn't."

"Well then, you must. Please, come into the breakfast room."

"Is Eve coming down, or shall I go to her?" Doris said.

"She'll be down. She's really not been herself lately, though. Maybe your little visit will cheer her up."

"I really am here on business but I'll admit, I do miss her," Doris said, smiling at him softly.

He placed his hand firmly on the small of her back and swished her forward to the place where he wanted her. He held out a chair for Doris and then turned to pour her a cup of coffee.

"So tell me, how did you know Eve was sick? You know it completely slipped my mind to phone you," he said.

"It was one of our clients. He was with her when she first showed signs," Doris said.

"Signs? What kind of signs?" he asked, moving toward his chair.

"You know, signs of not feeling well."

"And which client was that, if I might ask?"

"Certainly," said Doris. "It was a man by the name of Kyle Jordan. He had come to Innis to settle his father's estate." She paused while he shifted in his seat. "He's gone now, though."

"I see," said the Judge, seemingly disinterested. "So? What kind of business are you here to discuss today?"

"Oh, you know. The usual humdrum details of running a legal practice. There are a million scheduling questions —."

"Hi, Doris."

Doris turned. Eve stood in the doorway barely able to hold her head up. She jumped up and went to her quickly.

"You poor thing," she said, calmly. "Come on, you're going back to bed."

Doris turned back to the Judge.

"We'll just go right up to her room," Doris said. "I'll only stay a little while. She really looks like she needs to rest."

With a wave of her hand and a jingle of her jewelry she and Eve disappeared.

Doris held her arm around Eve all the way up the stairs. Once they were in her bedroom Doris closed the door. She walked over to the bed and sat down. She stroked Eve's hair for a while, then lowered her head onto Eve's. She slowly rocked her back and forth, placing little kisses on the top of Eve's head.

She gently laid Eve down onto the pillows.

"It's good to see you," Eve said, nearly whispering.

"I wish I could say the same," Doris said. "You look horrible. What am I going to do with you?"

Eve smiled.

Doris took her limp hand.

"What's happening to me, Doris?"

"You're waking up, child."

Eve began to cry and she reached out to Doris for comfort. After a while she pulled away and asked for Peter, then Kyle. Doris took Eve's sad face into the palms of her hands.

"A lot has happened, Eve," she said. "The important thing right now is to get you back on your feet. Would you like to come to the office for a while? It might do you some good to get out of here."

Eve shook her head.

"How about going outside then?" Doris said. "It's beautiful today."

"Alright," Eve said.

Doris smiled and helped Eve to her feet.

As they walked arm in arm around the grounds of her father's estate Doris thought about how much she should tell Eve. She looked at her; her face had brightened some with the morning light. She's showing signs of life, thought Doris, I don't want to destroy that. She pulled Eve close.

"Thanks for coming," Eve said.

Doris stopped and turned to face her.

"I care about you, Eve. I want to help you. Will you let me?"

Eve looked away. "I appreciate everything you've done to keep the office running smoothly," she said.

"I'm not talking about the office," Doris said. "I'm talking about you and your skinny little body that looks like it's about ready to disappear."

Eve laughed and then suddenly her eyes filled with tears.

"Sometimes, I'd like to disappear," she said.

"Why?" Doris said.

"I don't know," she said, "I just do, that's all. If Peter were here he could give me a treatment and I'd feel better."

Eve dried her eyes.

"Something has happened hasn't it? Please tell me. And Father seems so detached, I just don't understand what's going on. You'll tell me, won't you?"

Doris opened her arms wide. "Come here," she said.

Eve hid her face in the crook of Doris' neck. Doris smoothed and stroked her hair. "I'll contact Peter for you. But he and your father have had a misunderstanding. It may be difficult for you to see him, unless we can keep it a secret," she whispered, as though the Judge may have planted hidden microphones in the garden.

"Where's Kyle?"

"Your father is trying to run him out of town."

Doris felt all the weight of Eve's slight body merge into hers. She stood firmly to give Eve the foundation she needed until she could no longer hold her. She lowered them both down onto the grass where they huddled together.

"Why wasn't I told?"

"No one wanted to upset you."

"But you did."

"I want you to get well and how can you ever be well, if you don't know the whole truth?" Doris said, gently.

"What's going to happen? How will I manage without Peter? He's more of a father to me than Daddy. He's always there for me but he never asks for anything back."

"And your father does?" Doris said.

Eve dropped her head and began yanking at the thick, even blades of well-cared-for grass. As Doris watched her she felt a tightness building inside her chest.

"What does he ask for?" Doris said.

Eve let out an odd, forced laugh. "Nothing, really. Just my whole being, my entire life," she said.

"Eve," Doris said, "it's going to be alright, trust me."

"Shall we go inside?" Eve asked. "Suddenly, I'm starving."

Doris sat with Eve in the breakfast room while she gorged on two muffins, two eggs, and a croissant. They talked about things at the office as though everything were perfectly normal while Mrs. Bristol cleared away the dishes. She turned to them before finally leaving the room.

"Your father asked me to tell you to get some rest today and that he hopes you're feeling better. He'll see you tonight at dinner."

Eve nodded. "Thank you, Mrs. Bristol."

It was time Doris left for the office and she walked with Eve toward the door.

"I feel so much better. I'm so glad you came," Eve said.

"When are you coming back to work?"

Suddenly Eve was distracted. She began fidgeting with her hands and then began rubbing her thumb and forefinger together in little circles.

"What's wrong?" Doris said.

Eve blinked at Doris. Her milky green eyes grew larger.

Doris took hold of Eve's shoulders firmly. She was trying to draw Eve back from the scary place she had tumbled into. Doris reached up and brushed her cheek with the back of her hand.

"Eve?"

Eve's eyes turned to liquid and Doris knew that she was thinking of Kyle. She embraced her, trying to bring comfort where comfort could not go. Doris bent down to fish through her purse.

"I have something for you," she said, without looking up.

Eve straightened and wiped her eyes.

"I want you to listen to me," Doris said. "I'm going to give you this but you have to promise me that you're going to push this confusion aside and start pretending that everything is fine."

Eve's dark eyebrows wove together as she squinted at Doris.

"What I'm saying is that I want to see you at the office tomorrow morning at the usual time. Whether you do any work or not is beside the point. I don't want you hanging around this house any more than you have to."

"This is my home," Eve said.

"Do you trust me?" Doris said.

Eve's eyes went soft. "More than anybody, I guess."

"Guessing isn't good enough. I want you to feel it, in here," Doris said, placing her palm on Eve's heart. Eve put her own hand on top.

"Okay," she whispered.

Doris handed the letter to Eve and Eve gasped.

"I knew it wouldn't last," she said. "I knew he wouldn't stay."

Doris took back the letter, scowling at Eve. She raised a pointed finger at her.

"If I give this to you, you must keep your mind and heart open." Doris passed Eve the letter with a smile. "Keep this in a safe place. I'll answer all your questions tomorrow when I see you at work."

"Okay," Eve said.

Doris paused for a moment as Eve shifted her weight from side to side, feeling the envelope between her fingertips and chewing on the side of her lip.

As Doris walked down the steps, Eve shouted out, "Bye. See you tomorrow."

Unable to look at her again, Doris raised her arm and waved, moving quickly toward her little green car.

CHAPTER SEVENTEEN

SARA SAT UP IN THE BED tapping her pasty tongue inside her mouth as she looked around Peter's guest room. It had been a late night; Eve's case was so complex. She felt like she hadn't showered or brushed her teeth in a week. Her breath smelled like rotten fruit. She wrestled with her wrinkled skirt which was twisted tightly around her hips. 9:42; she sighed deeply.

They were going to see Justin Templeten in less than an hour; she laid back down. She crossed her arms behind her head as images from her dreams drifted through her mind.

She had dreamed she was in a heavenly spotlight hovering about a foot above the ground. She wore a long flowing gown and her hair was much longer, swirling around her body and face from the wind she seemed to be creating. The woods around her were very dark. The light she brought was the only light and it penetrated a circle of white mist into the blackness.

There was a path in front of her and she was waiting for someone. Fat red robins spun a halo around her head, singing while they encircled her. She saw a girl coming toward her from faraway. She lifted her arms and reached them out which turned her arms into torchlights, illuminating the path more brightly so the girl could find her way, and so she wouldn't be afraid.

Just as she thought the girl would make it to her safely a man came suddenly between them. She couldn't see who he was; she only saw him from the back and he was blocking the girl.

She waited for as long as she could, unable to move from that spot where she was for some reason. Then the man tipped his head back and let out a horrible, sinister laugh. The girl had disappeared and Sara drifted sadly away, taking the light with her, leaving the girl and the man in the dark woods until her image completely faded and everything went black.

There was a knock on the door.

"Sara?" Peter said. "We should get going if we're going to make this appointment. You up?"

"I'm up," she said.

PETER GLANCED ACROSS the front seat at Sara.

"You okay?"

Sara nodded.

"You seem preoccupied," he said.

"I had a strange dream last night. Like I was an angel trying to save a girl from this horrible man."

"What's strange about that. Seems obvious, that's what you're dealing with right now."

"I know but there was something more to it. I couldn't save her from him."

"You put too much pressure on yourself Sara. You've helped hundreds of patients—."

"This was more personal. I can't explain it," Sara said, looking out the window as they drove through town.

"And I can't explain what I'm doing here, in the driveway of a man's cottage who claims to be psychic," Peter said, grinning at Sara.

"Oh come on, this'll be fun," she said, slapping his arm before getting out of the car.

Justin Templeten met them at the front door. They followed him down the hallway and into a sunny room lined with books. He showed them where to sit and asked how he could help.

Peter leaned back in his chair to observe this tall, dark man.

"Well," Sara said, "we're psychiatrists. I heard you speak a couple of months ago out in San Francisco. I thought of you because Peter's doing research on the affects of using music in healing patient trauma." She looked at Peter who remained silent and stiff.

Templeten nodded graciously.

"The primary reason we're here is to discuss the possibility of collaborating with you, based on your knowledge of how music can help in the healing process — since that's what the lecture was on when I heard you speak. As far as I can tell, from the little that Peter's explained to me about his work," she shot another look at Peter, "you both seem to be on the same track. Using music to affect and heal the human energy field."

"Is there someone in particular for whom you have concerns? Or, are you just looking to enhance your practice in general?" Justin said.

Peter and Sara both began to speak at once. Justin turned to Peter.

"This is a fishing expedition, of sorts," Peter said, clearing his throat. "We're just interested in comparing our theory with yours, to see if there are ways to improve upon some pretty startling successes we've already seen."

"So you won't be using this information to assist someone right away?" Justin said.

Sara looked at Peter.

"You tell me," Peter said pointedly to Justin.

Justin smiled at them. "Something to drink? Tea, or juice?" he said.

"I'd love some tea," Sara said. "Peter?"

"I'm fine."

While Justin was out of the room, Sara whispered to Peter. "Stop being so suspicious. He won't even want to help us if you keep acting this way."

"What way?" Peter whispered back.

They heard footsteps coming down the hallway. Sara frowned at Peter and mouthed for him to be nice.

"Here we are," Justin said. He sat down, crossed his long legs and brought his hands together in his lap. He smiled at Sara then turned to Peter again.

"I understand your concerns," Justin said, quietly. "You have not experienced much in the way of what some might call spiritual confirmation in this lifetime."

"You don't know anything about my life," Peter said. Realizing the hostility in his voice, he glanced quickly over at Sara.

"May I?" Justin said, opening his hands in unison.

"May you what," Peter said, squinting at him.

"May I tell you what I know about your life?"

Peter cleared his throat. "Why not?"

"You are a good man, with a good heart but your life has not been without its difficulties. You have a keen mind and your abilities to help others heal is well noted —."

"Well noted? By whom?" Peter said.

"By the angels, the gods and the guides."

Peter laughed. Justin gazed softly into his eyes which caused Peter to cut his laughter short midway through a note.

"May I continue?" Justin said.

Peter shifted in his seat and sat up straighter.

"I thought we came here to talk about music therapy?" he said. He looked at Sara who shrugged. "Fine," he said. "I don't have anything to hide anymore."

"True. It's time for you to take a stand. We see the way you've been trapped as a result of your actions with your fiancée, but remember, no one is held captive without first choosing that on some level."

"Oh, now wait a minute," Peter said, standing up. "I never chose to be so filled with rage that I sent my own fiancée to her death." He turned abruptly back to Justin.

"Please," Justin said, who was also standing, "sit down. I'd like to help you, if you'll let me."

Peter and Justin returned to their seats. Sara reached across the table to rub Peter's arm.

"Your choices involved walking away before the violent act, and then, facing up to the consequences of your own actions. So you see, you did choose."

"What are you saying?"

"I'm saying that the time has come for you to forgive yourself. And to forgive Robert Whitman for the role he has played as well. You have paid for your mistake by using Eve as the pawn, by giving away your own dignity, by selling your soul in a manner of speaking. It's not too late to undo the damage."

Peter's eyes were red behind his tears. Sara scraped her chair closer to him.

"How can he know this?" Peter said to Sara, who smiled sympathetically. "I don't know what to do anymore. Everything is coming undone, and poor Eve, she has no idea —."

Peter's shoulders shook as his words broke apart. He took off his glasses, rubbed his eyes and looked back at Justin.

"How do you know about all of this?" Peter said.

"Let's just say, it's my job. I have unusual hearing and sight and I try to put it to good use," Justin said.

"Can you help us?" Peter said.

"I know that's why you're here. But first there are some things I'd like to share with you." He turned to Sara. "It's a big day, today."

Sara eyed him suspiciously.

"In what way?" she said.

"In the way that can change the course of a person's destiny. Or, in this case, several people's lives. Would you like me to explain why you're so affected by this case with Eve?"

"I'm not sure, would I?" Sara said, looking at Peter for reassurance.

"I think you're ready," Justin said. "And you have Peter with you."

"Okay," Sara said.

"You are Carolyn Whitman," Justin said, matter-of-factly.

Sara blurted and turned to Peter whose jaw was hanging open.

"That's ridiculous." Peter said.

No one said anything for a moment, then Peter said, "You know, she does look a lot like Carolyn, I've always thought so." Peter looked back and forth between them. "This time, I was really struck by it when I saw you at the airport."

Sara scowled at them both in disbelief.

"What did you just say?" she said, looking at Justin.

"You are Carolyn Whitman."

"That's what I thought you said, but that's impossible," Sara said, shaking her head.

"Why is it impossible?" Justin said.

"Because it is. I'm Sara Daniels. I'm absolutely no relation to the

Whitman's. I grew up in a completely different part of the country and I'm young enough to be Eve's sister."

"That's all true," Justin said, quietly. "Do you remember when you were six years old after your sister died?"

Sara nodded slowly, then looked to Peter for support. He moved closer putting his arm around her shoulder. She pulled away.

"Remember how you decided that you didn't want to live anymore? How you didn't want to be part of that family any longer?"

"I don't exactly remember making that decision but I remember not wanting to be there," Sara said.

"Exactly. And, do you remember how people used to say how you seemed to have changed overnight?"

"Of course I changed. My sister killed herself, because my father was molesting her and my mother refused to believe her. Who wouldn't be changed after that?"

Sara's breathing had grown shallow, her chest rose and fell rapidly. Her face was flushed.

Justin leaned across the table and reached his hands over to place his palms along her jaw bones. Gently he pulled her head toward his until their foreheads met. He breathed dramatically in and out, long slow, deep breaths.

Sara's fear melted. The tension in her neck disappeared and her heart relaxed. He released her forehead slowly and looked deep into her eyes still holding gently onto her face.

Sara reached up and covered his hands with her own, then slowly pulled them away from her face. There was something in all of this which felt okay, even though it seemed absurd. It was not believable, too many questions planted seeds of doubt, but if she let it rest gently, just there upon her heart, it almost made sense. Besides, how would he know about her childhood? She held his hands for a moment, not wanting to let go.

She looked over at Peter.

"Okay, I'm listening," she said. "Tell me what you think I should know." She looked into Justin's dark, sunlit eyes.

"It's not about what I think you should know, Sara. It's what you've asked to learn. You brought me here."

"Me?" she said grinning. "I had no idea I was so powerful... ."

"After you told your father you would never speak to him again, the people around you began to comment on how dramatically your looks were changing, even the color of your hair shifted from blond to dark brown. And how unusual it was that a person's eye color could grow darker, as yours did."

"What are you getting at?" Peter said.

"Carolyn took over the body that belonged to the old Sara Daniels," Justin said, sitting back in his chair.

"Oh, Jesus. This is crazy," Peter said.

Sara stood up. She was trying to be open but this was making her edgy. She paced around the room until she stopped suddenly.

"Okay, let me see if I've got this straight because judging from the look in your eyes, there's more."

She raised one hand to indicate she wanted a response.

Justin nodded.

"So, I'm dead. I've left my daughter behind to live out a fate worse than death with an empty-hearted lascivious father. I panic, what's a mother to do? I begin searching the earth for a little girl body, preferably one who no longer wishes to remain on the planet because her own father is also a creep, and because of it her sister killed herself, and voilà, I find one. Over in the Sacramento area, California is a bit far away from Connecticut, but at least they both begin with C. I'll take it, after all—."

"Sara," Peter said, softly, "maybe we should hear the man out.

Come, sit down."

Sara walked over and collapsed into the chair. She looked at Justin, frowning.

"Listen," Justin said, leaning in. "There are no coincidences. Every day of your waking life as Sara Daniels you have been preparing for this moment. You and Eve and Peter will help each other be free, that's the gift of your reunion."

Sara moaned.

"Let me ask you this. Do you feel an unusual connection to Eve?"

"I haven't even met her yet."

"I know, but in learning about her life has it struck an emotional chord within you?"

"Yes," Sara said, lifting her chin slightly.

"And do you feel an inordinate amount of passion toward her father?"

"I wouldn't exactly call it passion," she said. "Hatred would be more like it."

"Hatred is a form of passion, Sara. It's the reversal of love. And if you had loved Robert once and he betrayed you, wouldn't you suppose the intensity of your once positive emotion could be reversed? Become negative?"

"If all of what you're telling us is true, why don't I remember any of it? Wouldn't it be much more cosmically efficient for me to have just plunked myself back into my life as Carolyn Whitman?"

"That would not have been possible. She died at Robert's hand. There are karmic debts which need to be repaid. It's not up to you to undo the damage he's done. Besides, what about the dream?"

"The dream?" Sara asked slowly, turning a wide-eyed gaze toward Peter.

"What if I told you that Eve had a very similar dream just before her breakdown? What if I told you that it was a reminder to each of you to find a way to unite? To conquer the man who stood between you in the path."

Sara was silent. "I can't believe you know about that." She swallowed.

"So it's up to me to undo the damage that's been done to Eve, that's why I'm here?"

"You weren't able to let go of being her mother. You loved her very much and were so grief stricken that you chose an immediate return to the physical plane."

Sara was almost ready to accept the whole thing, her heart was breaking but maybe this explained it. Suddenly, a little red flag waved proudly inside her brain.

"And where is the old Sara Daniels?" she said, smugly. "Did I just kick her out of this body, and send her tumbling into the cosmic void?"

"It was a mutual agreement," Justin said. "And she's much happier in her silent role as a guide to another sensitive child for now, until she's ready to try again."

Sara shook her head and turned to Peter.

"I'm speechless," he said.

"You know, part of me wants to believe you," Sara said to Justin. "But I'm an analyst. Someone who works with facts, the logical progression of events." She looked out the window.

"Your reentry has some dramatic circumstances surrounding it. Most people wait for a new body to house them, so they can reenter the physical plane gradually, as an infant." Justin paused. "Listen carefully. The information your higher-self sends is subtle, have faith when you do hear it. Let that be your guide."

"If there are all these divine action plans happening out there, why are there so many victims?" Sara said.

"Right," Peter said, "why do people hurt each other in these obscene and terrible ways?"

Justin Templeten drew in a deep breath and closed his eyes.

"For now, let me say this," he said. "Each life you come across is just a representational piece of that soul energy. That piece, contained within the individual personality, holds within its cellular memory stories within stories within stories. Some of these stories have happy endings, some do not. Some souls come into a life with karmic debts to repay and some come in with credits to spend. If a soul, such as the one of Robert Whitman, continues to make the dark choice the chain that links his soul with another's continues on until one or both of the two souls that created the link deliberately chooses a higher path, a lighter choice."

"Are you saying that on some karmic level, Eve is at fault for what has happened to her?" Sara said, incredulously.

"No. I'm responsible," Peter said, staring blankly at the floor.

Justin moved closer to Peter. "It's time to forgive yourself, Peter. Letting go, will help to break the chain."

The tears came again, and Justin reached up to guide Peter's forehead onto his. Peter felt himself release something far beneath the surface, something he'd carried there for a long, long time. When he looked up at Sara, she was crying, too. They smiled and reached for each other's hand.

"To answer your question," Justin said, "no one deserves pain. But Eve and Robert have suffered many unfavorable lives together, each one becoming increasingly more destructive. It's within Eve's power, as it is within Robert's, to release them both from the destruction of their relationship."

"How?" Peter and Sara said in unison.

"Forgiveness."

"That's it?" Sara said.

"It's more than many people can manage, I'm afraid. Think of all the disputes between groups with different beliefs, the countries at war because in their history someone along the way had done them wrong. But, when it comes wholly from the heart, and is felt deeply and genuinely, the release is instantaneous."

"It seems too simple," Peter said. "Are we all so blind?"

Justin let out a melodic laugh.

"You two don't ask simple questions, do you?"

They both smiled, still waiting for an answer.

"To forgive is to accept the truth. And the truth is often elusive to those with varying points of view. When you forgive someone you accept them and all their weaknesses and you give them love, no matter what they've done or how they think."

Sara nodded.

"Love is all it takes to heal any wound. For you, Peter, it is self love. For you, Sara, it is the unending love of a parent for her child and also of the ones who have hurt her. You've been able to forgive Peter, now you need to forgive Robert. Then you will be whole. Together, through the strength of your love for one another each of you will learn to forgive."

Peter and Sara sat very still.

"And now I must say goodbye," Justin said.

"Wait a minute. What about our discussion on music therapy?" Peter said.

"Another time. Meanwhile, listen to your hearts. You will know what to do. You have made some progress already, and when it's time I am available to assist with Eve, if you still desire."

"Can I just ask, how do I fit into all this from a reincarnation perspective? How did I manage to get so tangled up in Robert's web?" Peter said.

"The two of you have shared many times together. There was the time when you were the father to both Robert and Eve. You were a warrior who died in battle, and so never saw them grow up—."

"Who was my wife?"

"That would be the one who was Jennifer in this time."

"Oh my God."

Peter brought his hands to his face.

"There is much that is veiled in this existence. That does not mean however, that it does not exist, only that it can not be seen. Right now, the most important thing is for Eve to remember the death of her mother.

From there, all else will unfold."

Sara and Peter both nodded, feeling they'd been hit with a stun gun. They stood up to thank Justin and said goodbye.

Peter would drop Sara off at his condo and head to the clinic to deal with his regular routine and the uncomfortable circumstances he'd created by the Judge's fraudulent incarceration.

When they arrived at Peter's building, he leaned over to kiss Sara and she kissed him back.

"That was amazing," she said. "I mean, the session with Justin, not the kiss."

They both laughed.

"Yeah, but I have a splitting headache," Peter said. "I think it's going to take a while for all this to filter through. I feel better though. Just knowing that someone like him exists makes me feel safer, less afraid, you know? Especially when it comes to Robert. You don't think Templeten's a complete charlatan do you?"

"How could he have known all that stuff about us? He must be for real. It's going to be alright, I can feel it," Sara said.

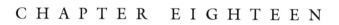

CHAPTER EIGHTEEN

E VE SLOWLY PUT THE PHONE DOWN
into its cradle. Her heart beat slow and hard.
Her father had not taken her call.

An hour passed and still she had not moved. Unanswered questions spun around her brain, like a whirlwind they were picking up speed. She was pulling on her hair now, trying to withdraw the pain. Her body began to quiver then shake. She began to scream — loud, shrill, agonizing cries which sounded as if she was being beaten or tortured.

Mrs. Bristol came running up the stairs toward her room. She stopped cold in the doorway when she saw Eve huddled in the corner, yanking on her hair, screaming. Her eyes had taken on a kind of fluorescence as they darted back and forth, up and down, as though frightening creatures surrounded her. She kept trying to push herself farther back into the corner, pushing against the walls, screaming and pulling on her hair.

This time, Mrs. Bristol was not annoyed. This time she was afraid. Her heart beat rose inside her head. She tried to swallow her horror and slid away from the door before Eve could see her. She hurried down the stairs and over to the phone where she dialed the clinic to ask for Peter. In a breathless voice she tried to explain the state that Eve Whitman had worked herself into. She was put on hold while the woman who answered went to find Dr. Weiss.

Mrs. Bristol smoothed her uniform over her hips nervously, first one hand then the other, again and again.

When she returned, the woman explained to Mrs. Bristol that Peter had not arrived, could someone else help?

Mrs. Bristol urged her to find Dr. Weiss, to have him come at once, all the while Eve's screeching grew more and more desperate in the background. The woman said they would need the Judge's consent. Mrs. Bristol told her she'd been unable to reach him.

She hung up the phone and urged the rest of the household staff to go home. She paced back and forth in the foyer, wringing her hands, trying not to hear the haunted screams wafting down the stairs. Something deep within Mrs. Bristol told her to give Eve this chance, that's why she didn't bother to call the Judge.

After nearly half an hour, the doorbell rang.

Mrs. Bristol scrambled to the door. Frazzled, she waved Peter, Sara Daniels and the two orderlies up the stairs without a word. She was so frantic that she didn't even notice the resemblance of this woman to Eve's late mother until Sara Daniels was inside Eve's bedroom, crouched beside her, cooing and shushing her as if she were an infant.

Standing quietly in the doorway, Mrs. Bristol tried to take in the scene inside Eve's bedroom. Seeing Eve and this woman together, close enough in age and appearance to be sisters, sent a shiver through her body. Mrs. Bristol rubbed her arms briskly but the chill remained long after they had all driven away with Eve strapped to a stretcher in the back of the white emergency van.

She stood in the foyer for a while and then walked directly to the desk in the Judge's study. She calmly pulled a sheet of writing paper from the top right drawer and laid it down on the padded blotter. She lifted the Mont Blanc pen from its pedestal and slowly and evenly wrote: Judge Robert Whitman, Here you have my resignation. Signed, Emily Bristol, March 27, 1996.

She laid the pen across the page and stared at the words, as if she herself was surprised by what they said. Then, feeling a lightness rise up from low within her belly she lifted her ample chin and turned to walk out the door of the study. As she moved through the house and toward the kitchen the sensation of lightness lifted her and carried her like the wings of a bird. She gathered her belongings, put on her hat, opened the back door and stepped out into the beauty of that fine Spring day. The robins seemed especially happy she thought, pausing for a moment to listen.

As she got into her car, she took one last look around the grounds. Twenty-two years, and she did not suppose that she would miss this place. Getting in her car and turning the key sent a wave of giddiness across her heart. The delicious sensation of freedom made her laugh softly. Smiling, she pulled away from the big house and down the grand drive.

ROBERT PULLED INTO THE GARAGE at the usual time. The staff cars were all gone. He opened the back door cautiously and stepped into the kitchen. There were no smells coming from the stove. There was an eerie silence as he moved slowly through the house. His blood pulsated through his veins as he moved methodically from one room to the next.

"Mrs. Bristol? Eve?"

He sneaked up the stairs with his back against the wall.

"Eve? Are you up here?"

His heart beat faster as he turned the corner toward Eve's room. A pain shot swiftly through his chest. Maybe she's sleeping and has sent the staff away so that they could have some privacy, he thought. He turned the corner to her bedroom.

All the air escaped his lungs, his shoulders and arms hung as though paralyzed. The room looked like a tornado had hit. Bed covers, clothes and shoes were strewn everywhere across the floor. Her bedside table had been knocked over and the lamp lay sideways against the wall. Shattered slivers of the light bulb shimmered in a stream of late afternoon sunlight. Robert stared at the tiny bits of broken glass. He slouched against the door frame. His knees went weak and his body slid down until he landed on the softness of the plush carpet.

PETER GAVE EVE a sedative to help her rest and once she was asleep left Sara to watch over her and went to check on his other patients. When he got to his office there were seven messages from Doris Stanley.

Peter picked up the phone.

"Whitman Law Office," Doris said.

"Yes, Doris. This is Doctor Peter Weiss, I—."

"Oh, good, Dr. Weiss. I'm so glad you called. I was out to see Eve this morning and she is not well. Not at all, and I was wondering if there is any way for you to—."

"She's here now," Peter said.

"Where?"

"Here, at the clinic."

"Oh, great. So her father can just walk back in there and take her out again?"

"Doris, I appreciate your concern, but this is a very complex —."

"Please, Dr. Weiss. She's right on the edge, I want to help. How can I help? Do you want to move her over to my place?"

"She really needs to be in a clinical environment, Doris. I think it's best if she stays here. Sara and I have agreed never to leave her alone, we'll take turns watching her."

"Sara? Who's Sara and you know Kyle was in that room with Eve before. A lot of good that did. Whitman almost killed him, you know," Doris said, breathing heavily into the phone.

"I didn't know that," Peter said, pulling off his glasses to rub his eyes. "Where's Kyle now? Is he alright?"

"He had to sail away. The Judge threatened to set him up for drug trafficking. Who's Sara?"

"Sara is an associate of mine, Dr. Sara Daniels, she agreed to come out from California to assist me on the case. Tell you what Doris, why don't you come in to see Eve in the morning. She'd like that and you could meet Dr. Daniels."

"Fine, I'll see you in the morning." Doris said, and hung up the phone.

THE NEXT MORNING Robert Whitman hummed a tune as he skipped down the stairs. He moved quickly and efficiently into his study to place a couple of calls before leaving for the clinic.

He spotted Mrs. Bristol's note of resignation on his desk.

You fat cow...don't think I don't know how you loved to listen to us from outside the door. Horny old bitch — I should have given it to you when I had the chance. He smirked as he crumpled up the paper and tossed it into the waste paper basket before picking up the phone.

He stopped briefly to inspect himself in the hall mirror. Satisfied, he stepped out the door and over to his pale green Jaguar. He had chosen the color precisely because it matched the extraordinary shade of Eve's eyes.

EVE SQUINTED FROM THE glaring morning sunlight. She was in the same room she'd been in before her father had taken her home. It reminded her of Kyle and that made her heart feel heavy. Her head pounded as tears began to flood her eyes. She was all alone. She had been alone for as long as she could remember. Even Kyle seemed like another one of her imaginary friends from childhood now. A fantasy she'd dreamed up so that she could pretend to have a happy life. She couldn't even think about her father; it was too confusing. She curled herself up into a little ball, hugging one pillow for comfort while soaking the other one with tears.

She felt the soft touch of a woman's hand against her wet cheek. She stopped crying enough to open her eyes. Things were blurry as she tried to focus first on the wall in front of her, and then at the woman standing beside her bed. Her eyes stung. She listened attentively to the footsteps which moved around the foot of the bed and then toward her again. The person sat down on the bed, the same way Kyle had done.

Who was this? Eve knew she wasn't a nurse. She wiped her eyes again and tried to focus through her foggy vision. She thought she was imagining the face she finally saw before her.

Eve blinked at the woman who was smiling kindly at her.

She blinked again.

"Hi Eve," Peter said, from the other side of the bed. "This is my friend Dr. Sara Daniels."

"Hello, Eve."

Eve's tears had cleared now but she still squinted at Sara.

"Are you feeling okay?" Sara said.

Eve shrugged a shoulder.

"I'll give you a little time to wake up. Would you like to take a shower? You could put on one of your pretty dresses and we could go out for breakfast."

Eve screwed up her face, closing one eye halfway.

"Why can't you just give me a treatment, Peter?" Eve said, after turning to look at him.

"Maybe later. Right now I'd like you to get to know Dr. Daniels."

"Come on then, up you go," Sara said, and pulled Eve's torso into a sitting position.

Eve fell into the woman's shoulder like a rag doll. The close contact with her felt good. She lifted her head and looked shyly at Sara.

Sara reached over and stroked her face.

Eve was surprised. She felt a tiny tingle inside her stomach. She imagined a butterfly tickling her with the soft fluttering of its velvet wings.

Sara looked softly at Eve.

Eve smiled at her like a child. Sara helped her into the bathroom and began to undress her. Eve had a strange sensation that everything about this person was familiar. She sat on the toilet with one foot on top of the other and watched herself sweep a strand of Sara's hair away from her face as if she was in a dream.

Eve giggled.

"What's funny?" Sara said.

"I don't know. You're so serious," Eve said.

Sara helped Eve into the shower and took Eve's place on the toilet. Eve was glad every time she peeked around the shower curtain to find that Sara was still there.

Just as Eve was stepping out of the shower there was a knock on the door. Sara wrapped her in a towel and went out to see who was there.

Eve was content, not the least bit curious. She heard mumbled words going up and down, back and forth, and all around. The tone of the muffled words made her feel a bit uneasy. She hummed softly to herself to cover up the sounds on the other side of the door. She began drying one arm then the other, one leg then the other, until her whole body was dry. She sat back down on the toilet cover with the damp towel rewrapped snugly around her and waited quietly for the butterfly lady to come back.

Eve watched the door handle turn to the right. Sara stepped through the door and Eve smiled brightly. Sara wasn't smiling.

"Your father is on his way over to see you," she said.

Eve's face went blank. She made tiny rhythmic circles with her thumb and forefinger.

"Eve...did you hear me?"

"Mmm," Eve said, staring down at the floor.

"How does that make you feel?" Sara said.

"Fine," she said, with a shrug.

Sara took a fresh towel to rub Eve's hair dry.

"Ouch!"

"Oh, Eve, I'm sorry. I guess I wasn't paying attention—."

"You were thinking about Daddy, that's why."

Sara dropped the towel and knelt down to come face-to-face with Eve.

"Why do you say that?" Sara said.

"Because, it's true...isn't it?" Eve said.

"It is true. But how did you know?"

Eve tilted her head and brought her shoulder up to meet her ear.

"Why do you think?" Sara said.

"I think you're kind of like my shadow," Eve said, and looked tentatively at Sara.

"I'm not your shadow, Eve. I'm your friend."

They smiled at each other; Eve lowered her eyes.

"I've never had a real friend," Eve said, so quietly that Sara could barely hear her.

"Sure you have. How about Doris and Peter, and Kyle?."

"Oh yeah," Eve said, sadly. "They don't like me anymore, though."

"Of course they do. In fact, Peter is very worried about you. And Doris is coming to see you today."

"Okay," she sighed and then stood up to get dressed.

WHEN ROBERT WHITMAN stepped off the elevator to the third floor he saw Peter leaning against the nurses' station with a woman he thought he recognized. He couldn't see the woman Peter was laughing with very well, but he tried to place her as he walked closer toward them, down the hall. As he approached them his stomach tightened. When Sara Daniels turned around to face him directly he felt his throat constrict. His nostrils flared involuntarily and he let out a small, dry cough.

"Hello Robert. Good of you to come, Eve gave us all quite a scare," Peter said.

Robert was staring at Sara.

"Oh, forgive me," Peter said. "Sara, I'd like you to meet Judge Robert Whitman, Eve's father. He practically runs Innis single-handedly. Robert, this is my good friend Sara Daniels who's come out all the way from San Francisco."

"To get away from it all," Sara said. "If you know what I mean."

Robert's mind's eye flashed unwelcome images of his dead wife. Smiling snapshots he'd thought he'd torn up and tossed away a long time ago flickered across his forehead. The resemblance of this woman to Carolyn was so striking that it took all his training to mask what he felt inside.

"Do I ever," he said, with his usual composure. "One really must get away — it helps to regain one's perspective."

"Absolutely," Sara said, smiling.

"Robert, about Eve," Peter said, "she's quite ill."

Robert cleared his throat and shifted his weight. "Yes, she hasn't been herself, the flu I suppose, she's been working too hard, got a bit run down, although I'm sure she'll be back at it very soon."

Peter and Sara looked blankly back at him.

Robert narrowed his eyes. "What kind of work did you say you were in?" he said to Sara.

"Sara is a brilliant musician," Peter said, quickly, "with the San Francisco Symphony Orchestra."

"Oh, really," said Robert. "What instrument?"

"Actually, my first love is the piano but I also play the flute, the saxophone and the guitar," Sara said, smiling softly.

"Fascinating." Robert said, flatly.

Robert turned his back on Sara and faced Peter.

"May I speak to you privately?" Robert said.

"Of course."

Peter led Robert further down the corridor where some staff people were working. Sara stayed at the nurses' station.

"What the fuck is going on?" Robert said, smiling through his teeth.

"Your daughter is having a breakdown. Didn't Mrs. Bristol tell you we came out to get her? She was severely distressed, extremely agitated, beyond any state she's ever been—."

"Yeah, I saw the mess. I'm taking her home."

Peter smiled broadly. "You're kidding, right?"

"How long?"

"A few weeks Robert. She's—."

"Like Hell. I'll be here to pick her up in two days, you see that she's ready. Maybe if you spent less time flirting with Little Miss Sara over there you could concentrate on what you're here for. Who is she anyway?

You've never mentioned her before."

"There are some things you don't need to know."

"We'll see about that, she's very familiar...," Robert said. "Tell Eve I'm tied up for a couple days, I'll see her on Thursday and I'll call her later. Get her better, Peter. I don't want people talking anymore than they already are."

Peter nodded and Robert turned away. When he stepped off the elevator into the lobby Robert bumped into a woman wearing a bright blue dress and big purple sunglasses.

"Doris?" he said.

"Judge Whitman. Nice to see you again," said Doris.

He reached out his hand to her. When she took his large, square hand he felt himself begin to perspire almost immediately. He quickly pulled it away.

"I really appreciate all you're doing for Eve. Perhaps I could repay you by taking you to lunch one day soon?"

"Aren't you nice."

The elevator bell dinged and the door slid open.

"There's my ride," Doris said. She stepped onto the platform smiling.

"I'll call you at the office," Robert said. He saw her nod just before the elevator doors closed between them.

DORIS STEPPED UP TO the third floor nurses' station to ask for the number of Eve's room. One of the nurses picked up the phone and whispered into it before telling her the room number. A second later a serious, dark-haired woman stepped out a door and into the hallway.

Doris was struck by the resemblance this woman had to Eve. Same body type, hair color, even the same style of dress. She seemed to carry a huge and heavy weight around her neck.

"Doris Stanley?" the woman said.

"Yes," Doris said, holding out her hand to greet her, "I'm Doris Stanley."

"Good to meet you. I'm Sara Daniels," she said, smiling back at Doris.

When their hands met, Doris knew that this woman was there to help. She was on a mission, no doubt about it.

"Before we go in to see Eve," Doris said, "could we talk privately for a few minutes?"

"Of course," Sara said, and led her into another room and closed the door.

"Here's the thing," Doris said, immediately, "you're going to need me on this one. I've been working with Eve for over a year now and there are things about her that I know that even she isn't aware of."

Sara smiled.

"I've heard about you from Peter, he thinks highly of you. I take it you and Eve are close?"

"You could say that," Doris said.

"I'll talk to Peter and see if I can get away this afternoon," Sara said.

Doris stepped closer and squeezed both Sara's hands. A split second later she had a strong image of a handsome couple on their wedding day. At first, she thought it was Eve and Kyle. But then she realized the man was a younger Robert Whitman. And the woman she'd mistaken for Eve looked almost exactly like Sara Daniels, with her distinctive pouty mouth and those intense eyes. Instantly, Doris saw that this woman was intimately linked to Whitman — she was his wife's incarnate, and he owed her a huge karmic debt. Doris smiled sadly, no wonder Sara Daniels seemed protective of Eve.

Doris let go of Sara's hands and stepped back.

"I'm glad you're here," she said.

Sara squinted curiously at Doris but then her eyes softened.

"So am I."

ROBERT FINALLY GOT THE call from San Francisco a few hours after he'd left the clinic. Sara Daniels was not a musician, but a psychiatrist. He also found out she'd made numerous phone calls to Peter, both to the clinic and to his home, within the last two weeks. Peter was still trying to beat him. He laughed. But then the unsettling image of Sara Daniels' face reentered his brain. It spooked him. *How could anyone look so much like Carolyn?*

He pushed the thoughts away.

As he idly rolled his Mont Blanc pen between his fingertips, his thoughts drifted away from Sara and landed on Doris. He'd only had one redhead before but that was so long ago he could barely remember. He pictured what Doris might look like naked, her milky white skin, a sort of canvas backdrop to those delicious crimson curls. He envisioned her with large pink nipples and wanted to pinch and pull on them just to hear her squeal. He squeezed the pen between his thumb and forefinger until the phone jolted him. He threw the pen across the room with such force that it broke apart, scattering in all directions.

"What is it Jane?"

"Sorry to bother you, Judge — your daughter is on the phone."

"My daughter? Take a message, I can't speak to her right now, and don't interrupt me again."

CHAPTER NINETEEN

DORIS HAD GONE and Eve was asleep. Sara sat in the rocking chair preparing for the session that she hoped would help Eve to remember. She rocked slowly back and forth trying to calm the raging rise and fall of sensations inside. She gripped the arms of the chair.

Eve opened her eyes softly and said, "Hello butterfly lady."

"What did you call me?" Sara said.

"Butterfly lady, because when you're with me I always feel this tiny tickle, in here," Eve said, rolling onto her back, and pointing to her stomach, "inside my tummy. It's like a pretty butterfly is in there, flying all around, and every now and then she touches me in there and it tickles."

Sara smiled and stood up. She walked over to the edge of the bed while Eve stared outside at the drifting clouds.

"How do you suppose the butterfly got in there?"

"I guess you put it in there."

"Me? Why do you say that?"

"Because I can feel it when you're around."

"Maybe you put it in there and then when I'm around she wants to get out," Sara said.

"I didn't put her in there," Eve said, adamantly. "I would've remembered if I did it."

"Well, as long as you like having it there, we won't worry about how she got there. How's that?"

"You're nice," Eve said.

"I like you, too."

"I'm hungry."

"Let's get you something to eat, then. What would you like?"

"Hmm," Eve said, tapping her index finger on her lips. "I would like…I think I'll have some…umm…I'm gonna get…hmm, what do they have?"

"How about some scrambled eggs and toast?"

"Okay." Eve shrugged.

After Sara had ordered Eve's dinner she walked in with a stethoscope and a thermometer. Eve's eyes grew very large and she pulled back her chin.

"What's that for? I don't want that. Get it away."

"I wanted to take your temperature, that's all. Then I was going to listen to your heart for a minute with this," Sara said, holding up the stethoscope.

"I don't care about that but you keep that other thing away from me. I've seen those lots of times before and I don't like them."

"It's just to tell me that you're feeling okay inside."

"They hurt. If you want to know if I'm okay, you can just ask. I know how I feel."

Eve's lower lip quivered and her beautiful green eyes grew watery.

Sara should have anticipated this. Eve's reaction to the thermometer was not unusual, she knew that. Many of her other patients refused to go to a dentist for the same reason. Lots of people who've been forced into oral sex had phobias about putting things inside their mouths. What if there was more to Eve's fear of the thermometer? Sara shuddered.

"Okay, Eve, it's alright. I promise you I will never do anything without asking you first. And if you're not comfortable with something, we just won't worry about it, okay?"

Eve wiped her tears away with the back of her hand.

"Does that sound alright?"

"I guess," Eve said, sniffling.

The nurse brought in Eve's lunch and set it up for her on the tray attached to the bed. Sara was relieved that Eve still wanted to eat. She could have sent Eve over the edge with that stupid move. But when she saw Eve diving into her scrambled eggs and chomping on her toast, she knew that it would be okay, at least, for now.

Eve and Sara spent the afternoon and evening together playing games until Eve became tired. Sara told her it was time for sleep and began picking up the cards and board games that were strewn across the bed.

"I'm going to give you something to help you sleep through the night," Sara said.

"What do you mean? Why wouldn't I?"

"It's just that I'm going to leave the clinic and I want to be sure that you get a really good sleep, because tomorrow we have a lot to talk about. But Peter is going to sleep in here with you on the cot just in case you wake up."

"What do you mean? Where are you going?" Eve said, frowning.

"I'm staying at Peter's house while I'm here."

"Don't you have a house?"

"I do but not here, it's in another town. So while I'm here visiting you, I'm staying at Peter's."

"You're just visiting? Nobody told me you were going to leave," Eve said.

"I'm not going anywhere for a while, we can talk about that tomorrow," Sara said.

"Let's talk about it now. I want to talk about it now," Eve said.

"Shh, alright, we'll talk about it now," Sara said, rubbing her arms until she had calmed down. "Would you like to come stay with me for awhile?"

"Really?" Eve said, beaming. Then, suddenly she was scowling.

"What's wrong?" Sara said.

"I don't think my Dad will let me."

Eve looked up at Sara quickly, her eyes flickered from side to front, side, then front. She pulled her mouth over to one side, chewing on her lip.

"We talked about it and since he has a lot of business right now, he thought it would be alright," Sara lied.

"He's gone away?" Eve said, in a very tiny voice.

"Not yet," Sara said. She stroked Eve's face, smiling down on her. Her heart had never been so full of love and hate and pain and anger and fear and love.

Eve smiled back.

"Get a good night's sleep, have sweet dreams, and I'll see you in the morning, okay?"

Eve nodded, still smiling as she watched Sara walk toward the door. Just as the door was about to close behind her, Sara heard Eve's small voice say, "Night, Mommy."

Sara closed her eyes when she heard those words and her knees went weak. She held onto the wall for a moment. She was exhausted, she hadn't eaten much, she told herself, refusing to let the words enter into her heart. She walked over to the nurses' station, left instructions for the evening and went to find Peter.

She found him in his office.

"It's good to see you," she said.

"You look beat."

"Eve just called me Mommy," Sara said. She tried to hold back the tears, but when Peter looked at her sympathetically she let go.

"I'm not sure we can bring her back. She's pretty far away right now," she cried.

Peter stood up and walked around to the front of his desk. He took Sara's hands in his.

"Tomorrow we'll do the session about her mother's death. We'll see how she responds, then we'll take it from there. That's all we can do."

"What about her father? He's supposed to come pick her up on Thursday, there's no way —."

"Come here, you need a hug."

Sara fell into him. She wanted to stay like that, letting his warmth slide over her and wash her clean.

The phone rang.

"It's for you," Peter said, holding up the receiver. "It's Doris."

Sara hung up the phone slowly and turned back to Peter.

"She says she has something important to tell me."

CHAPTER TWENTY

S ARA STEPPED INTO EVE'S ROOM
and found her staring out the window
at the field below.

"How's my favorite patient today?"

Eve shrugged.

"Where's Peter?" Sara said.

"In there," Eve said, pointing toward the bathroom door.

"What are you looking at?" Sara said.

"I'm just watching the grass."

"Let's go down, want to?" Sara said.

"I don't know," Eve said, sadly.

"It's beautiful outside, let's go breathe the air and see if we can hide in the field for awhile."

Eve's face brightened. "Okay," she said.

"First," Sara said, "let's get you out of that damned nightgown."

Eve brought her hand to her mouth and gasped.

"What?" Sara said.

"You just said a swear."

Sara laughed.

"You're funny," Eve said, giggling.

"It's good to hear you laugh," Sara said. "Now let's get you changed."

"Okay," Eve said, skipping past Peter and into the bathroom.

"I guess you don't need me hanging around," Peter said.

"We're going out for a walk before the session," Sara said.

"Okay, I'll see you when you get back."

"Also," Sara whispered, "I want to tell you what Doris told me last night."

Eve came out in a lavender and teal flowered dress. Her hair was brushed and she looked radiant.

"You are so pretty, Eve. Do you know that?" Sara said.

"You look beautiful," Peter said, bending down to kiss her cheek.

Eve dropped her head; Sara took her hand and led her out the door. The nurses all stared.

"We're just going for a little walk," Sara said, with her back turned she waved her right hand.

"I can feel the butterfly," Eve whispered to Sara.

"Oh good," Sara said, smiling.

In the elevator they both stared straight ahead. Sara's mind refused to be quiet. The ding of the elevator turned the tape off inside her head and Sara led Eve outside. When they first stepped out, Eve stopped cold and lifted her chin up to the sky. After taking in a deep breath of warm April air and spinning her body around, she stopped to look at Sara.

"What an incredible day," she said, her voice was strong and clear.

Sara was struck by the transformation. Instantly, Eve had become confident, cool and collected. She had all the mannerisms and presence of a healthy twenty-eight year old woman. Where was the little girl, who was present just moments ago? Maybe it had something to do with getting outside, maybe this was Eve's well-trained public persona.

"It's good to be outside," Sara said. "Come on, let's go find the field."

"What field?" Eve said.

"You know, the field with the waving grass. The one we're going to hide in."

"I don't know about you, Dr. Daniels, but I don't want to go sit in some field and have ants and mosquitoes crawling all over my legs," Eve said.

"You've got a point," Sara said. "Let's just take a walk, instead."

They admired the bright yellow splashes of early April. The forsythias and daffodils brought a sunny hope to the day.

"I would love to go to the beach. We could both use a little color in our cheeks — don't you think?"

"Maybe tomorrow," Sara said.

Eve dropped her head.

"It's just that we've got some work to do this morning, and we need to start making plans," Sara said.

"Can't we just forget about all that for one day? It's a perfect day, not too hot, there's a nice southwesterly breeze."

"Why do you want to go to the beach so badly?" Sara said.

Eve shrugged.

"There's someone I was hoping to see, that's all."

Sara realized Eve was thinking about Kyle Jordan, the sailor that Peter and Doris had both described to her.

"Who were you hoping to see?"

"The most wonderful man," Eve said, dreamily. She looked at Sara sadly. "Daddy sent him away."

"How could we see him, then?" Sara said.

"I don't know. I have this image of him anchored out there somewhere on the horizon, waiting for me. It's stupid, I guess, just some kind of fairy tale fantasy."

"Come on," Sara said, putting her arm around Eve's back. "Let's go back to the clinic."

As they walked, Sara spoke slowly and gently while Eve listened.

"I think it's wonderful that you're thinking about Kyle. It's a very good sign. And I want you to know that Peter has told me how much the two of you were drawn together. He said it was the kind of love that's rare — and he wants very much for you to be happy. But he feels, as I do, that before you can be happy with someone else, you must first be whole, yourself. That's what I want to help you with. And I know you can do it, you have more power inside yourself than you realize."

Sara squeezed her a little closer and Eve dropped her head onto Sara's shoulder.

"Do you think he's forgotten me?" she said, in a small voice.

"Never," Sara said. "Not in a million years."

When they were back inside the clinic, Eve turned the corner leading to the elevators but Sara stopped her.

"This way," she said, pointing down the hallway that led to Peter's office. "It's time for our session."

"Oh," Eve said, without moving.

"Trust me?" Sara said.

"Yes."

"So there's nothing to worry about, right?" Sara said, reaching out her hand.

"I guess not. It's just that the only person I've ever been in session with is Peter. It feels strange, that's all," Eve said.

"Peter will be there, too."

Sara guided Eve down the long corridor toward Peter's office. They entered Peter's office and then stepped into the soothing darkness of his private session room. Eve walked automatically to the couch and laid down on it. Sara had memorized the words that Peter used to bring Eve into a trance state, and repeated them to her now.

"All settled in?" she said.

Eve nodded with her eyes closed. Sara glanced at Peter, who was standing over by the bookcase.

"Now, Eve," Sara said, "I'm going to bring you back in time, and then I'm going to ask you some questions while you're there. Peter and I are both with you, we're here to protect you."

After a slight pause she began again.

"I want you to go to that secret place, that private place within where you feel safe. Do you feel yourself moving there now?"

"Yes," Eve said.

"Just let yourself go, bring yourself to your secret hiding place and tell me when you're there. That's it, go further down the path. You're not afraid, we're with you and we'll keep you safe."

She looked at Peter while they waited for the signs. Once the small smile appeared on Eve's face, Sara paused while Peter quietly left the room. He returned with some video equipment which they quickly set up.

"There we are, Eve. How are you feeling?" Sara said.

"I'm fine. It's nice to be here, I've missed it," she said, her voice was light, dreamy.

"Okay, Eve. I want you to go back to a time when your mother was alive. Do you remember what your mother's name was?"

"Carolyn."

"Good. Now let's move back in time, when you were just a little girl. What do you see around you?"

"I'm in my bed. I just woke up and I'm hugging my funny bunny," she said.

"Good. What else?"

"Well, the sun is shining in through my windows, it's making squares on my purple rug."

"What else?"

"I can hear the birdies singing. Mommy loves them, she says the robins are magic because they bring springtime when they come."

"Where is your Mommy, is she nearby?"

"There she is. She's coming through the door."

"Tell me about her. What does she look like?"

"She's the prettiest Mommy. She's always smiling at me and she makes me feel happy. Hi, Mommy. We're going to the beach, we're going to the beach! Can we make a sand castle?"

"Okay, Eve. Let's move ahead in time. Let's go to the day when your Mommy went away. Can you tell me where you are now?"

"I'm with Daddy, we're in his special room where he doesn't like to be bothered," she said. Her voice sounded a little older.

"Is Mommy there, too?"

"Oh no. Daddy just likes it to be the two of us."

"Go on. Tell me what's happening."

She giggled.

"Don't, Daddy. Stop tickling me," she said, still laughing.

"He wants me to sit on his lap now. I can feel a bump beside my leg. What's that Daddy?"

Sara looked at Peter; he nodded.

"What does he tell you?" Sara said, leaning in slightly.

"He says, that's because I love you, want to see?"

"What do you say?"

"I say, okay."

"Then what does Daddy do?" Sara said.

"He's unzipping his pants."

"How are you feeling right now?"

"I feel funny. I don't think he should do that, but Daddy says how much he loves me, so I guess it's alright."

"What's he doing now, Eve?" Sara said, her heart pounded so fast it hurt. Perspiration dampened her armpits.

"He pulled his thing out. Oh it's ugly. I don't like it and I back up so I don't have to be so close but Daddy grabs my wrist. Ow! You're hurting me."

Eve began to pout, as if she was about to cry.

"What does Daddy do now, Eve?"

"He's pulling me closer and he's whispering in my ear."

"What's he saying?"

"This will be our little secret, okay?" Eve was whispering, trying to make her voice sound low. "Now you do just what Daddy says and everything will be alright. But if you tell Mommy, or anybody else, we won't be happy anymore."

"What's happening now?"

"I ask Daddy, 'why won't we be happy?'"

"And what does he say?"

"Because," Eve says, whispering again, "somebody might hurt one of us, or try to take one of us away. You wouldn't want that to happen, now would you my little princess?"

Eve shook her head vigorously, her face was scrunched up.

"Then what? What does he tell you to do?" Sara said.

"He said to pretend that it's a popsicle, he wants me to lick it up and down, and suck on the end to get all the juices out."

"Then what happens?" Sara swallowed hard and looked at Peter for the courage to go on.

"I didn't want to do that," Eve said, "but then he started to get mad, and I remembered what he said, so I did it."

"How do you feel?"

"It tastes yucky, not like a popsicle at all, it's salty like the ocean."

Her lip started to quiver and she trembled.

"I have a tummy ache, I think I'm going to throw up."

"Do you tell Daddy?"

"Oh no. He seems so happy. He's smiling at me, now he lifts me up and says he wants me to show him."

"Show him what?"

"He wants me to pull my panties down, but Mommy told me to never do that, she said that's my special spot and I didn't have to show it to anybody."

"What's happening now?" Sara said.

"Daddy's mad at me again. He said it's not fair, he showed me his so I should show him mine."

"Then what?"

"I guess he's right," Eve said, reluctantly, and she began to yank at her underwear.

"What happens after your panties are down, Eve. Does he touch you there?"

Eve giggled self-consciously.

"What's he doing, Eve?"

"He's tickling me," she said, twisting her body from side to side.

"Has Daddy touched you there before?" Sara said.

"Not without my panties on."

"How did you feel those other times?"

"Fine. Daddy always told me that he knew it felt good, and there was nothing wrong with making me feel good."

"How do you feel now?"

"I'm scared," Eve said, frowning.

"Why?"

"Cause Daddy looks different, and he's breathing funny."

Suddenly Eve gasped and she was rolling on the couch, extremely agitated.

"What is it, Eve? What's happening?" Sara said, quickly.

"They're yelling at each other."

"Who?"

"Mommy and Daddy. Mommy came in and she's very angry with us. I'm sorry Mommy, I didn't mean to —."

Eve was sobbing uncontrollably. She had curled her legs up to her chest so she could hug her knees. Her breathing was very rapid and then she began to scream.

"Stay with me," Sara said. "I'll protect you. Tell me what's happening."

"Daddy's grabbing her and, and, and his hands are squeezing her neck, I think he's hurting her, Mommy?"

Eve was crying now, very quietly.

"What's the matter with Mommy, Daddy? She's not moving."

"Where's Daddy, now?" Sara said.

"He's standing there, rubbing his head. There's blood coming out of her head, Daddy, do something Daddy, she's not moving."

Eve stopped suddenly and then threw herself onto the floor where she laid motionless, her breathing was very slow, as if she were in a very deep sleep.

Sara couldn't move. She looked at Peter who stood behind the video camera with tears streaming down his face. Sara bent down and scooped Eve into her arms, lifting her back up onto the couch. She watched Eve's breath slowly rise and fall while she fought back her own tears.

She knew there were risks involved with going further but she decided to take things one more step. She looked at Peter behind the video camera. He nodded. Sara went back to her chair and took in a long deep breath.

"Tell me where you are after everything is over."

Eve began to suck her thumb.

Sara remembered how Peter had described Eve's catatonic state when he first began working with her.

"Okay, Eve," she said. "We're going to move forward in time. Everything is all better now and it's two years later. Where are you now?"

"I'm out in the garden, playing with my friends," Eve said, happily.

"That's nice. What are their names?"

"Oh, I have lots of friends. But nobody else can see them, they're my special friends. They're the only ones my Daddy will let me have over. Today I'm playing with Sally and Roger, we're having a tea party."

"That's nice. Where's your Mommy?" Sara said.

"She died," Eve said, casually.

"I'm so sorry. How did it happen?"

"She was in a terrible car crash, I was sad for awhile, but now I don't remember her that much."

Sara swallowed. "Did your Daddy tell you about the accident?" she said.

"Yep. But he said we could never talk about it again."

"Why not?"

"Because it's too sad. And besides, we still have each other," Eve said, her voice was hollow.

"Did you ever talk to anyone else about your Mom's accident?"

"My big friend Peter used to talk to me about it, a little."

Sara had heard enough. She looked over at Peter whose face was drained white. But it wasn't over yet. She had to decide whether to let Eve remember. When she looked back at Peter, he seemed to know what she was thinking. He nodded for her to go ahead.

"It's time to come back now, Eve. I'm going to count to ten and when I get to ten you will be fully awake. You will remember all that has been said during this session and you will understand that these memories are the keys to your wellness, and even if they hurt now, eventually they will help you to become whole. Do you understand?"

Eve nodded slowly.

When Sara reached ten, Eve opened her eyes. Sara was silent while she watched the panic contort Eve's face. Her chest heaved uncontrollably. Sara stood up to comfort her when suddenly Eve rolled to the side of the couch and vomited violently.

Sara's white blouse was splattered with orange and yellow curdled chunks. She rubbed Eve's head, holding her hair away from her face. When there was nothing left in Eve's stomach she began to cough and gag.

Peter gently lifted Eve up. Sara sat down beside her, cradling her. She rocked her back and forth and whispered in her ear that everything would be alright. Eventually Eve's sobbing hushed and her breathing mellowed. But still they rocked while Sara tried to ease Eve's pain.

Eve looked at Sara.

"What the hell am I doing on your lap?" she said, laughing through a continuous flow of tears.

They both laughed. Eve tried to stand up but her foot slipped in the mess and she fell back onto Sara.

"Shit," Eve said.

"Good swearing," Sara said. She helped Eve over to the side of the couch and looked down at the floor. "What's a little throw up between friends?"

"Nothing, compared to all the rest that's gone on in here today," Eve said, sadly.

Eve's lips quivered; she squeezed her eyes shut. Sara took her hand and rubbed her arm, waiting for Peter to come back from hiding the video equipment.

He sat down on the other side of Eve.

"Is it my fault that my mother died?" Eve said, through her tears.

Sara felt a hatchet gouge her heart.

"It's not your fault. You were just a baby," Sara said.

Eve opened her eyes and frowned at Peter.

"How long have you known?"

"Oh, Eve," he said. "I just found out."

She turned away from him and looked at Sara.

"Thank you," she said, in a squeaky whisper.

Sara saw the reflection of betrayal in Eve's face. Her eyes looked like they stung from shock and disappointment. She glanced past Eve to Peter who suddenly looked like a very tired, very old man. His rounded shoulders seemed barely strong enough to keep his head from hanging to his knees. Sara tried to deflect all the pain hovering around them in that room. She had to be strong enough for all of them.

Since Peter was paralyzed, Sara helped Eve get cleaned up and took her back to her room. Eve was slipping away again, back to her childhood. Sara asked her if she wanted something to eat. Eve shook her head. Sara asked if she wanted to play a game. Eve shook her head. Sara asked if she wanted to lie down and Eve walked over to the windows and stared down at the field. Sara sat quietly in the rocking chair in the corner of the room watching Eve stare out the window. After a while Eve turned and climbed onto the bed.

She fell asleep and Sara watched her.

Sara slipped her hand into her jacket pocket and found Justin Templeten's business card. She inhaled deeply then stood up and walked to the windows. The late afternoon sun had woven an undulating pattern of light and shadows across the graceful field below. She stared at the dancing shafts of tall grass, their feathered tops taking turns in the sun's spotlight. She focused wholly on the beauty, the absolute perfection that lay in that pastoral scene out there, on the other side of the glass. As she watched the field sway in unison back and forth, back and forth, moving to the glorious harmonies of its own secret orchestra, she felt herself swept up by the flowing rhythm.

She remembered Peter's theory. She would go to him, convince him to keep trying, not to give up on Eve — or, himself.

But she was so tired.

She turned to look at Eve, now sleeping like a baby, and carefully pulled the blankets up around her. She smoothed them across her back and went over to sit in the rocking chair in the corner of the room.

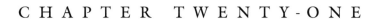

CHAPTER TWENTY-ONE

SARA SLIPPED AWAY and went downstairs to convince Peter to go home and get some rest; they needed to get through tomorrow when Robert would try to take Eve away again. Exhausted, she went back to Eve's room for the night.

She stepped quietly into the darkened room, relieved that Eve was still asleep. She laid down on the thin cot, too tired to care that her back would surely ache in the morning.

Sara awoke with the first breath of morning's light. Today Eve's life will start over, she told herself trying to alchemize the iron weight of fear she felt solidly in her stomach.

ROBERT WHITMAN WAS CHEERFUL and poised, greeting the staff along the way. They were cordial in return.

He opened the door to Eve's room.

Sara jumped up at his abrupt entrance.

"Don't you ever knock," she said.

"Fuck you," he said. "Where's my daughter?"

"She's in the bathroom. Or don't you give her permission to pull down her pants without you watching?"

Robert rubbed his hands together in front of his chest, looking squarely at Sara.

Eve appeared quietly.

"You look beautiful," he said, reaching his arms toward her.

"Hello, Daddy," she said, shyly. She lowered her head and stared at the floor.

Robert stepped toward her despite the rage he sensed in Sara Daniels as she stood behind him. He knew the power of such depths of anger. Suddenly he felt tired, and old.

He put his arms around Eve and she stood stiffly, holding her arms tightly to her sides. He lifted her chin.

"Daddy's going away for awhile. Want to come?"

Eve shook her head. Beneath her beauty, Robert saw the frightened little girl she had always been.

He was acutely aware that the doctor observed his every move. He took Eve's head in his large, square hands and tipped it downward, kissing her forehead firmly.

"What will I do?" Eve said. "How can I practice law...what have you done to me?"

Eve crumbled in his arms, pushing her body into his. She pulled and grabbed at his expensive suit coat.

"Eve," Robert said, calmly, "get a hold of yourself."

Sara stayed in the corner of the room without moving or speaking. He was trapped, and tried to calm Eve to no avail.

Eve was sobbing now, her face was screwed up as she begged and pleaded with him to explain her confusion. She yanked on the front of his jacket lapels. She began to slide her body slowly down in front of his then turned slightly, placing each of her legs around his thigh, until her crotch made firm contact.

Robert felt himself slipping into the flame. When she reached down with her right hand and began rubbing him just the way he'd taught her, he moaned. The sound of his own voice woke him up to the reality that they were not alone.

Suddenly, the door swung open.

Peter marched into the room; there was another man behind him.

The fucking sailor.

Robert and Kyle had a standoff with their eyes.

"Get your hands off her or I swear, I'll kill you," Kyle said.

Robert stiffened and grabbed hold of Eve's wrists, shaking her slightly.

Sara jumped and Peter took her hand.

"Eve!" Robert snapped, "you are my daughter and you will do as I say. Now get hold of yourself."

Eve went limp. All the desperation and agony disappeared. Her hands dropped loosely to her sides, dangling and her chin dipped slightly forward.

Robert stepped away from Kyle careful not to make eye contact with anyone in the room.

"Come on Eve," Kyle said, "I'm taking you out of here."

Peter stepped over to face Robert who refused to look back.

"It's over, Robert," Peter said. "You have no rights where Eve is concerned. You will not come near her again, is that clear?"

"Fuck you," he said, piercing Peter's eyes. "You have no power in this town and you certainly don't have any power over me."

Peter held up a video cassette. Robert squinted.

"What's that?"

"This, my old friend, is proof. It's a video-taped session of Eve relating the entire sequence of events leading up to the moment you murdered Carolyn."

Robert laughed.

"Under hypnosis?" he said. "Oh Peter, you'll never learn. That won't hold up in court, you know this recovered memory bullshit is completely unreliable where the law is concerned."

"I have a corroborating witness."

"There are no witnesses—." He crossed his arms, then said, "Bristol."

"No, Robert, not Mrs. Bristol. You."

"What?"

"I have it on tape. Let me refresh your memory. I asked, 'What happened to Carolyn?' You said, 'I put her out of her misery.' I think these two pieces of evidence are convincing, don't you."

Robert clenched his jaw.

"Leave Eve alone, Robert, that's all we're asking."

"That's all we're asking." Robert mimicked. "Who the hell are you, anyway," he said to Sara.

Robert brushed past Peter on his way to the door.

"I'm your reminder," Sara said.

She walked over to him.

"You're a sick man. But, I want you to know that I forgive you for all the horrible crimes you've committed against your own daughter —."

"Who the fuck are you to forgive me?" Robert scoffed.

"I'm the one who's going to do everything I can to get her well. But if you ever go near her again, without her awakened consent, I will personally see to it that you rot in jail."

Sara stared right through him, he flinched slightly before pushing her aside.

"You'll pay for what you've done to her," Sara said, as he moved quickly toward the door. "I don't know how, but this will all come back to you."

He walked out the door without looking back.

Sara and Peter looked at each other.

"It's done," Peter said.

Sara shook her head.

"It's only just beginning," she said.

Peter nodded and moved over to the phone to let Kyle know he could bring Eve back into the room.

Eve was in a daze; Kyle was holding her up with his arm around her waist. Sara helped bring Eve over to the bed and lay her down. She pulled a blanket over her and stroked her face. Sara's heart ached as she thought about the days and weeks and months ahead.

She turned to face Peter and Kyle who looked like two lost boys. She needed to get out of the clinic.

"Will you stay with her?" she asked to no one in particular.

Peter nodded, then Kyle said, "I'd like to stay. I'll look after her. You guys look like you could both use a break."

Peter said he had some patients to check on, and Sara said she was going to take a drive.

After driving for awhile, Sara parked the car and wandered around the streets of Innis. Eventually she found herself looking up at the sign which read: Eve Whitman, Attorney at Law. Amazing, she thought, and went inside.

She found Doris sitting at the desk with teary eyes and a runny nose. Crumpled tissues were all around her, on the desk, in her lap, on the floor.

"It's finally over," Doris sniffled.

"I'm going to help her," Sara said. "But I can't do it here. I'll have to bring her back to San Francisco with me. It'll be better for Eve to get away from this town."

"His secretary just called," Doris said, and joined Sara on the couch. "She said the Judge had instructed her to tell me to pack up this office within the week. I'm supposed to box up all the files, everything, and make complete status reports for all her current cases. Then, I'm to bring them directly to his secretary. She'll be sure that they're all assigned new, competent lawyers, and will hand over a severance check to me, signed by the Judge himself."

"So that's it?' Sara said. "He's just making that decision?"

"You don't really believe she could work, do you? I mean, let's face it—."

"No, of course she can't work — probably not for some time but he just walked away from her. Walked out the door and turned his back."

"Hello?" Justin said, as he stepped through the door.

"What are you doing here?" Sara asked, incredulously.

"Justin and I go back a long ways," Doris said.

"Amazing," Sara said, shaking her head in disbelief. "It's good to see you," she said, politely, "but I can't stay, I've got a terrible headache, I have to get back to the clinic."

Sara felt tears rising up from the lump inside her throat. She turned away from these two people whom she hardly knew.

"Can I help?" Justin said.

"That depends on what you mean," Sara said, feeling a rush of adrenaline.

"I might be able to bring some relief from your headache."

Sara turned to look at Doris who smiled gently. She turned to Justin and gazed into his dark and shining eyes. When he placed his hands over the crown of her head she felt heat pour in. The warmth seemed to slowly swirl like liquid gold into every crevice of her brain.

Sara let out a deep sigh.

Justin's hands traveled down the sides of her head, over her ears and cupped her neck and throat. Even after he had stepped back, she still felt the soothing heat melt her tension away.

She opened her eyes suddenly when she realized Eve would be waking soon. Sara felt disoriented, but more centered than before. She smiled at Doris, who had been smiling at her since she'd opened her eyes. She scanned the room for Justin; she wanted to thank him.

"He left. But he asked me to give you a message," Doris said.

"Oh?" Sara said, hopefully.

"Yes. He said to tell you that your sister wants you to let go of her death."

Sara scowled at Doris.

"He also said that taking her own life was her choice, it was part of her journey. She's very proud of you, glad you're going to help Eve, and love her — like a sister."

Sara stared at Doris, trying to blink back the burn of more unwanted tears.

"How did you meet him?" she said, after a minute.

"I've known him all my life," Doris said, with a wave of her hand and a curious grin.

When the phone rang Sara whispered that she'd let Doris know what was happening, waved and left the office.

"Whitman Law Office," Doris said in a professional tone.

"Oh good, you're still there," the man said.

Doris didn't need to ask who was calling. She recognized the voice and felt a cold current rush down her spine.

"Hello? Who's calling, please?" she said.

"Doris, this is Robert Whitman."

"Yes, Judge Whitman. What can I do for you?"

"I was wondering if you were free for dinner?"

"No, actually, I'm not," she said.

"Oh, too bad. I had a little proposal I wanted to run by you."

"If your little proposal has anything at all to do with some fantasy you might be having about getting me into bed, I can save you a lot of time right now by telling you that you're not my type."

"But Doris, how can you say that? We hardly know each other."

"I know all I want to know about you, sir."

"And what, may I ask, do you suppose my type is?" he said, in a charming voice.

"You're the type who molests his own daughter when she's five years old, then gets rid of her mother so that you can have complete control of her through a variety of sick manipulative techniques, including threats, hypnosis and drugs. Then when you've reduced her to a near non-human state, you turn around and walk the other way. Does that pretty much nail it for you Judge?"

There was silence on the other end.

"Have a lovely time in Europe and don't ever call me again."

Doris slammed down the phone. Her heart was racing. She stood up and walked into Eve's office. Sadly, she flopped down into Eve's chair. She sat there for a while, watching the harbor like Eve had so often done. She watched the setting sun brush strokes of pink and purple onto the crisp white sails.

Doris decided it would be good to take a break — to get away from all the confusion of being human for awhile.

CHAPTER TWENTY-TWO

T HE NEXT MORNING Sara entered Eve's room and found her weeping. She went to her quickly and sat down beside her on the edge of the bed.

Eve didn't notice her.

"Eve?" she said, softly.

Eve opened her eyes. Seeing Sara made her cry harder.

"Where's Kyle?" Sara said.

"He went to get coffee."

"Why are you crying?"

"What's going to happen when he finds out who I really am?"

Sara knew it would be difficult for Eve. She would feel like other incest survivors: undeserving, unwilling, and undesirable.

Sara dropped her chin. She needed to get Eve to the clinic in San Francisco. Other than the music therapy session she and Peter had planned, she wasn't going to attempt any further work while they remained in Innis. She hoped that when Eve got around other survivors she'd handle her recovery with less trauma. She knew it would be a long dark tunnel, with or without Kyle.

"I'd like to leave for San Francisco as soon as possible," Sara said.

"Why are you ignoring me?" Eve said. "You're just ignoring me."

"You'll be fine. But you have to trust me because I know what's best for you right now. I want to get you settled in San Francisco where there are a lot of wonderful people who can help."

"Everything is falling apart," Eve said.

"I want you to get some rest. I'm going to send the nurse in with your medication. I'll be up to check on you later."

"Where's Peter anyway? Seems like he's avoiding me, too," Eve said.

"He's not. He's just sad right now, he'll be in to see you. Right now I want you to get some rest. Okay?"

Eve shrugged.

Sara pulled her close, held her for a moment then stood up to leave.

AFTER LUNCH, Sara and Peter went to see Eve together. When they walked in, Kyle was reading a magazine and Eve was sleeping.

"She's been asleep all morning. I couldn't even wake her up for lunch," Kyle said.

"Why don't you take a break and come on down to my office for a bit," Peter said.

Kyle stood up.

"What if she wakes up?" he said.

"I'll have someone come and sit with her, they can call us if she does," said Peter.

On the way down the corridor to Peter's office, no one said a word.

When they got there Peter sat behind his desk and Sara and Kyle sat on the couch facing him.

"We know you've risked a lot to come back here Kyle, and I'm sure Eve is pleased—."

"But?"

"But, well, she's very unstable right now. We need to keep her as emotionally steady as possible. Frankly, having you around is confusing her," Peter said.

"I know, I've seen it coming. I just wanted to stay with her a while longer. I've got a good crew together, I'm ready to set sail for Tahiti anytime. If you both think it's better that I leave, I'll go tomorrow." Kyle turned to Sara. "But I'm coming out to San Francisco right after the trip."

Sara smiled.

"By then we'll have done some work," she said. "It will be good for Eve to see you then. You should understand, though, it's going to be a long road."

"I know," he said.

They all looked at each other solemnly. Peter stood up and Kyle left to go back to the room with Eve. When he got there, he sat down to write her a letter that might convince her that he loved her...that he wasn't disappearing, they'd be together, and happy, someday.

Afternoon turned to evening and Kyle left the clinic to go see Doris. He told Peter and Sara that he wanted to say goodbye to Doris for real, to thank her for all she'd done to help him and Eve. He knew he'd probably never see her again.

Sara walked into Eve's room slowly. She was standing in front of the windows even though it was pitch black on the other side. The nurse on duty had told Sara that Eve hadn't spoken all day and that she hadn't eaten either. She just stares out the window, the nurse had said.

"Hi, Eve," Sara said, walking towards her.

Eve continued staring straight ahead.

"It's pretty dark out there," Sara said.

"No darker than it is in here," Eve said, quietly.

"You had me going for a minute. I thought you weren't speaking to me."

She looked into Eve's eyes. She's drowning, Sara thought.

"I wish I could take away your pain," Sara said.

Eve's lip trembled and Sara reached out to her. When Eve was quiet, Sara lowered them both down onto the bed and began to tell Eve about her plan.

"Anyway, if you're feeling better tomorrow we'll get you out of here; you can come stay with me and Peter for a few days." Sara paused, then said, "We'll need to go to the house and pack your things."

Eve frowned, fidgeting with a wet tissue.

"I don't want to go back there," she said. "I can buy some new clothes."

"Isn't there anything you want to have with you?"

"Nothing matters. There's nothing there for me."

"Okay, but what about your purse, credit cards, that kind of thing?"

Eve shrugged.

Sara realized it was too soon to talk to Eve about revisiting her father's house.

"Have you ever been to San Francisco?" she said.

"I went there with Daddy once on a business trip." Eve stopped, and frowned. "Oh, my God," she said.

"Tell me," Sara said, putting her arm around Eve.

Eve gasped and brought her hand to her mouth as if she had just received some horrible news. She shook her head from side to side and stood up to pace back and forth. When she turned back to Sara her eyes bulged out.

"I just had a flashback. We were at this romantic candlelit table together as though we were lovers or something. I had on a low cut navy blue dress, a lot of make-up—."

She turned quickly to Sara.

"Could that be real?"

Sara inhaled deeply.

"Sara? Is there more? Is there something you're not telling me?"

Sara squinted at Eve.

"Oh God, there is."

Eve spun around and walked over to the windows; she stood stiffly, staring back out into the darkness.

"You're dealing with a lot right now. Let's try to take this one step at a time, okay?" Sara urged.

"I just don't know how much more I can take. I mean, my God, what kind of life is this? I'm some kind of—."

"Oh, Eve. Come on, sit down."

"I don't want to sit down," Eve said, pulling away from her.

Sara tried to reach for her but Eve ripped away.

"Fuck you, Sara. Just get away from me. Leave me the fuck alone."

Sara's eyes grew narrow. Her chest heaved.

"What the fuck do you know about any of this, anyway?" Eve said. "You think you can just waltz in here and put poor Eve back together? What's your gig anyway? What's in this for you?"

"Bobbie?" Sara said.

Eve snorted.

"You think you know it all, don't you? Let me tell you something, sister, the party's just beginning. I'm getting the fuck out of here to get myself a good, stiff drink. I could use something else stiff, too. Where is the old man, anyway?"

"Shut up, Bobbie," Sara said.

"Aren't you tough. I think you're clueless. You haven't got any idea how to handle us. You're in way over your head."

"What do you want?"

"I told you. I want a good drink and a good fuck —you got a problem with that?"

"Your private life is just about over. Your creator has dumped you. He's gone off to Paris or someplace sexy for some new blood, I suspect," Sara said, calmly.

"What do you know about it?"

"Without him, you're history. You even said so yourself once."

Eve spit at Sara.

"Oh, that's pretty," Sara said, her voice rising. "Don't mess with me, Bobbie. I can be nasty when someone I care about is in trouble."

Sara walked quickly out of the room, ordered some medication and a 24-hour watch on Eve's room. When she came back in, Eve was rocking back and forth in the chair. Sara walked past her to the bed and sat down.

"Do they have hot chocolate here?" Eve said.

"Is that you, Eve?"

"When's Daddy coming back? I miss him," she said.

Sara watched Eve rocking slowly back and forth.

"We talked about that, remember? Daddy's gone for a while and I'm going to take care of you, remember?"

Eve turned slowly to look at Sara, then suddenly burst out laughing.

There was a rap on the door.

"Come in," Sara said, without moving.

The nurse walked in holding a syringe in her right hand.

"What the fuck is that?" Eve said.

"That's to help you sleep, Bobbie."

"No way. No one's sticking that thing into me."

The nurse looked at Sara who nodded then stood up quickly. Sara grabbed Eve's arms, pulled them around the back of the chair while the nurse injected the needle.

Eve screamed and kicked and then slumped into silence. Her eyes were dull and her mouth hung open as she stared out into the room.

Sara told her to get into bed and she did. She stayed until Eve was asleep and then left.

She insisted that Eve be guarded every minute, around the clock, and instructed the staff to reissue the sedative every four hours. She walked down the hallway feeling their eyes follow her.

Sara went down to Peter's office and locked the door from the inside. She went slowly over to his desk, sat down and lowered her head onto the desk. She couldn't get Bobbie's words out of her head: *You're in way over your head.* Maybe Bobbie was right.

CHAPTER TWENTY-THREE

PETER HAD SPENT THE night before walking alone on the beach. The sounds of the waves reminded him that there are cycles to everything, including grief. That eventually the pain of these last few weeks would ebb and flow and he would find a way to get past it all.

He'd left his pager in his car so it was eleven-thirty by the time he saw that Sara had been trying to contact him for hours. When he got her message he went straight to the clinic. Sara had dozed off in his chair behind the locked door of his office. When she awoke, she was angry with him, felt she was carrying too much of the load, was tired of his guilt getting in the way. He knew she was right; he had to stop feeling sorry for himself.

That morning, driving to the clinic in a soft spring rain he thought about Eve. He had never meant to hurt her. He frowned, thinking about how Bobbie had spontaneously appeared. He gripped the steering wheel tighter. His stomach thrashed like a fish on deck.

Peter walked into the clinic and went directly to Eve's room. He knocked lightly on the door and stepped through. Eve was sitting on the bed, hugging her knees and humming as she rocked back and forth, back and forth.

"Good morning," Peter said, gently.

She didn't look at him. She just kept humming. Peter walked quietly toward her.

"Can I sit down?"

She didn't respond.

"Eve, it's me, Peter. I'm here to help you. Can we talk?"

She jerked her head away from him and stared out the window continuing to rock herself back and forth.

He reached over to rub her back.

"I'm sorry—," he said.

She pulled away from him violently, jumping to the floor on the other side of the bed.

"Don't you touch me," she said. "You're just as bad as he is."

Peter stared at her. He swallowed hard.

"I know you're in a lot of pain right now but I'm going to say what I came here to say." The lump in his throat almost choked him; he coughed, awkwardly. "You're like a daughter to me, Eve. The closest thing to family I'll ever know. Please believe me, all I've ever wanted was to help you. It's just that your father, well, he has a way of getting what he wants."

"Oh Jesus. So you just let him. Let the big powerful Judge have whatever he wants? Is that it?" Eve's laser-like glare burned a hole in his heart. "You're pathetic," she said.

"Eve. Please, listen to me."

She raised her hand up, palm out and bit her lip.

"I can't Peter. At least, not right now. I hurt all over. I'm bleeding and I can't find the source of my injury. I can't stop the blood because I don't know where to put the bandage—."

"I can help you with that. I've known you since you were born. I can help you put the pieces back together."

She sat down on the bed and rubbed the covers between her fingers. Peter could see that she was fighting tears.

"Why now? Why are you so willing now when you could have helped me years ago?" She began to sob.

Peter took the risk and sat down on the bed beside her. He put his arms around her. He felt her cries entering him and knew he would carry her grief with him until the day he died. He rocked her slowly from side to side. She let go further, wept forcefully onto his shoulder like crashing waves. Caught up in the current, Peter broke down, too.

"I know what I've done is wrong," he said, meekly. "But there's a lot about your father that I've just learned in the past few days. I don't want to get into all that. You need to take this slowly. Besides, a lot of it is between him and me. What I want to say to you is that I tried my best to protect you over the years. I believed that I was keeping you safe somehow. I see now how terribly wrong it was, for both of us." Peter looked at Eve through watery eyes. His lip quivered. "I'm so sorry, Eve. I love you."

She reached around and hugged him tight.

"I forgive you, Peter," she whispered.

He felt as though he'd finally been set free.

"You're a beautiful, talented young woman," he said. "You have your whole life in front of you. You can choose to be happy, I want you to be happy. That's all I want."

"Happiness seems absurd to me right now," she said.

There was a knock on the door and Kyle poked his head around.

"Good morning," he said.

Peter stood up and wiped his eyes. "I'll leave you two alone."

"Hey," Kyle said. He sat down and kissed Eve. He stroked her cheek with the back of his hand.

"I've got something to tell you," he said.

Eve's shoulders fell.

"I'm leaving for Tahiti today," he said, looking deeply into her eyes. "How do you feel about that?"

She shrugged. "I knew you'd leave."

"But, I'll be back. Sara's given me your new address in San Francisco, and I'm going to sail straight up there after my trip. You didn't think I'd really leave you, did you?"

Eve shrugged again.

"There's a lot going on for you right now. The doctors think it would be easier for you to work through some of this stuff on your own, without me around. I think they're right. But please don't think I'm not here for you. If you want me to stay, I will."

"Are you sure you're coming to San Francisco?" she said.

"I'm there," he said, smiling. "Just as soon as the winds can carry me." He lifted her chin. "Trust me?"

She smiled into his eyes.

"God," he said, "it's good to see you smile."

Kyle spent the next hour with Eve. He was trying to breathe her in, her face, her eyes, her essence, so that he could take a piece of her with him. He knew she was confused and that she had a long way to go before she was healthy, but he finally knew peacefulness.

"Where's Sara? Is she around today?" he said.

"I haven't seen her yet," Eve said, "she'll probably be here any minute. She doesn't seem able to let me out of her sight for more than four hours at a time."

Kyle smiled. "You're lucky to have her," he said, remembering how Justin Templeten had said that luck didn't have anything to with it. He wondered who Sara really was to Eve.

"Where'd you go?" Eve said.

"I'm not sure," he said, "but I just got this really peaceful feeling...like everything's okay."

She looked at him quizzically.

"Just a feeling."

He leaned over and kissed Eve long and hard. He wrapped himself around her, his heart overflowed. He held his face close to hers.

"No matter what happens," he said, "no matter how tough it gets, remember this moment. I'm strong enough for both of us, lean on me. I promise you, we're going to have a great life."

Eve's eyes filled with tears.

"I'm scared," she said.

He held her close, stroking her head.

"You've got me. You've got Sara, and Peter. That's more than some people. You're going to get through this Eve, you are. Believe in yourself."

She nodded, trying to fight back more tears.

"I have to go now," he said, softly. He took her face in both hands and kissed her tenderly on the lips. "I love you, Eve Whitman, and I'm going to marry you."

Eve looked back at him with the eyes of a child.

He stood up, wiped her tears with his thumb and bent down for one last kiss.

"I'll go find Sara for you. Take good care of yourself. I'll see you in a few weeks."

"Okay," she squeaked.

Kyle forced himself to turn around and walk out the door.

"I'M TAKING YOU OUT OF HERE TODAY," Sara said, bursting into the room. "Come on, let's get you cleaned up."

"I don't know," Eve said.

"Don't know what?"

"If I'm ready to leave. I feel safe here."

"Trust me, Eve. It'll be better this way. Besides, it's a beautiful day, don't you want to get out and feel the sun on your face?"

Eve shrugged.

"Kyle's gone."

"I know," Sara said. She rubbed Eve's shoulder. "But you'll see him soon."

"What makes you so sure?"

"Because something tells me he's a man of his word."

"He said he wants to marry me. He doesn't even know the truth —."

"Come on," Sara said. " There's someone Peter and I want you to meet."

"Who?" Eve said.

"I met him in San Francisco. And ironically, Doris knows him, too. She even introduced Kyle to him."

"Who is it?"

"Someone who's going to help us," Sara said, gathering Eve's things together.

"Help us do what?" Eve said, watching her.

"We'll explain it later. Right now, I want you to get ready."

Sara yanked on Eve's arm, until she finally gave in and went to take a shower. While Eve was getting dressed Sara went to the station desk to fill out the release forms. She took a moment to slow herself down. What if it doesn't work? she thought. She forced herself to move the pen across the page then went back into Eve's room hoping it would be the last time she'd ever see these four walls.

"Okay," Eve said, looking down at the floor, "I'm ready."

Sara picked up the suitcase and held the door for Eve. She stepped through slowly. The nurses looked up from their work, smiling.

Eve looked at Sara who was smiling, too.

"Why is everybody smiling?" she whispered.

"Say goodbye, Eve," Sara said.

Eve waved and the nurses all said goodbye. At the elevator, Eve lifted her hand to wave again but they were already back to work. Sara put her arm around her and squeezed, she was happy enough about getting out of there for both of them. Eve looked down at her shoes until the ding of the elevator made her look up.

Sara drove to Peter's condo, explaining that Peter and Justin were going to meet them there.

After Sara and Eve had settled into Peter's, the intercom speaker in Peter's kitchen buzzed. Eve flinched at the abrasive sound. Sara answered the door and escorted Justin into the kitchen to introduce him to Eve. She swept him away quickly and showed him upstairs to the room they planned to use for the session. Peter had called Eve out onto the balcony to join him there while they waited.

"Eve," Justin said, joining them, "I know you're not feeling your best, that's why Sara and Peter invited me here today. Peter and I have been working on the same type of work. Did you know that?"

Eve shook her head.

"We've been working on a way to help people take away the hurt they feel inside. We've found a method that helps unlock pain. Because when you let it stay in there, even if it's hidden, it will get in the way your whole life. Do you understand?"

"Not really," Eve said.

Justin glanced at Sara, then Peter.

"I mean, what if you don't feel anything at all?" Eve said, trying to cooperate.

"It's the same thing," Justin said. "The pain is what's preventing you from feeling. In order to heal, you must allow these feelings to come to the surface, to bring them out of the darkness and into the light. Sometimes they show up as grief, or loss, sometimes as anger and even outrage. But once you're able to really look at your feelings honestly, that's when you can start making decisions. I know it sounds complicated, but we'd like to take the first step today. Are you willing?"

"I'm not sure. I don't really understand what you're going to do."

Justin looked at Sara.

"Let's go upstairs, we'll show you," Sara said.

"This seems spooky," Eve said, looking at Peter.

"Eve," Justin said, softly.

She looked into his black, shiny eyes and her shoulders released. Suddenly, though, she looked away pulling her hand to her temple and let out an excruciating moan.

"What is it?" Sara said.

"It's Bobbie," he said. "She's resisting. We need to tell her—."

Sara lifted her hand to cut him off when she saw Eve's pain subside.

"Are you alright?" Peter said.

Eve nodded, then broke into tears.

"Come on, up you go," Sara said. "Let's go upstairs and lie down."

Without hesitation Eve stood up with Sara and went with her into Peter's bedroom.

"How do you want to proceed with this?" Justin said, when Sara had returned.

"I'm not sure," she said. "Maybe it's too soon. What do you think Peter?"

"You're the conduit for Eve," Justin said, looking at Sara. "You must make the choices for her that she can't make on her own."

"In my experience," Peter said, "if we bring the patient under hypnosis and focus on the information critical in that moment, we'll get the best results."

"Bobbie," Sara said.

They both nodded.

"You must understand that like any healing, this is a process. We aren't going to cure Eve in one day. She has accumulated years, over many lives, of unresolved emotion. We can help her unlock one doorway at a time so she's free to walk through, to clean up and throw away what she doesn't want and then finally to close the door on it for good, if she chooses."

"Maybe Bobbie was right, maybe I am in way over my head," Sara said.

"You are exactly where you belong. Trust yourself. You know Eve better than you think. Let go, and listen to your heart," Justin said.

Sara turned to Peter.

"I agree," he said. "I think she needs to eliminate Bobbie's negative force, before anything else can be addressed."

"It's going to be overwhelming for her," Sara said.

"In the long run she'll be whole, that's what we need to focus on," Peter said.

"Alright," Sara said.

They reviewed the procedures before going upstairs to Eve. When they walked in, she was lying on her side, staring at the wall.

"Hi," Sara said.

Eve was silent.

Justin held up a wand-like instrument to show Eve. Sara hoped it wouldn't set her off like the thermometer had.

"Eve?" Justin said. "This is a kind of measuring stick, it helps me to map your energy field so we can find the music that's best suited for you. After I wave this around the outside of your body, then we'll put some headphones on your ears so you can listen to some music for a while."

"Okay," she said, looking to Sara and Peter for reassurance.

"Can you stand up for me, please?" Justin said.

Eve closed her eyes and put her hands over her face while Justin waved the wand around her body and then told her to go back and lay down. The computer screen indicated very low frequency vibrational patterns. He put on some headphones and began clicking buttons and keys until he found a match.

"Brahms," he said.

"Oh," Sara said, "I love Brahms."

"We'll start with the first passage of Serenade Number Two for small orchestra in A major, the Allegro, and then we'll skip the second piece and go straight to the Adagio non troppo. There will be a pause between the two passages, so you'll have an opportunity to guide Eve, and to receive feedback from her at that time."

Justin passed the headphones to Sara and she helped Eve relax. He passed another set of headphones with an attached microphone to Peter so his voice would be heard directly through Eve's earphones.

Justin nodded for Peter to begin.

Peter brought Eve under hypnosis in the usual way. Once she was fully under, he began.

"I want you to go back to a time when you were very happy. So happy that you danced around all day, your heart was light and you loved everything about your life. Are you there?"

A small grin spread across Eve's lips and she nodded.

Justin began the Allegro with the volume up at first then lowered it so Peter could speak over the sounds of the music.

"Tell me where you are Eve, what's happening?"

"I'm in the garden, I love this garden, it's magic. I love to spin around in my pretty dress while Mommy works on her roses. She has on a big straw hat and I tell her she looks like a rose underneath a mushroom."

Eve giggled.

"Is Mommy happy?" Peter said.

"Oh yes! We're always happy when we're together."

"Stay there with Mommy for awhile Eve and let yourself remember what it feels like to be so happy."

Sara took in some deep breaths as she observed. Her heart was pounding too fast and her head hurt.

"Now Eve, let's go to the time when things are not as happy. Something happened and even Mommy isn't as happy anymore. Are you there?"

"Yes," Eve said, sadly.

Justin tapped Peter on the shoulder to indicate they needed to let Eve ride the wave of emotion as the tempo and volume of the music built.

Within seconds, a steady stream of tears spilled out the corners of Eve's eyes, pouring over her cheeks down her neck and onto the pillow. They were silent tears, no other signs were present except for the endless flow of tears. Peter looked at Justin before continuing. Justin nodded and lowered the volume so Peter could speak.

"Okay, Eve, tell me where you are now," he said.

"I'm hiding in the back stairway. Mommy and Daddy are fighting."

"What are they fighting about?"

"Daddy says she keeps me all to herself, that she won't let him get close to me. Mommy says that's silly and starts to laugh."

Eve gasped.

"No Daddy. Stop it!"

Eve covered her ears and began to sob.

Sara turned quickly to Justin who held his hand up, letting her know it was okay. Eve's crying slowed as the music softened and then she smiled.

"Why are you smiling, Eve?"

"Mommy's tucking me in, she says everything is alright and not to worry. Daddy didn't mean to hurt her, it's just hard to be a grown up sometimes."

"Okay, let's go further. Your mom is gone now and it's just you and your father. Tell me how you feel."

"I'm fine. Daddy gives me everything...a pretty home, ballet and piano lessons, he's even going to buy me a horse. My daddy loves me very much."

"Do you have lots of friends?"

"No, but that's okay. Daddy and I like to be together."

"What do you do when you're together?"

"We talk, eat dinner, sometimes he helps me with my studies."

Justin tapped Peter again to let him know that the first passage was almost over.

"Does he ever touch you when you don't want him to?"

"I suppose. He says I'm his girl."

"Do you tell him if you don't want him to touch you?"

"Sometimes, but then he gets mad."

"What does he do when he's mad?"

"He says, Eve Whitman, you are my daughter and —."

"And what?"

"I don't know, that's all I can remember."

"Try harder. Remember the rest of that sentence and what happens after he says it. Go back Eve, remember now."

"You are my daughter...and you...will do...as I say."

Eve was squirming on the bed. She covered her chest with her arms. She pulled her knees up and held them tightly, all the while flailing her head from side to side.

"What's happening?" Peter said.

"Daddy took off all my clothes and he's rubbing his scratchy hands all over my body — and...and...I'm just standing there."

Eve was sobbing hard as the music reached a crescendo. After the passage had fallen to a soft conclusion she lay perfectly still, stretched out flat on the bed.

Peter pulled the headphones off, not sure if he could continue. Justin reached over and placed his hand on the back of his neck, infusing him with strength.

"Have courage, Eve needs you to help her through this next part," Justin said, quietly.

Sara nodded to Peter and he put the headphones back in place.

"Alright, Eve. You're all grown up. Remember when you started college? I want you to go back to those days during college and law school and recall what happened with your father. What happened, Eve, when he wanted you to start taking vitamin B-12 shots?"

Justin started the Adagio from Brahms' Serenade and immediately Eve began to frown. They could see her stomach pumping as she gasped for air. As the music grew more and more intense she moaned loudly and harshly. She thrashed her body from side to side.

"What do you see, Eve?"

"He gave me a shot, some kind of drug that turns me into a prostitute or something. I dress up for him, we go out to dinner, we, we... ."

Powerful waves of pain rose up through her body. Her chest heaved so hard she was lifting off the bed as she struggled for air. Deep sounds of grief were escaping through her mouth. They were so low, so trapped, there seemed to be no end to their flight.

Sara and Peter turned to Justin. He shook his head no, they should not stop, and Peter whipped off the headset.

As the Brahms passage reached the middle it became dark and foreboding. Eve's body went stiff, every muscle was engaged, the cords in her neck protruded as she clenched her jaw so tightly Sara was afraid she would hurt herself.

Peter quickly replaced the headset.

"Talk to me, Eve. What's happening?" he said.

"It's someone else...it's not me. There's someone else inside my body," she said.

As the music reached its crescendo, Eve was screaming.

"Tell her to go away and never come back," Peter said.

"GET OUT! GET AWAY FROM ME!" Eve screamed. "DON'T COME BACK! GET OUT!"

Sara swallowed hard, tears rushed down her face. Justin nodded for Peter to continue.

"Okay Eve, she's gone," he said. "Relax, let your breathing come back to normal, that's it. Let your muscles relax, listen to the sounds of the music and let each instrument be a tool for healing, each note you hear is mending your soul, your heart and your innermost being. Allow the music to transform you, and help you to let go of all this pain. Tell yourself as you listen that you are whole, you are in control of your own life and that you deserve love and peace.

"When the music is over you are free to open your eyes. Embrace your own courage as a gift toward health and wholeness. That's it, Eve, breathe deeply, just relax."

Sara gasped quietly trying to conceal her cries. Peter wrapped his arms tightly around her. When he let go she felt a whole new beginning was now possible. She smiled at Justin.

"Thank you," Sara whispered, still crying.

Eve had opened her eyes and was staring up at the ceiling. She sat up, looked at Peter then Sara, then Justin. Her lips trembled and they all gathered around her like petals on a flower.

"We are all connected," Justin said, "and when we work together, all things are possible."

CHAPTER TWENTY-FOUR

E VE AWOKE TO THE SOUNDS of clinking dishes and shuffling feet. Sara had given her Peter's guest room and taken the couch. Eve listened for awhile to how normal these sounds must be. People everywhere were waking up, moving through their usual morning routines. She realized she had none of her own. She had never really learned how to take care of herself, even when she was in college and law school her father had hired people to cook and clean for her. I'm pathetic, she thought, and a single tear rolled down her cheek.

Eve laid in bed for hours. Occasionally, she would drift off to sleep. She felt empty and hollow like an endless tube. She was not connected to anything. Her whole life, she realized, had been one, long sleepwalk.

She sat up. Her body ached. She tried reaching up, then out, with her arms but she didn't have the strength. She laid back down. She turned onto her side, then rolled over to the other side. She could not get comfortable. Now that her thoughts had landed on her father, no position on that bed, no place on this earth, she thought, would ever bring her comfort again. *I have no reason to live.*

There was a light tapping on the door.

Sara stepped in and walked over to the bed. She sat down and rubbed Eve's back. Eve looked away, hoping she would stop.

"It's three o'clock, want to come out to the kitchen? I'll fix you something to eat."

"Not hungry," Eve said, rolling away.

Sara got up and left the room, quietly closing the door behind her.

When the light was gone from the windows and darkness came, it was easier. Eve felt comfortably wrapped up in the darkness. She heard whispers hissing through the line of light that was trying to get in underneath her door. She let the distant voices soothe her until she heard Peter say he'd seen her father...something about how he had canceled his plans to Europe.

The next morning the sun came screeching through the windows once more. Eve put her pillow over her head to block out the noise. The words father and Daddy kept slipping into her brain like an insidious infection. She knew they would not leave her alone until she paid attention.

She sat up suddenly and whipped the covers back. She thumped her feet to the floor and stomped out to the bathroom. As she marched down the hallway she felt Peter and Sara watching her from the kitchen.

In the bathroom she dared to look at herself. She was pale. There were half moons of darkness beneath her drooping eyes. Her breath was horrible and when she bent down to splash her face with some cool water, a wave of nausea forced itself up through her chest into her throat. She dropped to the floor to vomit into the toilet.

She heard footsteps rushing down the hallway. The door flung open. Sara was beside her, trying to lift her up. Peter hung back in the doorway.

"I can do it," Eve mumbled.

"Up we go," Sara said.

Eve yanked her arm away.

"I'll get up in a minute," Eve said.

"Come on, I'll help you," Sara said.

Eve slapped her hand down on the floor.

"I can *do* it," she said.

"Okay," Sara said. She stood up, stepping back.

"Just leave me alone," Eve said.

Sara and Peter left her and closed the door.

Eve stood up, took some water into her mouth from the faucet and spit it out into the sink. She looked up in the mirror. *You can do this.* She turned on the shower and peeled off the night shirt she'd been wearing for two days. When she finally came out fully dressed, Peter and Sara stood up from the balcony, smiling a little too much.

"Well hello," Peter said and gave her a hug.

"I want to go see my father," she said.

"Oh?" he said.

Eve nodded adamantly.

"Let's sit down for a minute and talk about this," Sara said.

"Alright," Eve said.

After some tea and toast, Eve said she was ready to go. She needed to get it over with.

They drove over to the Whitman estate in silence. Peter and Sara sat in the front, Eve in the back — like a real family, she thought. She stared out the window looking at the town of Innis as though it were her first time through. When they pulled into the long drive leading to the house where she had grown up, Eve's heart grew tight. Sara turned around to look at her.

"You sure?" she said.

Eve swallowed and nodded.

They walked up to the main door, Eve in the center, Sara and Peter flanking her left and right, and slightly back. Eve reached down and turned the door knob; it was open and the house was quiet. They stepped through the door searching each room for some sign of her father. In the breakfast room, Eve heard the rumple of newspapers outside. She inhaled deeply and walked out to the back patio.

Her father sat at the patio table with coffee and croissants, he had his reading glasses on and looked up up over the frames when Eve appeared.

Eve sighed heavily.

"Just another pleasant Sunday morning at the Whitman Estate?" she said.

He didn't move.

She stepped closer and ripped the paper from his grip.

Startled he leaned back in his chair.

"Eve, you're back," he said, taking off his glasses.

"No, I'm not. I'm never coming back. I came here to say goodbye." She looked down on him.

"I'm still trying to grasp all that I've learned about our lives together. So far it's not going too well. Mostly I just want to sleep and throw up. But I wanted to see you, to tell you that I think you're sick. I think you should get some help. In fact," she said, "Peter?"

Peter stepped out onto the patio. Eve put her arm around him.

"You know Peter, don't you Daddy? He's a wonderful psychiatrist, but you probably only know him as the other person whose life you wanted to destroy."

Eve stood there for a moment breathing heavily. Her father was not looking at her and Peter's head hung down as he stared at the bricks beneath their feet.

"Well that's about it, I guess," she said. "Oh, wait. Sara?"

Sara stepped out onto the patio and went to Eve's other side. Eve put her arm around her.

"I just wanted you to have the chance to see what real love is."

Eve's father stared up at the three of them. He looked into Eve's eyes.

"Goodbye, Father," she said, and turned away. She walked numbly through the house, up the stairs and into the room where safety had only been an illusion. She grabbed clothing and threw it into suitcases angrily while Sara tried to help. When she could no longer bear the pain she slammed the suitcases together and latched them closed.

"That's it," she said. "Let's go."

Sara nodded and lifted the other bags to follow her down the stairs. Peter was waiting at the door and they all walked out and got into the car. On the way to Peter's, Eve cried quietly in the back seat while Peter and Sara looked straight ahead.

DORIS KNOCKED THREE TIMES on the door marked number 843. She thought about the positive vibrations of that number as she waited for someone to answer.

"Doris," Sara said, "what a wonderful surprise. Eve will be so glad to see you."

"How's everything?" Doris said.

Sara shrugged.

"Where is she?"

"Come on," Sara said, "I'll take you to her room, she's been in there since we got back from her father's house."

"Oh," Doris said. She nodded at Sara and knocked on the bedroom door. Doris didn't hear anything so she slowly opened the door and popped her head through. Eve was lying in bed with a book in her hands.

"Good afternoon, my lady," Doris said, bowing slightly.

"Doris," Eve said.

"You know," Doris said, waving her arms around, "this isn't too bad. Could use a little color, but it's kind of cozy. The apartment number is very good."

Eve began to laugh then cry.

"Oh, sweetie," Doris said, and rushed over to her. "Do I look that bad?"

Eve laughed again, through her tears and said, "It's so good to see you."

"I've missed you, too."

They held each other tight. Even when Eve tried to pull away, Doris held her tighter still. It might be the last time she'd see Eve and she wanted to make it memorable.

"Okay, Doris, you're choking me. I can't—."

Doris released her.

"There," Eve said, letting out a great sigh, "that's better. Now what were you saying about a number?"

Doris went into fine detail about the numerological characteristics of the number of Peter's condo which reduced to the compound number of fifteen, and then reduced further to the single number, six. Doris said that six was the number ruled by the planet Venus, which symbolized love, and that was extremely positive. When she finished her dissertation on the power of numbers, and more importantly, the power of love, she stopped abruptly and tossed her hands into her lap.

"So, tell me, what's been happening with you?" Doris said.

Eve's eyes glazed over. She began rubbing her thumb and forefinger together in tiny, rapid circles.

Images of the memories she'd uncovered during the past several days flew through Eve's mind. So too, did they flood Doris's internal eye. Without a single word, Doris had received the entire meaning of that day, and of the few days before. She moaned in agony, and raised both hands to her temples to push the pain away.

"Doris," she said. "What is it? I'll go get——."

Suddenly Doris burst into hysterical laughter.

Eve froze midway across the room. She turned back frowning.

"What's so funny?"

"I'm sorry," Doris said, still laughing.

Eve looked confused and when Doris saw her face, she stopped laughing.

"Come here," she said, kindly.

"What happened to you?" Eve said.

"I read your mind."

Eve looked hurt.

"I wasn't laughing because of what I saw, you poor thing. Come over here."

Eve sat down across from Doris on the edge of the bed. Doris reached up and stroked her cheek with the back of her hand.

"The truth doesn't always tickle," Doris said, lifting Eve's chin to meet her eyes. "But it does set you free."

"I don't feel very free," Eve said, quietly.

"I didn't say it happened over night," Doris said, tapping Eve lightly on the knee. "Besides, you've got to have the whole truth before it can do its thing. You've got to be like a warrior, who never gives up until you fight the big buffalo, face-to-face, eye-to-eye. Then, after your victory, you'll get one of those big, fancy headresses with all the beautiful feathers."

Eve smirked.

"Won't that be nice?" Doris said.

Eve looked at Doris with tears streaming down her face and Doris leaned over to wipe them away.

"I'm not a warrior, Doris. I just feel like a scared, little girl."

"Well, it's time to grow up," Doris said, sternly. "You'll make it to the other side, Sara will help you. I have faith in you Eve, I always have. You just wait, there's a whole world out there, you'll see."

Eve managed a slight smile.

"What was so funny before, anyway?" Eve said.

Doris flung her hand toward her.

"I was so thrilled to have received my first telepathic experience. I've been working on that for awhile now. It's very exciting for me. And to think, it was you who gave it to me... ."

Doris paused to sigh at the wonder of it all.

"So there was that part but it really took me by surprise. I had no idea it would hurt."

"Doris, you're rambling."

"Sorry. The funny thing was, and you might not think it's so funny, but the thing that struck me as funny was that you were running to get me a psychiatrist."

"That's it?"

"I told you, you wouldn't find it funny. It's just that most of my life people have thought I was crazy, just because I know more than they do about the things that really matter. So when I have this monumental breakthrough, where I am seeing, feeling, and hearing someone else's thoughts at the same time and intensity that they are, you want to run and get me a doctor who'll want to put me in a straitjacket and prescribe me some downers. Don't you see the irony?"

Eve shook her head.

"It's way beyond me, Doris."

"I know, I know," Doris said. "I brought something for you."

"You're changing the subject."

"The subject is complete. Discussion over, finis, finito. There is nothing left for either one of us two exceptional and gorgeous women to say on that matter. Zero. Zed. Nada. Nil. Now, do you want your surprise, or do you want me to bring it back tomorrow?"

Eve laughed.

"That's better," Doris said, fishing around inside the huge sack she called a purse. She pulled out an envelope, crumpled and stained with a ring of coffee.

"Oh, look," she said. "It's got a zero on it. That's Pluto's vibrational number. Very powerful. Do you understand the significance?"

Eve shook her head.

"Zero is the symbol of total harmony, no opposing forces, eternity."

Eve squinted at the back of the envelope.

"That's a coffee stain," she said.

"Oh, ye of little faith," Doris said, handing the letter to Eve. "Go ahead, turn it over."

Eve took the letter and turned it over. She gasped and looked up quickly at Doris.

"It's from Kyle," Eve whispered.

"Of course it is," Doris said, as she stood up. "And I'm going to leave you to read that privately. Besides, your father has instructed me via his most professional secretary, to break down the office. Did you know that?"

"No," Eve said, sadly. "But it makes sense. I'm going to San Francisco with Sara."

"Yes," Doris said. "I'll miss you terribly but I know that's where you belong."

"What are you going to do now? Do you need money?" Eve said. "I haven't taken very good care of you."

"My dear, it was always meant to be the other way around."

"I see that now," Eve said, her eyes brimming with tears.

"I don't need any money. Money doesn't matter to me, it always arrives when I need it. I'm going to take some time off from people for awhile, write some poems maybe, color some pictures with my children at the hospital. I've got some money saved so I won't need a job for a while."

Doris laughed her deep, rich laugh and handed Eve a small package, beautifully wrapped. Eve took it from her and unwrapped it. It was a book of poems by Maya Angelou.

Doris sighed and touched her hand to her heart.

"Whenever you're not sure you can keep going, I want you to open this book and read 'And still I rise.' That way, I know you'll be just fine."

"Okay," Eve said, her voice cracked.

Without another word, the two women embraced and kissed each other. Doris turned and walked out the door leaving Eve alone with the book and the unopened letter in her lap.

EPILOGUE

Hope

Hope is the thing with feathers
That perches in the soul,
And sings the tune without the words,
And never stops at all

~Emily Dickinson

E VE TOOK THE MAIL out of the small black tin box at the base of the stairs. She ran up and pushed the door open.

"Sara," she called, breathlessly, "a letter from Kyle!"

Sara smiled from the kitchen where she was just finishing the dishes. She had her ear cocked for the news on Kyle's arrival. Thinking it was too quiet, she walked through the arched doorway into the living room. Eve was limp on the couch, her eyes flooded with tears. Her face was strained as if she were pushing herself through a cold harsh wind. She brought her hand to her mouth when she saw Sara.

"Oh God, oh Sara," Eve said, her shoulders shook as she fell back.

"What?" Sara said, rushing over to Eve.

Eve opened her hand, unclutched the crumpled letter and let it fall to the floor.

Sara didn't know which to do first, pick up the letter and read it, or try to comfort Eve. She reached for Eve while looking down at the page. *Heather is pregnant,* she read, *can not leave.* Sara turned to Eve.

"I have nothing now, my life is over if I don't have him."

Eve sobbed, intensely.

"That's not true," Sara said. "You have yourself and you are extraordinary. You will get through this."

"I can't...I can't do it," she cried.

Sara sat quietly beside Eve and then reached down to pick up the letter. He did not want to repeat his father's mistakes. Couldn't bear to leave a child in the world the way he'd been left. Hoped she could find a way to understand, to forgive. At least he knew she was safe, out of harm's way now. He would always love her.

EVE STOOD UP STILL CRYING and looked around the room.

"What do you need?" Sara said.

"What I need, I am never going to get, I'm going out—."

"You sure? Want me to come?"

Eve shook her head, and fumbled with her jacket as she walked slowly out the door.

She walked the streets of San Francisco for hours and hours trudging up and down Nob Hill, passing by all the places she had dreamed of bringing Kyle. There was no stopping the river of tears so she just let them flow, she didn't even see the people as she walked by them.

She found herself at Fisherman's Wharf. She was cold, even though it was still August she felt the chill of the approaching winter, the wind cut through her. She found a spot along the water without too many people. She stood firmly with her feet planted on the concrete; her hands were lonely in their pockets. She raised her head to the ocean air, breathing in and out, feeling the foggy mist as it gently veiled her face.

She could not blame him for his decision. It was why she loved him;

how could she hate him for wanting to care for his own child? But her heart was broken, maybe for good this time and she didn't know how long she'd be able to carry around the crushing weight inside her.

She had Sara, that was good. In six or seven months Spring would come again, the robins would come back. It's not really an ending, she argued, it's a new beginning. If she kept telling herself that (she would have to say it every day over and over like a mantra) by Spring when the robins sang again, she might be able to smile. She could learn to live with half a heart the way some people learned to breathe with just one lung.

But for now she still felt the strength of Kyle's arms around her, still smelled the sea upon his skin, and her desire for him crippled her. She imagined him standing on the beach somewhere in St. Thomas, gazing out at the water like she was, and lifted her fingertips to her lips. She blew a kiss that would skim across the ocean waves on life's ever-changing winds. Someday, she knew, it would reach him. Maybe not in this lifetime, but someday.

Something behind her beckoned, like a whisper trying to get through the crowd. She turned around, scanning the Saturday shoppers seeing nothing she turned back towards the water, but the moment had passed.

She took in a deep breath, wiped her tears away, and turned to walk some more. She would keep walking until being still was more bearable.

Someone tapped her shoulder, she turned around, frowning.

"Hey gorgeous," Doris said.

JB

JUPITER BRAHMS
P U B L I S H I N G

Jupiter Brahms Publishing is a division of ISIS 2000, LLC, dedicated to providing a voice for new writers. The focus of our work is creative self-expression around the themes of empowerment, freedom and personal truth. We are committed to cultural, social and age diversity; we welcome all writers whose work speaks to our mission. For more information on Jupiter Brahms, please visit our web site.

www.isistudios.com